AFTER THE CRASH

EMMA ALCOTT

To Courtney Bassett, Lori Parks, Jill Weller, Lynn Van Dorn, and Lucy Lennox, who inspire and encourage me. I couldn't do this without you.

And to my husband for understanding why I often need to camp out in my office until all hours of the night.

PROLOGUE

FOX

Marshall Lloyd hit the floor with the same fleshy sound as the purple jelly dildo that had appeared out of nowhere one lunch period back in December, and if he'd been made out of glittery PVC instead of flesh and bone, Fox might have laughed.

But Marshall wasn't.

He'd never been.

The kid would never sparkle. Not like this.

"What's the matter, Marshall?" Hayden sneered as he dragged Marshall up from the floor and shoved him against the lockers. Marshall opened his mouth, but before he could talk, Hayden slammed his knee into Marshall's gut. Upon impact the air burst from Marshall's lungs, and he sputtered and gasped in an attempt to get it back. "Too much of a coward to fight back?

Fox, who stood several feet away, closed his locker with his hip. When Marshall said nothing, Hayden drove his knee into Marshall's stomach again.

"He might break a nail if he did." Peter, the little shit that he was, laughed. "Little princess would rather save her manicure than her life."

"She's probably waiting for her prince to come save her." Hayden

1

grabbed Marshall by the hair and wrenched his head back, then leaned in so his lips were by Marshall's earlobe. "You want that, Marshall? You want some man to sweep in and save you? I bet you'd get on your knees and suck his dick if he did. Is that what you want? To swallow some guy's load?"

"P-Please stop," Marshall wheezed. With his neck stretched like it was, his skin was taut enough that his pulse visibly raced beneath it. "It hurts."

"Why don't you make us?"

Hayden raised a knee like he was going to pummel it into Marshall's gut for a third time, but as soon as Marshall braced for the attack, he stopped. Peter took over, catching Marshall across the jaw with a right hook while Marshall was least expecting it. The crunch of knuckles against bone rang down the hallway, followed closely by Hayden and Peter's laughter. Marshall grunted in pain and wilted, his legs shaking so much, Fox doubted he'd be able to stand without Hayden there to hold him up. It was a miracle he'd made it as far as he had—Marshall was small and wiry, all bones without any muscle. Every hit he took had to be devastating. The only saving grace was that he took them so often, he likely knew what to expect.

Most days Fox was able to ignore what was happening, but now that he and Marshall were seniors, he'd been having more of a problem pretending not to notice what was going on. Hayden and Peter were juniors, for fuck's sake.

It was sad.

All of this was sad.

And Fox was done standing around and doing nothing for the sake of popularity.

"Hey! Fuck off."

Peter glared at him. "Are you fucking serious right now, Fox? I'd ask who put that stick up your ass, but it's not a stick, is it? Sounds like you're sitting on an entire fucking tree. Calm your tits. We're just having fun."

Hayden rolled his eyes and dropped Marshall, who slid down the locker and curled into a ball. "It's scientifically proven that Marshall doesn't have a backbone, so it's not like he feels anything. It's like beating up a slug. Besides, you never gave a shit before. Why do you care now?"

"Does it really fucking matter?" Fox stepped forward, wedging himself between Marshall and Hayden while keeping an eye on Peter, who looked like he might want to get a cheap shot in on Fox for interrupting their fun. "I decided that I'm sick of this, so I'm putting an end to it. Go kick around a hacky sack or snort some Pixy Stix or something."

"Looks like Fox wants his dick sucked." Peter jerked his head in the direction of the foyer. "Come on, Hayden. Let's give the *lovebirds* some privacy. Maybe when Marshall's drained Fox's balls he'll come back to his senses and start being fun again."

Fox's lip twitched. "Get the fuck out of here."

"Have fun with your girlfriend," Hayden sneered. He stepped back without turning, keeping his eyes on Fox in a bid to intimidate him, like Fox could ever be scared shitless by what a junior thought of him. "Hope that mouth is worth it."

"We'll tell Elijah you say hi," Peter added before he and Hayden split.

Fox stood in place and watched until they'd made it from the hall to the foyer, then turned to face Marshall. He hadn't moved.

"Hey, look…" Fox pushed his tongue against the roof of his mouth while he contemplated what to say. It wasn't like he and Marshall were friends. Marshall likely hated him after what he'd done. "I'm sorry about what happened. It's bullshit. Are you going to be okay?"

Marshall said nothing.

"Hey, I'm talking to you." Fox glanced at Marshall, then looked up and down the hall to make sure the coast was clear. If Mr. Horner caught him engaging with a kid who'd clearly been roughed up, he'd be locked up in ISS quicker than Sherry Campbell had been expelled for lighting up a doobie in the middle of the cafeteria. Once he was sure that nobody was around, he squatted beside Marshall and laid a hand on his shoulder. "Are you going to be okay?"

"Yeah," Marshall said in a small voice.

"Good. Just... I don't know. Go to the library or something. Mrs. Crummit will keep you safe if those goons show up. Not that they would. I'm pretty sure the last time Hayden read a book, he was in second grade."

For a long, awkward moment, Marshall didn't react. Right when Fox was certain he'd decided life was safer on the ground and that it was in his own best interest to leave, Marshall unfurled and propped himself up on his elbow. He looked up at Fox with glistening gunmetal-blue eyes. "Thank you."

A feeling wrapped itself around Fox's stomach and squeezed. He couldn't name it—didn't *want* to name it—but acknowledged it all the same. "It's no big deal. Just... don't mess with those guys, okay? Head the other way if you see them. Elijah, too. They're only going to cause you trouble."

"Okay." Marshall looked away and smoothed a hand nervously over his long hair. With his dainty features and his big thick-rimmed coke-bottle glasses, his sense of style did him no favors. He'd never escape the "princess" moniker if he didn't get his hair cut, but the fact that his hair was an issue at all was such bullshit. Everything in Bulrush was such bullshit. Fox couldn't wait to get out.

"I'll talk to Elijah and see if he'll ask the guys to knock it off. Just... lay low or whatever. If you see any of them coming, go the other way."

The glimmer in Marshall's eyes didn't fade, and for a treacherous moment, Fox found himself thinking that if Marshall had been born a girl, they would have been eyes he wouldn't have minded losing himself in—the kind that could make his heart beat in time to the batting of their lashes.

Fox cleared his throat. "You got that?"

Marshall nodded.

"So… be careful, I guess." Fox tucked his hands into the back pockets of his jeans and took a step back. If he stuck around any longer, Hayden and Peter would bring Elijah around, and Fox would have to answer to him. Telling two juniors to fuck off was no skin off his back, but Elijah? No way. Fox wasn't going to stick his neck out if Elijah was around to behead him. Until their senior year was over and Fox left for basic training, he needed to keep himself in the good graces of the King of Bulrush High. The last thing he needed was to draw the spotlight onto himself.

Not that Hayden and Peter weren't going to do their best to make sure that happened, anyway.

"Fox?" Marshall asked in a small voice that made Fox pause.

"Yeah?"

"Thank you. Again. I really mean it."

"It's whatever. If you're really thankful, don't talk about it, okay?" Fox didn't look at Marshall's face, because he was sure that if he did, he'd get sucked in by his stupidly sweet eyes. "I've gotta go."

"Okay." Marshall rose shakily to his feet. "I—"

"See ya."

Fox couldn't stick around to hear what Marshall had to say—there were footsteps in the distance, and alongside them, the piping voices of two pissed-off juniors who no doubt wanted to flaunt their authority.

Whatever.

Fuck them.

Fox didn't care much for what Hayden and Peter thought. They orbited Elijah like sickening satellites, waiting for their shot at being the big man on campus, but as long as Elijah was still around, it would never come. It was how it'd been since preschool, when Fox's uneasy friendship with him had begun.

"Fox," Elijah called from the foyer as Fox strolled toward it. "Hayden and Peter say you're being a pussy. What the fuck is going on?"

"Nothing." Fox didn't look over his shoulder to see what Marshall was doing, but he heard scrambling footsteps growing fainter by the second. If the kid had any brains, he was hightailing it to the staircase at the other end of the hall. "I was looking for change in my backpack when I saw Hayden getting in real close with Marshall. Pulled him back and whispered in his ear and everything. I figured if I didn't step in, Hayden was going to start making out with him."

"Fucking *liar!*" Hayden seethed.

Fox shrugged. "I saw what I saw. You *were* talking about how he likes to suck cock more than I'd consider normal. You got a fantasy, Hayden? Maybe you and Peter could—"

"I swear, if you say one more word—"

"Boys, boys. Calm down." Elijah waved a hand. By then, Fox had made it to the foyer, and Elijah clapped him on the back, steering him toward the upper gym. Hayden glared at him, but didn't push the issue. "Who cares? We've got bigger things to worry about. Fox, word just broke that Morgan is having a house party this weekend. Her parents are going away. According to my sources, not only will she have access to enough booze to kill an elephant, but Rico's going to be bringing some dank bud. You're coming, right?"

"Sure."

Fox was only half listening—his ears were trained on the hallway, listening to make sure Marshall had got out safely. The guy was a dork, but he didn't deserve Hayden and Peter's cruelty, and he certainly didn't deserve what Elijah would do to him if he got it in his head that Marshall needed to be taught a lesson.

Elijah clapped him on the back. "That's my boy."

"But only if you listen to me." Fox brought Elijah to a stop, effectively stopping Hayden and Peter as well. "Look, it's nothing against Hayden or Peter, but the way Hayden was touching Marshall made me sick."

Hayden puffed up his chest. "You're so full of it! Stop fucking lying!"

"Like you didn't lean in close and speak into his ear like you were trying to get him all hot and bothered?" It was a risk, but Fox wasn't going to let it stop him. Marshall was the weird kid, but that didn't mean he deserved to have the shit kicked out of him. "Peter?"

Peter crossed his arms over his chest and looked off to the side. "I mean, he did, but like, it wasn't *that*."

"Only it was." Fox met Elijah's gaze, keeping his expression as neutral and unperturbed as he could. He only had one shot to get this right. "I think it'd be a good idea if we all left the princess alone for a while. I don't want any of us to start getting... *ideas*."

Elijah held his gaze for a long moment, then glanced at Hayden, who looked ready to start throwing punches. "You think it's contagious?"

"I'm not saying that. All I'm saying is that it's better to be safe than sorry. It's our senior year. We don't want anyone talking about us."

"You're right." Elijah nodded in the direction of the gym, and without a word, the group continued walking. "Hayden, Peter, leave the weirdo alone."

"But—"

"If you're rolling with me," Elijah's voice was slick ice—the kind you didn't notice until it was too late, and you were already careening off the road, "you need to maintain certain standards. One of them is not putting yourself in a position where people are gonna start to talk, because guess what? It always gets reflected on me, and I'm not going to tolerate people thinking that something gross is going on between me and the princess. Got it?"

"Fine. Whatever. I'll leave him be." Hayden glared at Fox, but his ire was the least of Fox's worries. The sickeningly tight feeling in his stomach eased, and for the first time since he'd witnessed Hayden slam his knee into Marshall's gut, he was able to properly breathe. Somehow he'd managed to do the impossible—he'd bought Marshall time.

"So, now that that's settled, what do you boys say to a little trip

7

to Love's before lunch is over?" Elijah took a sharp left in front of the upper gym and headed for the staircase. It was the fastest way to get to the student parking lot. "I heard Rico's going to be there. We can skip the rest of the afternoon and get wrecked."

"I'm out." Fox stopped in front of the door leading into the stairwell. "I've got a math test this afternoon, and if I fail it, they're not going to let me graduate."

Elijah shrugged. He pushed the door open and held it for Hayden and Peter. "Sucks to be you."

"Yeah."

"Guess we'll catch you tomorrow." Elijah held his gaze for a second longer than was necessary, like he saw through Fox's lies and knew the truth. Then, with a telling smirk, Elijah winked. "Peace."

"See ya."

The door shut. Fox watched through the small window on it as Elijah, Hayden, and Peter roughhoused their way down the staircase. When they were gone, he slumped against the wall next to the door and heaved a tired sigh.

There were just three months, two weeks, and six days until graduation.

Two thousand, six hundred and forty hours with weekends included.

One thousand, eight hundred and seventy-two without.

He could do this.

He could make it through.

And once he did, he'd leave Bulrush for good.

1

MARSHALL

Phone calls were the bane of Marshall's existence. Well, maybe that was being unfair to Alexander Graham Bell. It wasn't like a telephone had ever gone out of its way to spite him. There were worse evils in the world. Cold cat puke strategically placed where his bare foot would land in it first thing in the morning, for one, which only narrowly beat out cliffhanger season finales. In all honesty, phone calls typically ranked fifth or sixth on the bane-o-meter, sandwiched between motorists who neglected to use their turn signals and produce going bad a day after bringing it home.

But today's phone call was different.

It left Marshall glowing.

With all the rhythm of a pasty white beanpole from the Midwest, Marshall danced—in other words, wiggled—into the kitchen, where a bottle of champagne was waiting on the counter. This morning had been the result of years of hard work, and he was ready to celebrate with a little day drinking.

For the first time in almost a decade, he was free.

"Get your drink on," Marshall sang under his breath as he struggled to pull the cork. It came as a surprise to no one that he was not

Missy   Elliott.   "Getchur-getchur-getchur-getchur-getchur drink o—"

The cork shot out of the bottle with such force that Marshall shrieked and leapt back from the counter. His flailing luckily failed to knock the bottle, but it did put a stop to what would have been the hottest remix of 2019. When his heart came back from orbit, he approached the bottle and poked it, just to be sure it wasn't packing any other surprises, then poured himself a glass. In the silence that followed, he whispered an apology to the gods of early 2000s music, grabbed a box of Lucky Charms from the pantry, then slunk into the living room and lay on the couch. Now that the last pesky phone call was out of the way, he could enjoy something he hadn't been able to do in years.

Nothing.

Absolutely nothing.

It was going to be *glorious.*

Marshall fished his wireless mouse and keyboard from the bottom shelf of his coffee table and streamed the first decent-looking movie he found on Netflix, then yawned and settled in with the intention of zoning out. With the box of Lucky Charms between his thighs and his champagne in hand, he had everything he needed. There wasn't a cork in the world that could harsh his mellow. Not with the plans he had.

One marshmallow at a time, Marshall picked all the fun out of his cereal. When there were no colorful bits left on the top layer, he took a sip of his champagne, glanced furtively across the room to make sure Missy Elliott wasn't watching, then downed the glass and set it aside. The buzz did away with the last of Marshall's worry, and he spent the rest of the movie sifting through cereal to find the pieces that mattered.

By the time the credits were rolling, Marshall had come to two conclusions—the first was that, despite the low alcohol content, the bubbles had definitely gotten to his head; the second was that doing nothing was dull as shit. He'd been moving mountains since graduating high school, doing anything and everything he could to establish himself as a force to be reckoned with in Silicon Valley's tech industry, and now that he'd succeeded, time off felt... empty.

At least, emptier than he'd expected.

What was it that people did when they weren't working? Television wasn't going to cut it. A glass or two of champagne would be fun, but Marshall hadn't gone through the logistical nightmare that was taking a year off from his business so he could become an alcoholic. When he'd imagined what life would be like after making it, he'd never pictured the bottom of a bottle... but he'd never pictured anything more substantial than "freedom," either.

Wrinkling his nose, Marshall shook his Lucky Charms to farm for any remaining marshmallows, then unlocked his phone as he snacked on his harvest. Phone calls might have been fifth or sixth on the bane-o-meter, but he could text all day long and not feel like he was one more awkward silence away from shriveling up and dying. Better yet, he had exciting news to share with the most important person in his life—his mom.

Marshall: Brace yourself for the biggest news of 2019
Momzilla: omg! Ready!
Marshall: But first, tell me what's new with you
Momzilla: that's not fair!!
Momzilla: Okay, okay
Momzilla: I've got "groundbreaking" news
Momzilla: I'm in the middle of preparing the flower beds for planting!
Marshall: I love you
Marshall: I'm literally laughing out loud.
It was true.
Momzilla: Good :) then my job is done
Momzilla: Tell me about your news!!
Marshall: Well...

This was it—the moment he'd been waiting for. Marshall bit his lip and held back a laugh that had nothing to do with his mom's play on words. It'd been a long time coming, but all the details had finally fallen into place.

Marshall: I'm stepping down
Momzilla: NO!!!
Momzilla: OMG!!
Momzilla: Are you serious???
Marshall: It's just for a year
Marshall: I needed a break before I burned out
Momzilla: But what are you going to do with a whole year off? I know you. You can't just take it easy
Marshall: Well, that's part of why I decided it was so important for me to take a break
Marshall: I've been so focused on professional success that I've been ignoring who I am as a person
Momzilla: Okay, so is that code for backpacking through Europe or what??
Marshall: Interesting that you should ask...
A grin cracked his face.
Marshall: You know that old Victorian house off highway fifteen?
Momzilla: MARSHALL LLOYD
Momzilla: YOU DIDN'T
Marshall: I did

Marshall's phone lit up with an incoming call—it was from his mom, who undoubtedly had decided that texting wasn't enough, and that he needed his eardrums thoroughly shattered.

"You did *what!?*" she gushed as soon as the call connected. "*Marshall!* Karen Winthrop has been telling everyone that some coal industry bigwig from Harrisburg is moving into that house. You're telling me it's actually you?"

"Hi, Mom." Marshall tried to resist a laugh, but it bled into his voice regardless. "Yep."

"You're serious?"

"Dead serious."

"You're not pulling my leg?"

"Mom, it's not a joke! I promise. I'm the one funding all the renovations, and I'm the one who's going to be moving in. I spent the last ten years of my life focused on my career—it's time I switched gears and focused on me. Part of that means spending more time with you. I miss you."

"Marshall." It sounded like she was seconds away from sobbing. "Baby, I love you. I can't believe you're coming home."

"Me neither."

"Is there anything I can do to help you?" She sniffled. "Do you need me to go over there and make sure the construction at the house is going okay? It's so old and overgrown. Are you sure it's going to be safe?"

"It will be. By the time I move in, the house is going to be like new. The yard is another story, but it should be knocked back enough that I won't need a machete to get inside."

"When are you coming?"

"Friday."

The shriek of delight he earned in response for his answer almost broke his phone's speaker. Marshall held it away from his ear and laughed while he waited for her to calm down. While she laughed her excitement away, he fished one last marshmallow from his box of Lucky Charms, then closed the flap and set it aside.

"Do you need me to pick you up from the airport?" she asked as Marshall headed into the kitchen in search of more champagne. "What time does your flight arrive?"

"It doesn't. I'm driving."

"From *Silicon Valley?*"

"It's thirty hours. I'm going to take it slow and do it over three, maybe four days." Glass in hand, Marshall leaned against the counter and watched the television screen from across the room. The credits had ended, and Netflix was aggressively trying to push another movie on him. "It'll give the interior designer time to set up all the furniture and make sure everything that I order has been delivered and installed. Besides, I'm not in a rush. I've got time. It'll be nice to see the world from the ground for once."

"I just... I can't believe you're coming home. I know I keep saying it, but I really can't. I'm so happy you're coming back, even if it's just for a little while."

"Yeah. Me too." Done with the kitchen, Marshall headed for the patio. The heavy glass door slid across its track with a satisfying whoosh, and he stepped through the open space onto the stone steps waiting on the other side. The heat they held soaked through the soles of his feet, hot, but not unpleasant. Still, by the time he made it to the closest patio chair, he was glad to be able to sit. Despite his honorary vampire status, the sun bolstered his resolve and improved his spirits. It was encouraging to hear his mom gush about his sudden return to home, but Marshall had mixed feelings about it.

"I should plan you a party." She hummed in thought. "Or maybe a nice dinner. I think that makes more sense. We could go for steak. I can make reservations. Are you planning on arriving Friday afternoon, or are you only going to be getting in late at night?"

"I don't know." Marshall tipped his head back and watched the cloudless sky. Sunshine saturated his hair. The world remained unchanged no matter where he went, but the sky was always different. Would he miss it here? It was hard to say. "Why don't we wait and see what happens with the move? I don't think anywhere near Bulrush is going to be busy enough that we'll need reservations, but I appreciate the thought."

"Oh, I know. I'm just so excited to see you. Can it be Friday yet?"

Marshall closed his eyes and focused on the way the sun kissed his cheeks and shone red through his eyelids. The concept of Friday was simultaneously a delight and a terror, but nothing in life worth doing was ever easy. "It'll be here before you know it, Mom," he promised. "I'll be home soon."

2

FOX

The small house from Fox's childhood was different. Too small. Too dark. Too cluttered. Trinkets he didn't recognize clustered the mantle—dainty porcelain dolls with pretty faces and vacant eyes, pillar candles in varying sizes, and miniature Christmas trees whose bristle branches were tipped with artificial snow—and the old coffee table by the couch was stacked with magazines and used glasses with milky rings staining their insides.

It was wrong.

All of it.

The mess swelled in Fox's head like an ever-growing blob, swallowing everything in its path until there was nothing left to feast on but the air itself. Fox's throat tightened. His lungs burned. The air was too thin, and he needed someplace safe to hide—someplace where the chaos wouldn't follow. That someplace turned out to be his bedroom, where he hid for a whole day before finding the will within himself to venture out again. It was a short excursion—to the kitchen and back—but it was enough for him to know that things here were off.

Or maybe, he realized as he lay in bed and watched shadows cross the ceiling, it was that *he* was off.

There was no coming back from that.

On the second day, when he felt composed enough to leave bed and head into town, he confirmed his suspicion. The downtown strip looked the same, but it was pocked by changes that made it wrong, like he'd stepped onto the plane coming home and landed in an alternate dimension. With his heart in his throat, he dodged the stares of people he knew and ducked back into his old truck, only to slam his fists against the top of his steering wheel in a fit of rage.

Why did it have to be like this?

Why did *he* have to be like this?

It'd been too much, too soon.

Bright and early the first Sunday morning of Fox's return, there came three rhythmic knocks at his bedroom door that startled him out of his sleep. Heart pounding, he pushed himself against the wall and squeezed his eyes shut, cognizant that he was home, but scared shitless all the same. When he didn't answer, Fox's mother opened the door and stepped inside. "Good morning, Frederick." She swept across the room and parted the curtains with enthusiasm. Light spilled across Fox's bed, temporarily blinding him. With a grunt, he hooked his arm over his eyes and fell back into bed. "It's time to get up and get ready for church. Pastor Barton is looking forward to seeing you."

"I'm not going."

"Frederick!"

That name. Fuck, did he hate the way she said it. Fox let out a breath and pushed the thought aside. If he got off topic, she'd find a way to weasel him into doing what she wanted regardless of how it would affect him. "Tell Pastor Barton I say hi and that I'll see him some other time."

With his eyes covered, Fox couldn't see what she was doing, but he could imagine it. With her arms crossed over her chest and her lips pursed, she'd either glare hard enough that he'd get out of bed to do her bidding or she'd end up hospitalized from sudden corneal hemorrhaging. Fox hoped she'd reached her deductible, because he had no intention of cracking.

As a teenager he'd bowed his head and done everything she'd asked, but he was a grown man now. The subservient son she knew was gone.

Not that she'd cared to notice.

When Fox didn't budge, she cleared her throat angrily and shuffled her feet. At least the click of her kitten heels on the hardwood hadn't changed—it wasn't a comfort, but at least it was familiar. "You've been living in your room for almost a week. Don't you think it's time you go visit the people who've been waiting to see you?"

"Not yet."

"*Frederick.*"

"Not. Yet." Fox tried to keep his voice level, but failed. It came out growled, harsh enough that his mother gasped and took a few steps back. But not even that was enough to keep her from trying to get her way.

"You have to come," she insisted. "I wasn't going to tell you because it was meant to be a surprise, but Jean and Scott Wilder are hosting a brunch in your honor. The whole congregation is going to attend."

"Then you can give them all my regards. I'm not going."

"Why are you making this so difficult?" While Fox's frustration was snarled, his mother's was high-pitched and quivering—the kind of tone often accompanied by clenched, trembling fists and thin facial expressions. "Everyone loves you. Everyone is so happy to see you back, and you're treating them like they don't matter."

"So what?" Fox tore his arm away from his eyes and sat up, his temple twitching. It was wrong of him to lash out and he knew it, but he couldn't stop himself. If she would fucking listen it wouldn't have to be so bad, but she wouldn't. She never would. It had been that way since forever, and apparently coming back from war broken hadn't changed that. "So I can show up so I can have a panic attack in front of all your friends? I'm sure Pastor Barton would love seeing me curl up under the pews during worship. Is Jean ready to serve brunch through the bathroom window? Because if you make me go and I break down, I'm going to be locking myself in there and you won't be able to get me out."

"What's wrong with you?" A cloud passed over the sun, stealing the light from the room. With it his mother had looked angelic—her blonde hair lit up from behind like a halo and her white floral dress a billowy dream—but without it, she lost her grace. All Fox saw was anger. "Why can't you make an effort? All we're trying to do is help you feel welcome. No one's going to try to make you do anything you don't want to do."

Guilt. It wrapped itself around Fox's stomach and squeezed, then curled upward until it found his lungs and heart. Fox placed a panicked hand firmly on his bare chest, but not even external pressure was enough to prove to his anxious mind that he was still breathing.

All of this was his fault, wasn't it?

Everything.

With one deep breath after another, Fox tried to override the crushing dread taking over his brain, but it wasn't so easy to shake. His thoughts spiraled. A play-by-play of what he knew would happen unraveled behind his eyelids.

Conversations. So many conversations. Painted faces and prying eyes. All of them would want to tell him the same thing—that he was a hero and that he was brave. Bullshit. All such bullshit. They'd build him into something he wasn't, revere him like he was something he'd never be. None of them would want to listen. None of them cared about the truth. The lies they believed were perfect and pretty, and they'd never let them go.

While Fox struggled to calm himself, his mother went on the attack. "So are you going to get up and join us?"

Pinpricks of pressure pushed against the inside of Fox's eyes. The darkness in his head ballooned, then shrank.

Twenty-eight years old.

He was twenty-eight years old, yet she was still treating him like a child.

One breath. Another. He urged the air to lift him out of the dark place his mind threatened to push him into, but all it did was prove how bottomless the void really was.

"Frederick?"

Fox opened his eyes. The sun had returned. His mother stood by the door, irritation pinching her lips and narrowing her eyes. If he said nothing, he'd topple into the dark place hidden inside of him, but if he replied, he worried the darkness would rise up and swallow him whole.

"I'm not going to church today." Fox let out a stale breath and drew another, coaxing himself away from the edge. "I know that disappoints you. I'm sorry. It's just how it has to be."

"So what? You're not going to go to the Wilder's brunch, either? You're just going to sit in your room all day doing nothing?"

"No." Fox closed his eyes. The darkness was receding, but he knew what a fickle thing it could be. "I'll come to the brunch. I might not stay long, but I'll show up at least long enough to thank the Wilders. Okay?"

There was silence, which was an answer in itself. Then, after a long while where nothing was said, his mother sighed. "I wish you'd reconsider. I know with your... condition... that you're not able to work, but it's not like going to church is hard. All you need to do is sit there and listen. I don't get why you can't bring yourself to do it."

"I know you don't."

"So?"

"You wouldn't understand no matter how many times I explained." Fox looked out the window at the fenced backyard and the monster weeds that grew where the mower couldn't reach. "I'll see you at brunch, okay? Text me the time and the address and I'll be there."

"Fine." She shut the door.

When she was gone, Fox stayed in bed a while longer, his eyes fixed on an unseen point beyond the window while he relived memories he'd never escape. No one would ever understand. Not his mother, not his father, and not any of the well-meaning people in Bulrush.

He was no hero, and it hurt like hell that none of them could see it.

"Why, if it isn't Frederick Fraser!"

A hand collided with Fox's back, knocking him forward. Instinct reared up inside him, and Fox had to fight to keep himself from spinning and incapacitating his attacker—which wouldn't have gone over too well, considering he was in the Wilders' backyard. His restraint proved to be a blessing for Kevin Acton, Bulrush's resident widower. For as long as Fox could remember, Kevin had been living off his wife's life insurance payout, and he doubted that whatever was left would cover a broken arm.

In an effort not to look like he'd been about to throw down, Fox tucked his hands into his pockets and straightened his back. Not that he needed to. Kevin had never been the type of guy who gave a shit about how other people appeared, and by the looks of it, he gave even less of a shit now. With his stained Hawaiian shirt stretched unflatteringly over his beer belly, the lit cigarette dangling between his fingers, and his sparse, messy nest of wiry hair, he looked one couch short of a *Baywatch* marathon—which would have been fine, had it not been for the beady, unscrupulous look in his eyes.

Fox didn't like what that look made him feel, but he minded his manners anyway. "Hi, Mr. Acton. It's nice to see you."

"Nice to see you, too, boy." Kevin scratched the patchy stubble on his chin and gave Fox a once-over like he was livestock yet to be appraised. Ashes tumbled from the end of his cigarette. "Looks like the desert stole your baby face. You see that, Sam? *That's* what a real man looks like. When you graduate, we'll ship you out and man you up just like this."

The Sam in question was Samuel Acton, Kevin's son. When Fox had left Bulrush for basic training, Sam had been seven years old, wide-eyed, and innocent. The teenager he'd become was a far cry from the boy Fox remembered. Sam's brown hair was black now—maybe dyed—and his face had lost its roundness. Like his hair, his wardrobe had gone dark. Apart from his black jeans, which were a little too tight, and his oversized Black Veil Brides hoodie, he wore plain Converse shoes whose white sides had been stained green.

"You think the military could make something out of my boy, Fraser?"

Sam's eyes, tired instead of innocent, dulled. "C'mon, Dad. Don't be like that."

A wraith of a woman Fox didn't recognize passed behind Kevin and tapped him on the back of the head. "Cut the kid some slack, babe. At least he's got ambition."

"To do what? Play video games? Spend his life online?" Kevin shot her a look as she cut through the crowd toward the banquet table. "Women."

When she was gone, Kevin rolled his eyes and shook his head, turning back to Fox like he expected him to laugh along. Fox didn't. Seemingly unperturbed by Fox's lack of support, Kevin shrugged and changed the topic of conversation like nothing had happened. "So, they put you through school while you were serving?"

"No." Fox glanced past Kevin at Sam, who looked like he wanted to escape as badly as Fox did.

"Yet you turned out fine. See, Sam? All colleges are gonna do is steal your money. Fox turned out fine and didn't sink hundreds of thousands of dollars into debt while doin' it. Anyway, it's good to have you back in town, son." Kevin clapped him on the shoulder, causing Fox to flinch. "Good to see one of our own out there and doing something with his life."

"Like Marshall isn't," Sam muttered.

The name took Fox by surprise. "Marshall?"

"Marshall Lloyd." Sam lifted his chin and came out of his shell just a little. "From your graduating class. All the teachers at BHS talk about him. He went out and—"

"Sam, shut it," Kevin snapped. "No one gives a fuck about Marshall Lloyd."

Except that wasn't true, because Fox did. Memories flooded back to the surface. Long hair. Thick-rimmed glasses. Gunmetal-blue eyes. After Fox had stepped in to get Hayden and Peter off his case, Elijah and his little gang of delinquents had lost interest in making his life hell, and Marshall had faded into obscurity. From time to time Fox had passed him in the halls, and every time Marshall had looked at him with wide, earnest eyes, like...

Like...

Fox swallowed and pushed the memory aside. It didn't matter. It'd been weird at the time, and it was weird now. It wasn't worth thinking about. "What happened to him?"

Sam beamed. "He moved to California and made a name for himself in the tech industry. He's worth billions. This week, he's—"

Kevin rounded on Sam and grabbed him by the shoulder, cutting him off with a squeak. Sam's whole body went rigid, which made it easy for Kevin to steer him around and shove him between the shoulder blades, sending him flying toward the banquet tables. "Go get yourself something to eat before you embarrass yourself. We ain't here to talk about Marshall."

Sam didn't fall, but he did have to windmill his arms to keep his balance. When he'd recovered, Sam looked over his shoulder once, mixed emotions rife in his eyes, then shook his head and disappeared into the crowd.

Fuck that. Fuck Kevin. Fox turned on Kevin, ready to grab him by the front of his stupid hibiscus-print shirt, when sense got the better of him. If he started a fight in the Wilders' backyard, his mother would make his life miserable until he found a way to move out. With how slim his prospects were given his condition, Fox couldn't risk it. What he could do was catch up and make sure the kid was okay.

"So, Fraser—"

"You know, I'd love to stay and chat, Mr. Acton, but I've gotta go." Fox offered no further explanation. He cut past Kevin and into the crowd in pursuit of Sam, but like a dream interrupted by an alarm, he was gone. With him went something of Fox's—a feeling he knew was missing, but that he couldn't hope to explain. It was like a hole had opened up inside him, different from the darkness he'd struggled with earlier that morning. It was a lack of something that had once been rather than the arrival of something new, menacing, and endless.

Whatever it was, it wasn't good. If he was going to keep his dignity, he needed to get out before it got worse.

While Sam had disappeared, the Wilders were easier to find. Fox thanked them for organizing the event, then left to sit in his truck, where he thought about Sam and Marshall Lloyd.

Marshall. Shit. It'd been so long ago. At the time he'd been so quiet and broken that Fox had assumed he'd disappear into the world and never be heard from again. It was what had happened to the other guys from high school—and what had happened to him. But the way Sam had spoken made it seem like Marshall hadn't just survived, but thrived.

Had he really made it? After everything he'd been through, he deserved his success.

For all the shitty things he'd done in life, Fox had gotten what was owed to him, too.

He rested his head on the headrest and ran his palm over the leather cover on his steering wheel, imagining Marshall as he remembered him, only grown up, his hair tied in one of those ridiculous buns while he rubbed elbows with Elon Musk and made plans that would shape the future.

For the first time since he'd come back to Bulrush, Fox smiled.

Marshall was an unlikely warrior, but he'd won the battle all the same.

3

FOX

An hour after Fox made it home from the Wilders' brunch, the front door slammed and the sharp click of angry kitten-heeled footsteps hurried their way down the hall. The abrupt noise set Fox on edge, and he flinched and tensed despite his best efforts to remain calm. Those efforts were dashed when his mother knocked three times in frenzied succession on his door, then wrenched it open and stepped into the room. Her face was twisted with rage. "Frederick Michael Fraser, what the *hell* do you think you're doing?"

"What?"

"Oh, don't pretend that you don't know. Kevin Acton told me how rude you were to him—how dismissive." Even through her foundation, his mother's cheeks burned red. Fox had never seen her so angry. "And apparently you said all of five words to poor Jean before leaving? You know better. We raised you better than that."

"Mom—"

"Don't 'Mom' me, mister." She took a threatening step into the room, which only served to spike Fox's pulse. No matter how he tried to calm himself and convince his psyche that there was no threat, he couldn't stop himself from panicking. Trapped, he pressed himself into the corner until his back was flush with the wall. At least there he was safe from two sides. "Your father and I have been doing everything we can to help you feel welcome since you've come back, and this is how you act? I understand that you went through a hard time when you were in service—"

"Shut up." Fox bared his teeth. His head pounded and his heart lodged itself in his throat, where it worked hand in hand with his pulse to choke him. "You need to *shut up.*"

"You will *not* tell me to shut up! I am your *mother!*"

"And I'm your son." Fox fisted his bedding in an attempt to ground himself, but the precipice inside was opening back up, and no matter how he fought for solid ground, the universe was starting to shift. Before long he'd lose balance and tumble into nothingness. "Don't talk about what happened. Don't tell me who I need to be."

"I'll tell you whatever I want, because you need a reality check. What happened was awful, but it's over. You went to therapy and you're home now. You have no reason to keep acting like everyone should pity you. You need to go on and live your life and be a productive member of society. Even if the plane hadn't crashed—"

No.

No. No. *No.*

The universe tilted on its axis, knocking Fox into the darkness.

Shifting pressure. The earsplitting screech of metal pushed beyond its limits. Pain. Pungent smoke. The smell of it flooded Fox's nostrils until it was all he could smell. Scorched hair. Burning chemicals. Fuel.

When he opened his eyes again, he was on his feet and had backed his mother into the hall. Her eyes were wide and her face had drained of color. Unable to form words and terrified over what he'd just done, Fox grabbed the doorknob and slammed the door shut before anything else could happen.

Breathe, he told himself, letting the command echo through his head so it could drown out the voice telling him to fight. *Breathe.*

"You need to leave," his mother uttered from the other side of the door. Her voice was steel—cold and hard, unwilling to bend. "I don't care where you go, but you can't stay here."

Fox squeezed his eyes shut and clenched his jaw, but not even that could keep his lips from trembling. It was his fault and he knew it. The mistake, the crash, the fucking impulses that had turned him from a man into a slave. He wanted it out. All of it. Every last horrifying memory that festered in his mind like cancer. But all he knew how to do was breathe and talk himself down, and even that didn't do shit half the time.

There was no point in saying sorry when it would happen again.

"I will not have you threaten me in my own house," his mother seethed from the other side of the door. "If you're not gone in half an hour, I'm going to call the police."

Tears of frustration leaked from the corners of Fox's eyes, spilling messily down his cheeks. All of this was fucked up and there was nothing he could do to fix it—not unless his mother decided she wanted to listen. It was more likely he'd be hit by a meteor.

When he said nothing, she continued. "When you've decided that you've calmed down enough to come home, then you can come back."

Only Fox didn't think he wanted to.

Ten years ago, he'd left town for a reason. Time had made him forget why, but he had no trouble remembering it now.

While the darkness tugged at his ankles and begged him to come back, Fox gathered the few things that meant something to him and set out on his own.

Behind the wheel of his Chevy, Fox had expected to find solace, but it never came. By the time he'd pulled down the driveway, his palms were sweating so badly he struggled to turn out onto the street. No more than five minutes later, in the heart of Bulrush's downtown district of all places, the inside of Fox's skull tightened. The world wobbled. With an airy gasp and a forced exhalation pushed between his teeth, Fox struggled to fight the pain and stay alert.

He couldn't drive like this. Hell, he could barely see straight. What he needed was somewhere safe—somewhere he could hide and not worry about what anyone thought of him—but without his bedroom to fall back on, he'd run out of options. There was nowhere left to go.

Another second ticked by. The python squeezing his brain constricted again. The world blurred, then sharpened.

Left without a choice, Fox pulled to the side of the street, left his car, and did what he needed to do.

4

MARSHALL

In news that surprised no one, doing nothing in Bulrush was every bit as boring as doing nothing in Silicon Valley. To keep himself from going insane, Marshall spent the first couple of days after the move sweeping up errant sawdust and repositioning his furniture until it looked just right, but there was a limit to how many times he could drag an end table across the room, even in a five-bedroom house. When the art of distracting himself lost its appeal, Marshall left his meticulously swept floors and perfectly placed furniture to head into town, where Main Street was sandwiched by brown brick businesses with old-school awnings that turned the downtown core into a relic of the fifties. Marshall parked not all that far from the local florist's shop, then strolled down the sidewalk to see what had changed.

Not much, really.

The same family-run businesses that had been doing well when he'd left town ten years ago were still there today. Some of the ones that had been struggling had closed—notably Albert Parker's travel agency, the athletic footwear business owned by an out-of-towner Marshall knew little about, and Cristine Larue's women's fashion boutique—but new businesses had arrived to take their place.

Marshall was set to investigate one—a coffee shop called Bean There that reminded him of some of the quirkier businesses in California—when one of the nearby bushes dividing the sidewalk from the street sneezed.

"Bless you," Marshall told the bush.

The bush didn't answer, but it did rustle a little bit, which might have been its way of saying hello.

Perplexed by what was going on, Marshall abandoned his quest to familiarize himself with the changes in town to investigate what was going on. A few passing pedestrians looked at him strangely as he stepped off the sidewalk and into the foliage, but it was their loss. Very few adventures started with sticking to the well-worn path.

The sneezing bush didn't object to being stepped in. It rustled again, then fell still. Marshall smoothed back several of its branches and unveiled its secret—the bush had swallowed a man. Not that Marshall could say he wouldn't do the same if he'd been in its place. From what Marshall could see of him, the man wasn't just a snack, but a whole meal. The main course was composed of a rugged jawline; crew-cut blond hair; a proud, almost hawkish nose; and a narrow but muscular build that suggested he was more than capable of fighting off a man-eating plant. Which made the situation all the more perplexing.

When the man refused to meet his eye, Marshall dropped into a squat and let himself be swallowed, too. That way they both had something in common. "Hey."

No response.

Marshall bit his lip and decided to risk making contact. He had every reason in the world to expect things to go poorly, but if he didn't try, he'd never know. Using minimal pressure, he laid a hand on the man's calf. "Hey?"

The man blinked, but didn't speak.

Perhaps he was being digested.

How unpleasant.

"Um, hey. So. I don't really know what's going on, but I have a feeling you're not in a good place right now, so I'm going to sit here and make sure you're okay until you tell me to go away." Marshall folded into a cross-legged position next to the man, and for a while, they sat in the bush together. No digestive acid rose up through the soil, which was a plus, but Marshall did notice a few other troubling things. For one, the way the man was breathing. Between periods of deep, mindful breaths he was hyperventilating. In conjunction with his refusal to acknowledge Marshall's presence, Marshall figured out what was going on—Mr. Plant Chow was having a panic attack.

Marshall's typically cheerful demeanor sobered. He took a moment to compose himself, then sucked in a breath and committed himself to what his heart urged him to do.

"How about we breathe together?" Marshall asked. He kept his hand on the man's calf, establishing an anchor point. There was no way to tell if it was helping, but Marshall knew it was what he would have wanted were he the one being digested, so he persisted. "I see you trying and you're doing a great job, but we need to take it an extra step. Focus on me and let's get through this together, okay? We'll take it one breath at a time."

Marshall counted out loud to guide his bush-sitting partner through an inhalation, then counted again when he was supposed to let it out. He repeated the process a few times, but it wasn't until his fourth repetition when he heard the man start to breathe alongside him. They sat together in the bush and breathed until the man's shoulders relaxed and his posture loosened.

"You feeling a little better?" Marshall asked.

"Yeah." The man's gaze flitted up to meet Marshall's, and with it came a crashing wave of familiarity that swept Marshall away.

Blue.

Sparkling blue, like the sky on a clear July day.

There'd been a time long ago when eyes like that had lingered in his mind and followed him into his dreams. But it...

It couldn't be.

There was no universe in which Fox Fraser would crawl into a bush and break down. Marshall, sure, but Fox?

No.

It was a pity Marshall's brain didn't share the conclusion with the rest of his body. A tingling sensation swept up his arms and tightened the space between his shoulder blades, and his heart beat like he'd just stepped out of a merger negotiation. At last, after a prolonged moment of silence, Marshall's tongue found the courage to bridge the divide between his mind and body. "Fox?"

"Marshall." Fox sat up slowly while keeping his eyes on Marshall. Worry marred his face. "I... ugh. Fuck, you must think I'm crazy."

"I don't."

"I don't normally hide in bushes."

"I figured."

"I..."

A cloudiness overcame Fox's eyes that set Marshall on alert. Before it could intensify, Marshall pushed past his awkwardness to take control of the conversation. "I know it's probably a little weird for you, but in the grand scheme of things, I climbed into the bush, too. That practically makes it a trend."

Fox blinked. The cloudiness dissipated.

"Besides." Marshall lifted his chin. "There are worse places to hide. Dumpsters, for one. Ask me how I know. Rose bushes, for two. In comparison, this regular bush could be considered luxury accommodations."

Another blink. Then, like the sun creeping out from behind a cloud on a rainy day, the smallest smile quirked Fox's lips.

"So... here we are." Marshall plucked a leaf from Fox's hair and cast it aside. It was a futile gesture, seeing as how the bush had no shortage of leaves to shed on both of them, but doing something helped distract him from the nerve-racking yet simultaneously wonderful way being Fox's object of focus made him feel. "Two guys making bush-sitting trendy. I'm totally fine with sitting here all day long and getting to know all the creepy-crawlies we're undoubtedly bunking with, but if you're getting tired of being fashion forward, let me know. Before this I was on my way to check out the new coffee shop. Not that I drink coffee, but... you know. I live with the delusion that one day I'll find a place that serves a quality cup of tea. If you feel up to it, you could come with me."

There was another lapse in the conversation, but even as Fox's smile faltered, his eyes didn't lose their shine. Whatever he'd been through wasn't over, but as far as Marshall could tell, it wasn't on the verge of debilitating him again, either. That was good enough for now.

"Why are you doing this?" Fox asked when the silence grew too thick.

"Doing what?"

"Helping me."

"Oh." Marshall smiled, and while it was small, he hoped Fox knew it was true. "Well, I may not know what's going on in your life right now, but I do know one thing—no one should have to go through what you're going through alone."

5

MARSHALL

Whatever kind soul had taken it upon themselves to open a trendy coffee shop in the middle of nowhere southern Illinois deserved a medal. Bean There was a nod to the small coffee shops and tea houses Marshall had loved while living on the coast, and the second he stepped inside, he felt at home. From its chalkboard menu with its quirky doodles and tongue-in-cheek selections to the tall chairs and taller tables that populated the sunny floorspace, it was a taste of sleek and efficient modernism in a town staunchly rooted in tradition.

Marshall was enamored.

His love only grew when he noticed the abundance of silver jars lining the shelves beneath the chalkboards, each labeled with a white sticker inscribed with the same meticulous handwriting: *Sakura Cherry Blossom Green; Black Dragon Pearl; South African Rooibos.*

He'd discovered the holy grail.

Bean There served and sold loose tea.

Marshall's excitement simmered into understated anticipation when he turned his head to check on his impromptu coffee shop date. Fox had come in behind him, but he lingered to the side of the doorway, his facial features tight and his posture rigid. When he noticed Marshall looking, he lifted his head in what appeared to be attempted confidence, but Marshall saw his Adam's apple bob as he swallowed lingering emotion.

Tea could wait. There were things more important to tend to.

"Hey." Marshall sidled up beside Fox, his hands in his pockets. He kept his gaze on the menu. "You have any idea what you might want?"

A beat passed. Marshall was about to glance at Fox when he responded. "Not yet."

"No big. I'm not in a rush. Before this, I was literally moving furniture around my house to pass the time." Marshall's lips quirked with the hint of an encroaching laugh. "Besides, I'm not too sure what I want, either. You'll probably end up waiting on me."

Fox made no comment, but his body language changed. The tension in his shoulders eased, and while it was hard to tell from the corner of his eye, Marshall thought he witnessed the beginnings of a smile. Not wanting to chase it away, he scanned the labels on the jars of tea and let Fox process his emotions on his own. It wasn't Marshall's place to ask what had happened, but whatever it was had twisted Fox up in knots. If he was ever going to come undone, he needed time to untangle himself.

After a long minute spent browsing and a curious look or two from the barista, Fox spoke. "I'm ready. You want to go first?"

Marshall shrugged. "I'm paying for both of us, so it doesn't matter to me."

"No, you're not."

"Well, I guess we'll have to see whose card makes it through the machine first." Marshall stepped forward, leaving Fox to follow. At the counter, the barista took their order and made their drinks—a Silver Yin Zhen Pearls tea for Marshall and an Americano for Fox. While she worked, she stole little glances over her shoulder at them, like it had never occurred to her that anyone could want a little caffeine on a Sunday afternoon.

When their order was ready, the barista set their drinks on the counter and gave Marshall a blatant once-over. With a pensive hum, she cocked her head and pushed her brightly painted lips to the side. "You're Marshall Lloyd, aren't you?"

"Um, yep."

She narrowed her eyes suspiciously. "The tech billionaire?"

"I prefer 'destroyer of worlds,' but I guess you're not technically incorrect."

With an indignant huff, she swept a lock of hair behind her ear and crossed her arms over her chest.

"It was supposed to be a joke," Marshall concluded lamely.

"You're *weird*." The barista took a step back and glanced at Fox, then back at Marshall. "What are you doing back in Bulrush, anyway? You've got swimming pools filled with dollar bills back in California, right? That's what everyone's been saying."

"Oh, that's just a rumor." Marshall palmed his cup of tea, which had conveniently been brewed to go. Heat seeped through the protective sleeve and into his skin. "People hear I installed a pool and they get all these outrageous notions in their head. I'd never fill something so big with money."

There was a brief pause during which the barista eyed him suspiciously. "Okay."

"It was much more economical to fill it with rubber ducks." Marshall switched the cup to his other hand and looked the barista in the eyes, keeping up his deadpan performance. "You get more bang for your bill."

The joke did not go over well. Not wanting to strike out for a third time, Marshall apologized by way of a ten-dollar tip, then directed Fox away from the counter.

"Rubber ducks?" Fox asked, half laughing as they headed for the door.

"I thought it was funny. Like a reverse *Duck Tales*. If ducks can dive into gold coins, then I can dive into ducks." Marshall held the door, letting Fox out first. The good news was that as badly as his humor had struck out with the barista, it seemed to have taken Fox's mind off whatever had caused him to shut down. The bad news was that if Marshall knew Bulrush half as well as he thought he did, by lunchtime tomorrow everyone and their mother would think he was actually in possession of a swimming pool full of rubber ducks.

"Do you want to go back to bush sitting?"

"No." Fox nodded toward the street where a silver Chevrolet Silverado was parked. "I'd rather sit in there."

"Oh." Like a balloon that had drifted into a field of cacti, Marshall's daydream met with a violent fate. Fox, who'd been popular and athletic in high school, wasn't his friend. The fact that Marshall had found him in a bush and helped him through a rough time didn't mean that they had any more in common than they had ten years ago. While Marshall had extended the offer, Fox wasn't obligated to spend the afternoon getting buzzed on caffeine, and he certainly didn't have to sit with Marshall while Marshall rambled about nothing and tried not to make himself out to be too big of a fool. Apart from their brief encounter in the bush, there was nothing between them. The silly crush Marshall had harbored in high school wasn't reciprocated, and it would never be. Theirs would be the shortest romance of all.

Boy meets boy (for a second time, but this time in a bush).

One of them is gay.

The other isn't.

The end.

Simple.

But by the way Marshall's heart deflated like the sad balloon who'd gone all-in on a hug with a prickly pear, that ending left much to be desired. If his dick had anything to say about it, the middle could use some work, too.

"Oh?" Fox echoed, snapping Marshall out of his personal pity party.

"I meant… n-oh." Because telling Fox he couldn't go sit in his car was so much better than casually observing it was parked nearby. If

Marshall had been in a conference call rather than a real-life conversation, he would have clawed his face in frustration over the hole he was digging himself into. Fox was looking at him like he was *insane*, which at this point probably wasn't all that far off from the truth. "And by that I mean, 'N-oh problem, you can definitely go enjoy your coffee in the comfort of your own car.' It was, um, it was nice bush sitting with... you."

Fox furrowed his brow. "I thought you said you didn't have anywhere to be."

"I don't."

"Then where are you going?"

The cactus needles skewering Marshall's heart withdrew, and hope pumped a tentative gust or two into its deflated corpse. "I don't know."

"Then come sit with me." Fox lowered his gaze so it was set on the lid of his coffee, but try as he might to hide what he felt, Marshall didn't miss the inkling of vulnerability in his voice. "I don't want to be alone just yet."

In the comfort of Fox's truck, Marshall removed the plastic lid covering his tea and breathed in the steam rising off the top. It carried delicate notes he appreciated—a hint of sweetness, an undercurrent of jasmine, and the tiniest bit of kick. The aroma grounded him much in the same way lavender did, distracting him from the very troubled, very handsome man sitting not more than a foot to his left.

The man Marshall had been crushing on since high school, and the one who'd just invited him into his private space.

No big.

As it turned out, that man had been watching him enjoy his tea. Fox furrowed his brow and fixed Marshall with a quizzical look. "Uh, did you just... huff that?"

"No."

"I'm pretty sure you did."

Marshall gestured at his cup. "Tea is not a thing that can be 'huffed.' I was simply appreciating it."

"Right." Fox plopped back in his seat, knocked back a good portion of his coffee, then let out a withering sigh that was so deep, it'd likely been rooted in his toes. "So what are you appreciating?"

"Silver Yin Zhen Pearls tea."

"In English?"

Marshall chuckled. "It's, um, a white tea. White teas are sometimes a little flavorless, but this one has an earthy taste with some residual sweetness. Some say it tastes like hay."

Fox turned his head slowly and fixed Marshall with a flat look. "You bought a tea... that tastes like hay?"

"It's good. I promise. And it's good for you."

Fox twisted the cardboard sleeve around his cup listlessly. He didn't reply.

"I take it you're not much of a tea guy?"

"No." Fox took another few mindful breaths, then looked Marshall over again. The blues of his eyes washed over Marshall's thighs, then followed the length of his body to his shoulders. By the time they had risen to Marshall's face, Marshall was convinced his cheeks were on fire. The intensity of Fox's gaze was like hot pavement on bare feet, innocuous at first glance, but superheated to those foolish enough to wander across it unprotected. It made Marshall want to squirm. "At least tell me you add milk."

"Are you a heathen?"

"No. I just can't imagine how else I could bring myself to drink hay." Fox lifted a brow, then turned his head and looked out the windshield. Without his eyes boring holes straight into Marshall's soul, the heat was off, and he was able to compose himself. Maybe it would've been for the best if they'd gone back to bush sitting—at least there the threat of spider attacks had distracted Marshall enough to keep him safe from spontaneous combustion.

There was silence after that. It wasn't awkward, but it was thick, and it turned the atmosphere in the truck from lighthearted to serious. Fox was the one to end it, both hands clutched around his cup of coffee and his focus set on a nebulous point in the distance. "I didn't know you were back."

"I got in Friday." Marshall worried his bottom lip with his teeth and traced the edge of his cup's sleeve with his thumb. While he spoke, he followed the zigzag pattern between the layers of cardboard with his eyes. "I spent the last two days cleaning up what little mess was left over from the renovations at my new place and arranging furniture an interior designer spent hours making just right. My mom brought over some groceries the day I arrived, so I haven't been out much. This is the first time I've made it into town."

"I didn't think you'd ever come back."

"Me neither, to be honest." Marshall inclined his head slowly until it hit the headrest. Once there was nowhere else for it to go, he fixated on the safety warning adhered to Fox's sun visor. "When I left after high school, I told myself that I'd never come back for anything, not even to visit my mom. But... things change, I guess. People change." Marshall swallowed the lump rising in his throat and counted down from three, grounding himself in the moment. Memories were destructive, but they couldn't hurt him. All he needed was the strength to acknowledge them and let them go. "It's messed up how you can spend a decade of your life growing into the best version of yourself, yet still feel like you're the unpopular, unwanted loser you used to be. I don't know if I'll ever forget how it feels." Marshall closed his eyes and took Fox's example—he breathed in deeply, drawing it to the depths of his lungs, then released it to a mentally measured count. "But that's why I'm back here. Why I *needed* to come back. I can wake up every day and take comfort in knowing that I'm Marshall Lloyd, the kid who beat the odds and achieved greatness despite adversity, but I don't know if that'll ever make me feel whole. It's like there's this... this gap. It's not front and center, but it's still there, covered in cobwebs and shrouded in darkness, waiting for me to trip up. And sometimes I do." It wasn't like Fox had a reason to care, but now that Marshall had started, he couldn't stop. In an attempt to keep his voice from wobbling, he read the safety warning on the visor again and again.

EVEN WITH ADVANCED AIRBAGS

Children can be killed or seriously injured

"So I'm here to try to close that hole." Marshall's nail caught on the edge of the cardboard sleeve.

The back seat is the safest place for children

Never put a rear-facing child seat in the front

"I don't think that it will ever really go away, but I do think that by confronting it, I can build a support system around it that will keep me from falling in."

Always use a seat belt and child restraints

See owner's manual for more information about airbags

"At least, that's the plan." Marshall cleared his throat and tore his gaze away from the warning. "Which is more than you ever wanted to know, I'm sure. I just... I don't know. I put my life on hold to come back here and work on myself, so I figured that here, with you, would be a good place to start."

Marshall didn't look at Fox. He couldn't bring himself to do it. Instead, he sipped his tea and thought about how big a spectacle he was making of himself. Fox was the one who needed help right now —it wouldn't have killed him to check his baggage at the door for long enough to make sure he was okay.

"Sorry," Marshall muttered. "I guess I needed to get that off my chest. Forget about it. Let's—"

"Don't apologize." The sharpness of Fox's voice was cut by the barest trace of vulnerability, like a steel beam engraved with the faintest floral pattern. Marshall, not sure how to reply, stayed silent. Fox didn't. "People were shitty to you. *I* was shitty to you. That's on them. All on them. If what you feel makes them uncomfortable, fuck them. You deserve to be heard."

It felt like there was something deeper going on, but what it was,

Marshall didn't know. He glanced at Fox—studied the stern line of his lips and the outrage in his eyes—and wondered what else had changed since high school. *Who* else had changed.

"You weren't shitty to me," Marshall finally managed, albeit in a small voice. "You were the only one who cared enough to help me."

"I could have done more. I could have helped you sooner."

"But you helped." Marshall's gaze dropped into the depths of his tea. "That's enough for me." Another few pumps of air inflated his cactus-snuggling heart, and after a pause, he added, "Of all the people in Bulrush I could have found in that bush, I'm glad it was you."

It was meant to have been an encouraging sentiment, but something about what he'd said did more harm than good. Fox slammed his drink into the nearest cup holder on the central dash, then ran his hand shakily through his hair. Hurried, shallow breaths took him over for a moment, then tapered off until they were level. The struggle was one Marshall recognized—a culmination of hopelessness, despair, and fear.

"I don't want you to think I'm a good person." Fox's voice was a low warning, chilling in the same ominous way as fog rolling across a gray lake. "I don't want you to think I'm someone I'm not."

"I don't."

"I'm fucked up, Marshall." Fox scrubbed his face, then dropped his hand onto his lap and sighed. "The things I did… if you knew them, you wouldn't say what you just said."

"I don't think that's true."

"Then you'd be the first." Fox's face hardened, his expression unreadable. "My Flight, this town, even my family… I fucked them all over. All of them. My own mother threw me out. If that doesn't tell you what kind of a person I am, then I don't know what can."

"I don't agree." Marshall set his tea in the cup holder next to Fox's and ran his hands nervously down his thighs. What he was about to do felt crazy, but what Marshall saw in Fox made his heart want to believe there were no coincidences—that he'd come across

Fox for a reason. "If you're so sure it's true, then I want you to prove me wrong. Come work for me. I've got a bedroom to spare and a vacant position for a groundskeeper I need filled."

"What?"

"You heard me." Marshall curled his fingers until the crescents of his nails bit into his palms. "There was a time when everyone told me I was worthless, too—when it felt like the whole world was against me. Look where I am now. You saved me when we were in high school, and now I want to return the favor. Come work for me. Be the best damn version of yourself that you can, no matter what everyone else thinks. Prove everyone who told you that you couldn't that they were wrong."

Wide-eyed shock replaced the desolation on Fox's face. "You're serious?"

"Yes." For a heart with so many holes, Marshall's still beat strong. "You know the old Victorian house off Highway Fifteen? I live there now. Come stop by at three this afternoon so we can get you moved in."

6

FOX

The old Victorian house off Highway Fifteen was a relic of Bulrush's most lucrative days, when the coal mines had brought men—and their money—to southern Illinois. While a mine or two remained and there was still money to be made, the industry had gone to shit, and the most entrepreneurial of the coal-rushers had moved on to other ventures, leaving their houses behind. Most sat empty, too large for modern families and too decrepit for modern renovation budgets. Apparently neither disadvantage was a concern for Marshall Lloyd, who'd taken a building better suited for demolition and turned it into a treasure.

On his drive up the gravel lane leading to the house, Fox took the changes in. The roof had been re-shingled, each chocolate-brown slat positioned with precision to be uniform and watertight. Pale bricks, either blasted clean of grime or newly installed, supported it from beneath. Fox counted no fewer than nine immaculate windows facing the lane. But what was most impressive about the structure was its central tower, which was connected to the main building by its back wall. With its arched windows and crown of ornamental piked iron fence, it demanded attention. If it weren't for the sad, shriveled, partially overgrown gardens which flanked it, it would have looked like something out of a magazine. That, Fox assumed, would be his job.

Great.

Without a clearly designated parking spot to aim for, Fox pulled in next to Marshall's car, grabbed his belongings from the back seat, and left the vehicle. He took a moment to appreciate the house, then glanced across the lawn. The majority of the property was wooded, tucked as it was into the Shawnee National Forest, but what time he'd save on mowing would be spent conquering the creeping ivy that wound its way up the surrounding trees and encroached on the house.

Was Marshall really trusting all of this to him? Apart from the mold he'd cultured on a slice of sandwich bread in science class during freshman year, Fox had never grown anything. Tearing shit up wouldn't be that hard, but trying to make something grow was a whole different story.

While Fox looked on, the front door opened. Marshall, wearing what Fox suspected might be his pajamas, stepped out. He took the stairs at a leisurely jog, then came to stand by Fox. The old house wasn't the only thing that had changed—Marshall was far from the kid he'd been in high school. Sometime in the last ten years he'd ditched his long hair for a stylish shorter style that showed off his jawline and added a much-needed touch of masculinity to his otherwise gentle face. While he was still slender, he'd gained defini-tion, taking him from awkward stick to sleek sophistication. His thick-framed glasses were gone, and while he continued to dress in comfortable clothes, they weren't quite as unflattering as they'd been before.

If Fox was being honest, he looked good.

"Hey." Marshall tucked his hands into the pockets of his sweat-pants. He was barefoot and had only come as far as where the grass met the gravel driveway.

"Hey."

"I'm glad you decided to come. Guess you can see why I need a groundskeeper." There was the perpetual suggestion of a smile on Marshall's face, but as he spoke with Fox, it bloomed. "This is some of what I need help with."

"Some?"

"There's a big section around the back of the house with a patio, a walkway, a pond... and gardens. I think. If you can call them that." He wrinkled his nose. "Right now it's not much more than a mess. It's going to take some full-time work to whip it into shape, especially if we want to do some planting. My mom's already getting her flower beds ready. I don't know all that much about plants, but I assume that there's a window of opportunity."

"I have no clue."

"Then we're in the same boat. Excellent." Marshall rubbed his hands together and took a look at the front garden. "Between the research you'll need to do, the supplies you'll need to pick up, and all the manual work that goes into this... how does five thousand a month sound?"

It sounded like Fox had heard him wrong. Too stunned to accept the offer at face value, Fox cautioned, "Five thousand?"

"It is a little low, isn't it?" Marshall hummed thoughtfully. "We can do six. I figured with room and board, five might be okay, but six is still within my budget. Would that be okay?"

There was a catch. There had to be. Marshall was rich, but he hadn't grown up that way. He understood the value of the dollar as well as Fox did.

So what was his game?

Fox glanced at Marshall's hands, which were hidden in his pockets, then lifted his gaze to read Marshall's face. There was no hint of deception or cruelty in his eyes.

He couldn't be serious, could he?

"Marshall, that's more than seventy thousand dollars a year."

"It's hard work."

Fox wheezed.

He *was* serious.

"Oh." Marshall blinked and pushed his lips to the side. "We can roll medical in, too, if you want."

There was something going on here. Nothing added up. Marshall had swooped into town after striking it big in California, bought a house in the middle of nowhere, and was now offering employment to old classmates he found breaking down in public. There were actual groundskeepers he could've hired for much less than he was willing to pay Fox, whose knowledge of horticulture was limited to an understanding that plants needed water to live, and that most of them were green.

Fox glanced at the wizened garden that framed the house, then looked over his shoulder at the long lane leading to the street. While parts of the house were visible from the highway, there was no way to look into the backyard without entering the property.

By "gardens," did Marshall mean…

"Okay, wait." Fox shook his head and looked back at Marshall. "Before we go any further, what kind of 'gardens' are we talking about? I'm not getting involved with a grow-op. That shit may be on the way to being legal, but I'm pretty sure harvesting it in your backyard will never be."

"Grow… oh." Marshall's eyes widened, and his voice took on an airy, alarmed tone. "No. I wouldn't."

"Then why the hell are you offering to pay me seventy grand a year?"

Realization overtook Marshall's surprise, and his small but cheerful smile returned. He held Fox's gaze for a second, the dark blue of his eyes lightened to near sapphire by the sun. In them, Fox saw what Marshall felt about the situation—or maybe what he felt about Fox.

Patience. Kindness. Understanding.

Then, like it was nothing, Marshall rewarded him with the full version of his sunny smile. "Because everyone should be able to afford to live comfortably from the work they do, and because I can afford it." He nodded in the direction of the backyard. "But before you let yourself think I'm mister generosity, let's go check out what's lurking out back. No grow-ops, I promise—just seventy thousand dollars' worth of labor pulling actual-weed weeds."

The backyard was rough, but not deserving of the salary Marshall was so set on paying him. After they'd scoped it out and Marshall had told Fox what kind of work he'd like to see done, they entered the house through the front door, and Marshall spent the next half hour showing Fox around. The ground floor had been gutted and remodeled, fitted with bright wood and light-colored walls that subverted the traditionally dreary mood most Victorian houses embodied. There was a parlor and a living room—Fox hadn't the faintest clue what the difference was, other than that the "parlor" seemed fancier—a kitchen, a dining room, two bathrooms, and a library stuffed with old books and perfumed by aged paper. Twin French patio doors in the kitchen opened onto a porch facing the backyard from which the back patio could be accessed. When the gardens were cared for and the dead shrubbery was pruned, the view would be lovely. Fox had his work cut out for him.

Upstairs were five bedrooms—one of which had been turned into an office—and another two bathrooms, with a third likely adjoined to the master suite. Fox didn't ask to look. It was Marshall's room, and asking to go poke around felt way too personal.

Fox selected one of the bedrooms as his own, then carried in his belongings from the truck. Despite Marshall's invitation to do otherwise, Fox chose the smallest room, but even it seemed too large for what little he'd brought. He spent a while placing his possessions where it felt like they belonged, then lay on his new bed and reflected on what had happened.

If it hadn't been for Marshall...

Fox squeezed his eyes shut and scrubbed his face.

He didn't want to think about it.

Time passed. The setting sun drenched the room in gold, then amber. Frogs croaked. Birds sang. There was no rumble of nearby engines or skid of wheels on pavement to detract from the surroundings. No aircrafts buzzed overhead. No pedestrians passed outside the window.

Years ago, Fox had thought that he'd spend his career as an Airman and follow opportunity wherever it might take him. He'd envisioned life in the city, the air choked with progress and industry. Fast cars, late nights, and pretty women. All things that would never be.

Marshall's footsteps passed by the door, and a moment later, Fox heard him head downstairs. The muffled sound of his voice rose through the floorboards, then faded into nothing. The house was still and silent again.

By no stretch of the imagination was this what Fox had wanted for himself, but there was a strange kind of comfort in the quiet that he hadn't thought to expect. The house was big enough that he could be on his own without interruption, and Marshall was respectful enough that Fox doubted he'd have to worry about melting down over an unexpectedly slammed door or a confrontation he didn't want to have. Maybe here, in the middle of nowhere, he could do what Marshall had come here to do—piece his shattered life back together.

7

MARSHALL

Fox was a quiet houseguest. On days when he wasn't up with the sun and out and about on the property, he kept to himself, preferring the solitude of his room to Marshall's company. Occasionally they met in the kitchen around mealtime, but apart from polite conversation, Fox did little to engage.

Which was fine.

Marshall wasn't paying him to socialize, and while he was thrilled that The World's Shortest Romance hadn't ended like he'd expected, he wasn't delusional enough to believe that Fox would ever be anything but straight. Sexuality didn't work like that. Marshall had harbored feelings for enough straight men when he was in California to be one hundred percent certain about that.

The only satisfaction he needed was knowing that he was helping the man who'd once helped him... and the prospect of a sweaty, topless Fox toiling in the dirt beneath the late-spring sun.

As altruistic as he was, Marshall was only human.

One week into Fox's stay, the gardens were already looking better. The errant ivy Marshall's landscapers hadn't been able to deal with had met its match—what hadn't been ripped out by the roots was now starting to shrivel and brown. While it did, Fox had begun thinning the overgrowth surrounding the perimeter of the property. Piles of desiccated twigs and branches cropped up near the driveway, only to disappear by the next day.

For someone who claimed he'd never done anything like this before, Fox was doing a great job.

Confident that Fox knew what he was doing and was self-sufficient enough to get it done, Marshall took off late one morning for town. It'd been a few weeks since he'd last worked out, and while Bulrush was too small to have a gym, it did have streets he could jog on. The only downside about living off the highway was having to travel for fitness. Marshall supposed he could jog down the shoulder if he was really in a pinch, but he preferred not to die.

Besides, there were other reasons heading into town was a good idea. Marshall had come back to confront the past, and he wouldn't be able to do it from his safe haven in the woods. If he could bring himself to feel comfortable jogging down the street, then he'd be one step closer to closing that hole inside of him. And so it was that Marshall took to the residential streets, passing by houses he'd once avoided while winding his way steadily closer to the high school. His Bluetooth earpiece chimed as his fitness tracker urged him to pick up the pace, so Marshall bowed his head and went for it. Back in California, he would have used this time to turn whatever issue he was having at work over in his head. There was always something. Botched investments, mismanaged resources, underperforming updates... when his little B2B startup, Luminous, had exploded into a multimillion-dollar business, it seemed he couldn't go a day without something going wrong. Not so in Bulrush, where the biggest disaster so far had been discovering there were no Lucky Charms in the pantry.

Left idle, Marshall's mind wandered. As his soles struck the pavement and his pulse rushed in his ears, he thought of the problem he couldn't fix—Fox—and wondered if his kindness wouldn't come back to bite him in the ass.

Wrapped up in his thoughts, he didn't notice the lone wanderer ahead of him until it was almost too late. Marshall snapped back to reality seconds before collision, cried out in surprise, and dove to the side to avoid impact. His success came at a price. Like an unwieldy lawn ornament caught by the wind, he tumbled onto the nearby plot of grass, where his fitness monitor chimed a few times in exasperation. They'd barely been together for fifteen minutes and it was already sick of his shit.

Startled but not injured, Marshall took a few shaky breaths, then rolled onto his back and sat up. The person he'd almost run over was unharmed. In fact, judging by the curve of his lips, Marshall would hazard that he was amused. "Hi."

"Hi."

Marshall ran his arm over his brow and sank back to support his weight on both hands. From there he looked his would-have-been victim over in full. The kid couldn't have been much older than sixteen, which would've made his untimely fate all the more tragic. He wore Converse shoes, dark-wash distressed jeans, and a too-big band hoodie unzipped to reveal a white V-neck tee beneath. Jet-black hair swooped over one of his eyes, hiding it, but the other was a charming blue emphasized by the tasteful application of eyeliner. In Marshall's high school days, the kid would have been pegged as "emo," but these days that probably wasn't a thing.

When the kid only grinned at him, Marshall supplemented his thin greeting with an apology. "For the record, while there isn't a public safety rule about me being outside, there probably should be. Sorry for almost running you over."

"You're fine." The kid held out his hand. "You're Marshall, right? Marshall Lloyd?"

"Yeah."

"The one with the pool filled with rubber ducks?"

Marshall snort-laughed. He'd called it.

"Yeah." Marshall shook his head and snorted again. God, some things really didn't change, did they? "And who might you be?"

"I'm Sam, Lord of Umbrellas."

"Umbrellas?" Marshall hitched an eyebrow.

"Yeah. I mean, I don't have a swimming pool filled with them yet, but it's on my bucket list." Sam cocked his head and jiggled his hand, which Marshall reached up and took. Once their hands were clasped, Sam helped him to his feet. "Everyone's been saying that you moved back to town. Are you really living here now?"

"I am."

"Why?"

"I have my reasons."

Sam scrunched his nose in dissatisfaction and crossed his arms over his chest, but otherwise didn't call Marshall out on his nonanswer. "That's fine, I guess—we've all got our reasons. You don't have to tell me anything. I know how the town talks." A hint of sorrow marred that last sentence, ending in a half-beat of silence before Sam added, "But just so you know, I'm not like them. I'm like you."

"Like me?"

Sam waved a hand. "Yeah. You know, *like you.*"

The second time was no more elucidating than the first. Marshall furrowed his brow, scrutinizing Sam's face for clues as to what exactly he meant, but came up short.

Sam sighed. "Whatever. It doesn't matter. What matters is that I'm not the kind of guy who's going to go around spreading your business, so you can trust me. Probably. If you want to."

The more Sam spoke, the more Marshall liked him. If there were ever a rift in the time-space continuum, his younger self and Sam's present self would be friends. "Why wouldn't I? Your name precedes you. The umbrella aristocracy has a long, proud history of honesty. To think you anything but would be an affront against one of America's greatest noble families."

Sam blinked, then grinned. With a low bow and a flourish of his hand, he spoke again, this time in an exaggerated British accent. "Indeed. 'Tis an affront that these local cretins fail to acknowledge such a glorious birthright." From his bowed position, Sam looked up at Marshall. He dropped the accent. "But, really, I mean it. So is it cool if I ask you a couple questions?"

"Sure."

Marshall's fitness tracker did not agree. It beeped several times in irritation. If it wasn't careful, Sam would send it to the pillory. Luckily for it, Sam hadn't seemed to notice its disrespect. He righted himself, shoved his hands into the pockets of his hoodie, and launched into a round of questioning. "You went off to Silicon Valley and got really rich doing tech stuff, right? Is it true?"

"It's not false."

The look Sam gave him made Marshall think his fitness tracker wasn't the only one in danger. "So is it also not false that you're not working right now? You're just hanging around town?"

"True."

Sam rolled his eyes. "And you're not like, working on any personal projects?"

"Not in a full-time capacity."

"Okay. So, would you be willing to mentor me?"

The question took Marshall by surprise. "Maybe?"

"You should."

"I didn't say no."

"I'll earn my place by offering you a trade." Sam lifted his chin and thrust out his chest, not that it made much of a difference. "If you can teach me how to program, I'll supply you with an endless supply of awkward sarcasm and other absurdities. And if you act now, I'll even throw in a mystery gift."

It wasn't the first time Marshall had been approached about a mentorship, but it *was* the first time anyone had offered to throw in a surprise for his efforts. "A mystery gift?"

"I can't tell you any more than that, or it wouldn't be much of a mystery." Sam cocked his head to the side, eyes locked on Marshall's with surprising tenacity. "So, what do you say? This is a limited time offer—a once-in-a-lifetime deal. There are only minutes left before yours expires. Act now before it's gone!"

God, the kid was weird. Marshall loved it. "So before I lock myself into a commitment, what kind of low, low price—"

"Hey! I resent that." Sam grinned. "I'll have you know that nothing about me is cheap, thank you. If you need to break this arrangement down into five easy payments, you probably can't afford my superior brand of snark."

Marshall snort-laughed again. "Fair."

"So anyway, what was it you were saying? What's stopping you from smashing that buy button?"

"I wanted to know what I'm getting for my purchase. When you say you want to learn to program, do you mean you've never done it before, or do you have some knowledge that you want to expand upon?"

"The second one." Sam took his hand out of his pocket to check his phone, then put it away again. "I mean, I already know how to code—sort of—and some programming languages, but I want to know *more.* One day I want to do what you did—get out of here and make something of myself. I'll be starting my senior year in the fall, so there's no better time to do it. If I can wow colleges with my extensive knowledge and killer connections, then I can do anything. Plus it means you get to hang out with me." Sam smirked. "Rubbing elbows with a member of the umbrella aristocracy has been scientifically proven to better your health *and* your career."

"Where were those studies conducted?"

Sam rolled his eyes. "Independently owned and operated labs. Duh. Do you think I'm playing games, Marshall?"

Snort-laughs no longer cut it—Marshall burst into laughter. When he composed himself, he held out his hand, palm up. "Give me your phone." Sam narrowed his eyes but didn't otherwise act, so Marshall curled his fingers a few times. "Gimme."

"What are you going to do with it?"

"Save my number to your contacts list. I want you to call me between seven and nine tomorrow evening, when I'll be at home in front of my day planner. We'll figure out a schedule from there."

Sam's eyes widened. "You're serious?"

"As long as you plan on bringing the same snark you are now, yeah."

The phone was unlocked and in his hand before he could finish the sentence. Marshall plugged in his details, then returned it to Sam, who was vibrating with excitement. "I can't believe you said yes."

"I can't believe that after a performance like that you think I wouldn't." Outraged by his lack of commitment to his cardiovascular health, Marshall's fitness tracker powered down. The string of notes as it shut off was judgmental. "If your coding is anywhere near as refined as your sense of humor, I don't know what I'll have to teach you."

"We'll find something, I'm sure." Sam checked his phone once more, dropped it into his pocket, and glanced over Marshall's shoulder. He took a small step back, then another, like he was ready to bolt, but didn't want to end the conversation so soon. "I'll call you tomorrow. I've gotta get back to school."

Marshall followed Sam's gaze, but all he saw were a few teenagers a couple streets down casually wandering in their direction. When he looked back, Sam was already halfway down the block. Marshall called out, "I'll be waiting. See you later."

"See ya." Sam lifted a hand in parting, then darted around a corner and was gone.

Marshall watched the place where he'd disappeared for a few seconds, then shook his head and turned his fitness tracker back on.

Lord of Umbrellas. He snorted.

With a mind like Sam's, he could only imagine what the "mystery gift" could be.

8

FOX

The smell of char. Sweltering heat. The crackle of fire as it consumed something that popped and spat. A scream rent the darkness, crisp with anguish that twisted Fox's heart and churned his stomach—then silence that did even worse. Heart in his throat, Fox tried to launch himself from where he was sitting, but failed. Thick nylon straps locked his body in place. They would not come undone. The scream of frustration that longed to rip itself free from Fox's lungs died in his throat, choking him. The grunt that emerged in its place was barely more than a whimper.

It wasn't enough.

Would never be enough.

Move, Fox urged himself. *Get out. Get the **fuck** out.*

But no matter how he struggled, the straps would not let go.

The crackling drew closer. Bitter smoke weighed down the air. Fox gritted his teeth until they scraped and strained, pushing forward with every ounce of strength he possessed, but there was nothing he could do. Heat swept forward. Sweat pearled on his brow and soaked into his eyelashes, stinging his eyes. Fox panted for breath, but it felt like every new lungful left him all the more starved for air.

This is where you die, Fox thought. *This is where it ends.*

The sensation of flame. Panic. The foul smell of his own fear.

Although he couldn't see it happen, the darkness swallowed him. It would never let him go.

Fox woke up in Bulrush screaming, his mind six and a half thousand miles away.

9

MARSHALL

A scream pierced the night, startling Marshall from his sleep. For a while he lay still and silent, focused on the rapid-fire beat of his heart while wondering if the noise had been real or imagined, when it happened again.

Fox.

Marshall threw off his blankets and sprang out of bed, but by the time he'd made it to Fox's bedroom door, Marshall's mind had poisoned his good intentions. If he barged into Fox's bedroom, then what? It wasn't like they were close. Fox wouldn't latch on to him for comfort and break down, and it felt just as unlikely that he'd open up. All invading Fox's privacy would do was make things more weird than they already were. He couldn't force Fox into trusting him. All he could do was show Fox that he was there—that he wasn't so alone.

Marshall rested a hand on the doorframe, struggling over the decision. His heart demanded he act, but his rational mind urged him to let Fox be the one to take the first step. There was no rushing recovery. Not for Fox, and not for himself. It had taken him years to find the courage to come back to town, and even then it had been a difficult choice. Who was he to force Fox to confront what he wasn't ready to face?

There came a low, tormented groan from the bedroom followed by one last scream. Marshall squeezed his eyes shut and let his heart override his mind, but as he raised his fist to knock, the bedsprings creaked. Bare feet hurried for the door. Marshall barely had time to step away before it was thrust open and Fox spilled into the hallway. He stumbled a few paces, then rushed to the bathroom. The door closed. A second later the taps squeaked and water began to run.

Marshall let out a breath and tucked his arms over his chest. An uneasy feeling gripped him. He lingered in the hallway for a short while, listening to the water run, then shook his head and made his way back to bed. When Fox was ready, he'd let Marshall in on what was going on. Until then, Marshall would wait.

Morning came. Marshall's alarm went off, but he didn't feel rested. With a yawn, he stretched out and worked the sleep from his limbs, then climbed out of bed and brushed his hair back from his face. Not bothering to dress, he stumbled into the bathroom to relieve himself, then headed down to the kitchen in his pajamas to start a pot of coffee. Most mornings he tried to stick with a green smoothie, but today he went straight for the Lucky Charms. Screw it. The spinach waiting in the vegetable crisper could wait. If he was going to make it through the day, he needed something magically delicious.

Fox came in through the back doors while Marshall settled on the couch with his box of cereal. He thudded around in the kitchen for a while, but came to a complete halt when Marshall started rustling the cereal bag. Marshall didn't let the attention stop him. If Fox wanted his Lucky Charms, he was going to have to wrest them out of his cold, dead, potentially clover-covered hands.

Fox poked his head into the living room. "Marshall?"

Anticipating breakfast sabotage, Marshall shoved the box under his shirt. "Yes?"

Fox squinted at him. "What are you doing?"

"Nothing. Definitely not harboring leprechauns."

"Right." Fox stepped into the room and leaned against the doorframe. Work had started early today—the knees of his jeans were caked in dirt, and a fine sheen of sweat set his skin aglow. The same sweat that turned him into a sun-kissed god caused his t-shirt to cling to his body, showing off his muscular frame. Marshall, who'd tensed preemptively in anticipation of a cereal thief, loosened. Fox was fucking gorgeous.

One boy is gay. The other isn't, Marshall desperately reminded himself. *He's straight, Marshall. **Straight.** Don't you dare catch feelings for him.*

Unfortunately for Marshall, feelings were tricky things which, unlike leprechauns, allowed themselves to be caught from time to time. These ones in particular relished it. A blush crept across Marshall's cheeks. It was like being back in high school and admiring Fox from afar, only worse. Furtive glances from across the hall and steamy daydreams where Fox pushed him against the lockers and did excessively inappropriate things paled in comparison to the Fox who stood before him now.

The one living in his house.

Working for him.

Marshall swallowed hard and shifted his thighs, hoping—and likely failing—to hide the stirrings of an erection he was ashamed to have. What was his problem? Fox needed a source of support, not a pillar of perversity. It was, frankly, rude of his dick to have become involved.

If Fox noticed his change in flaccidity, he didn't mention it. "Is that a box of cereal under your shirt?"

"Maybe."

"Are you eating it straight from the box?"

"Maybe."

Fox scrunched his face. "And you call me a heathen."

The joke was enough to snap Marshall out of his embarrassment. He laughed. "Hey, don't knock it until you try it. I'll have you know that dry cereal is about a thousand times better than soggy cereal. I'll take out of the box over in a bowl any day of the week."

"Uh-huh. You keep telling yourself that." Fox folded his arms over his chest, and although he smiled, there was the glimmer of something more serious in his eyes. "If, uh, you decide you're not interested in eating cereal the wrong way, would you have a second to talk?"

The box was out from beneath Marshall's shirt and on the coffee table in an instant. "Sure. What's up?"

"Did I wake you last night?" Fox scratched the back of his neck and dodged Marshall's gaze. "I, um, I was pretty loud, and I know the walls aren't the thickest."

Marshall bit the inside of his lip, unsure of what to say. On one hand, acknowledging what had happened might stress Fox out, but on the other, shrugging it off felt dismissive. Peopling on normal mode was hard enough, but doing it on little sleep while Fox was on the verge of opening up to him required superhuman skills Marshall just didn't possess.

Met with silence, Fox's lips twitched, and he lowered his chin. "I did, huh?"

"I wasn't going to bring it up. It's not a big deal."

"For now, sure, but what about tomorrow?" There was an empty quality to Fox's voice that voided his grittiness and broke Marshall's heart. Unsure what to do, he rose from the couch and took an uncertain step toward Fox, only to stop when Fox lifted his eyes and locked them on Marshall. Frustration burned at their core. It was like Fox was trapped in his own mind, his meaning muffled behind layers of armor his brain had erected around itself without Fox's consent. "What about next week? Next month? Next year? Don't tell me you bought a house in the middle of nowhere so you could be woken from your sleep by a man who can't get a grip."

Marshall took another step forward. "Fox—"

"It's bullshit."

Another step. "Fox."

"I don't understand why you let me stay." The frustration in Fox's eyes burned out all at once, like his mind had discovered the source of his insurgency and stormed its stronghold to shut it down. What remained was hollow, tired, and drained. "Not even my own parents could put up with me for more than a week. But you... you..."

One more step. Marshall stood in front of Fox, so close the smell of cut grass and geosmin from Fox's clothes and skin flooded his nostrils. So close Marshall witnessed the rise and fall of Fox's chest as his breathing veered toward panicked.

"Why?" Fox asked in the thin, breathless way of a man teetering on the edge of composure. "Why are you doing this? You don't owe me anything."

"That's not true."

"Bullshit. That's *bullshit*, Marshall, and you know it."

Last night Marshall had been too wrapped up in his own head to step in when Fox needed him, but here in the daylight, face to face, he had no such hesitation. Chaotic energy crackled and sparked in the air between them, but as unpredictable as it was, Marshall didn't fear it. All through high school he'd lived never knowing what might come next—whose fist might slam into his gut, or when, or where, simply because he was different—but now, faced with that same uncertainty as an adult, he refused to back down. It held no power over him.

This was what he'd come back to town to face, to overcome, and to conquer.

He wouldn't let Fox suffer in silence.

Not like he had.

Never again.

Daring to act, Marshall did the unthinkable—slowly but surely, he lifted a hand and brought it to Fox's cheek. The second their bodies connected, the chaos radiating from Fox dissipated. His shoulders slumped and his anxious tension left his body. Like a lion whose paw had been freed of its thorn, he mellowed for Marshall, and they spent a moment suspended in time, the only proof the world still turned the way they both drew breath.

At last, Fox closed his eyes and pressed his cheek into Marshall's palm. "They told me it would get better."

"It might."

"I don't believe that." Fox opened his eyes and looked at Marshall from beneath partially closed eyelids. Another feeling took the place the chaos had once occupied—chemistry. Goosebumps spread down Marshall's arms, and while his heart remained broken for the man before him, its pieces rallied to establish a frenzied beat. "Do you really think you can handle me? Do you really want me to stay here, as broken as I am?"

"Yes."

"You're crazy."

Marshall chuckled, but there was little humor in it. "I've been called worse."

Fox slotted his hand over Marshall's and took it from his cheek. He held on to it a moment longer than necessary, then crossed his arms over his chest and looked aside. "I might hurt you."

"You haven't yet."

"Don't be dumb. You're better than that. What you're doing is the same as letting a pit viper stay in your house because it hasn't struck you yet. You know the damage it can do. You know its nature. Marshall, screaming in my sleep isn't the worst I might do. If things get bad—"

"Then we'll deal with it when it happens."

Fox looked at him from the corner of his eye. Curiosity flickered in his gaze, but so did something far more difficult to pin. Something sharp, and wild, and dangerous.

Something that made the pieces of Marshall's heart yearn all over again.

"You're making a mistake."

"And it's my mistake to make." Every one of Marshall's instincts urged him to make his move now—to show Fox that he cared, and what he wanted—but the old narrative played in his head in nauseating repetition.

Straight. Straight. Straight.

Fox shook his head. "Fine. I told you. You can't say I didn't."

"Fox..."

"I need to get back to work." Fox moved past Marshall back through the doorway. He lingered there like he might say something else, but in the end kept his silence and left through the patio doors. Marshall stood where he was for a while longer, processing the conversation and the rampant emotions turning his head into a war zone. At last, he returned to the couch and plucked the box of Lucky Charms from the coffee table.

If Fox wanted to leave, he could, but that wasn't what he wanted. The broken part of him needed Marshall to push him away like everyone else had—to prove to what little was left of his confidence that he was the monster he made himself out to be. Marshall wouldn't let him think that. He knew what that voice was like, and he wouldn't feed it. Instead, he opened the cereal box he clasped between his thighs and poked through it for the marshmallows, which he ate without milk, thank you very much.

If Fox didn't like it, he could suck it.

Straight. Straight. Straight.

Except for the part of Fox that was shattered and jagged. The part that cut him, and everyone around him, by virtue of its being.

The part that time would wear smooth until it turned from jagged edge to gaping hole.

With a trying sigh, Marshall found a few more marshmallows and sank down to enjoy them. The sugar was much needed. If he was going to make it through to this afternoon's mentoring session with Sam, he needed to get Fox off his mind, and that called for all the sugary distraction he could get.

10

FOX

Dirt crumbled beneath the force of Fox's gloved hands as he ripped another vine from the ground. The effort shimmered on his forehead and burned muscle-deep, but still wasn't enough. Gritting his teeth, he yanked harder, dislodging more stubborn roots and unearthing portions of the vine previously buried. With a final jerk and an aggressive grunt pushed through his teeth, the vine snapped. Fox cast the refuse aside, drew a shaky breath, and dropped to his knees to search for what remained.

Throwing himself heart and soul into tending to the garden was all he could do to keep his mind off what had happened.

Off the look in Marshall's eyes.

Fuck.

Fuck all of it.

Fox grabbed the remnants of the vine and kept pulling. Dirt lifted and crumbled. Roots met the surface. The creeping ivy hadn't just consumed the surface of the property—it had wormed its way into its core, invading what couldn't be seen. Fox needed it out. All of it. Every last root. If he left even an inch, it would bide its time where no one could see, gaining strength until it was whole again and the lawn was consumed once more.

He couldn't let it.

Didn't want to feel it.

Wished he'd never felt anything at all.

Why the hell was he always such a jerk? The vine uprooted the rest of the way, and Fox tossed it into the pile with the rest. The young man he'd been before the crash... was he still there, buried and suffocating beneath the weight of what had happened? Fox didn't know anymore. The gardens of his soul were so overgrown that it was impossible to see.

All he knew was that whether that version of Fox was alive or dead, who he'd become didn't deserve Marshall's affection.

Fox found another vine of ivy and tore it viciously from the ground. All of it was a mess. If he could just *talk* to Marshall—hell, to anyone—maybe things would be better, but every time he tried, he shut down. The words wouldn't come. The reality of the situation and his emotions surrounding it choked him. The weeds rooted deeper.

Yet there was Marshall, on his hands and knees, digging through the overgrowth like it wasn't too late.

Like he knew Fox was still there.

A feeling gripped Fox's heart, raw, intense, and demanding. It swept through him like a monsoon, drenching every inch of his awareness with its presence.

After all he'd said and done, Marshall hadn't given up on him.

The feeling squeezed, and Fox's veins warmed from the tips of his fingers to the recesses of his heart. From somewhere deep within, the young man he'd lost long ago breached the surface and gasped for air before disappearing once more.

Disconcerted, Fox spent the rest of the morning at work and baked under the sun until he could no longer feel the kindness of Marshall's touch on his cheek or in his heart.

The doorbell rang while Fox was in the kitchen, his head under the stream of the kitchen faucet while he attempted to cool off. Fox jerked back from the sink and checked the time on the stove. It was three in the afternoon. Marshall hadn't mentioned that they were expecting guests.

When the doorbell rang a second time, Fox turned off the water and went to see who was there. The lock on the front door was stiff, and in the end, he had to push the door inward to get it to budge. It looked like Marshall's renovation crew hadn't replaced all of the old house's quirks.

On the front stoop stood none other than Sam Acton. He wore a zipped black hoodie and a tight pair of jeans, and—if Fox's eyes weren't deceiving him—eyeliner. There was an umbrella-shaped something tucked under his arm. Whatever it happened to be was hidden from view by shoddily assembled rubber duck wrapping paper. There were bits of tape everywhere, including several places on Sam's hoodie.

"Uh." Sam looked at Fox, heavily confused and slightly nervous. "Hi?"

"Hi." There was an awkward pause. "Can I help you?"

"Yeah. Is, um, is Marshall home?"

As far as Fox knew, Marshall had gone upstairs to do whatever it was that tech billionaires liked to do in their free time. Maybe fight crime. Fox hadn't thought to ask. After this morning's bout of emotional diarrhea, he figured Marshall wouldn't tell him, anyway. No one confided in assholes. "He know you're coming?"

Sam's brow furrowed. "Uh, yeah? Look, can you just go get him? I'm—"

"Sam!" Marshall called from deeper in the house. Fox glanced over his shoulder to find Marshall on his way to the door. "I was just booting up a couple programs. We're gonna start with some gamification to see where you're at, then take it from there. You ready to show me what you got?"

Fox, who had no idea what was going on, stepped aside. He

would have left had it not been for the fact that Marshall was blocking the doorway leading from the antechamber into the house. While he stood there, Sam entered the antechamber and continued the conversation. "Heck yeah. But first"—Sam extended the parcel toward Marshall—"your mystery gift, straight from the vaults of the aristocracy."

"I'm honored."

"As you should be."

Weird.

Fox tucked his hands into his pockets and watched the conversation unfold, not one hundred percent sure what he was looking at. The Sam on Marshall's doorstep was leagues away from the Sam he'd met at the Wilder's brunch. Plus there was the whole eyeliner thing. If Kevin knew about it, he sure as shit didn't like it... which, come to think of it, might explain why he'd been a royal asshat the one and only time Fox had seen him since coming back to town.

"Fox." The mention of his name snapped Fox back into the present. While he'd been reflecting on Kevin, Marshall had steered the conversation his way. "You remember Sam, right? Kevin Acton's kid?"

"Yeah. I'm familiar."

"He's going to be coming around every now and then." Marshall waved the gift-wrapped umbrella ceremoniously at Sam. "I offered to mentor him. We'll be working on coding, programming, and other suitably nerdy endeavors."

"The nerdiest," Sam confirmed.

"I'd wanted to tell you that he'd be coming over beforehand, but it kept slipping my mind."

Big fucking surprise after what had happened earlier that morning. Fox nodded. He figured the conversation was over and that Marshall and Sam would head to Marshall's Bat Cave, but to Fox's surprise, Marshall kept the conversation going. "Do you want to help?"

"What?"

"Help." Marshall rolled his hand like he was struggling to find the right words. "You know, with the mentorship."

"I don't know shit about coding."

"You know about other things." Fox stared blankly at Marshall. Marshall, apparently immune to disbelief, shrugged. "I was thinking it might be a good idea if Sam got a well-rounded education."

What was he getting at? Fox glanced at Sam, wondering if he was in on this, to discover he was just as mystified. Before Fox could reply, Sam held up a hand. "Uh, wait a second. Not that I don't appreciate what you're doing for me and all, but I'm pretty sure this limited-time offer was made to include programming and coding only."

Marshall shrugged. "Limited-time offers have all kinds of bonuses thrown in for free. Ultimately, it's up to you and Fox."

No pressure.

Fox glanced at Sam. The kid was scrawny—not much bigger than Marshall had been when he was in high school—and based on his style, probably just as much of an outsider. Fox hadn't liked the way Kevin had pushed him around, and if what he'd seen was to be believed, it was closer to a norm than an exception. Shit like that needed to stop.

"Sure." Fox locked eyes with Sam. "Go nerd it up with Marshall. When you're done, you'll be training with me."

Sam paled. "Training?"

"Self-defense." Fox slid his hands into his pockets. It was a bold move to offer his help when he felt so fundamentally helpless, but it felt right—like by doing this, he could repent for not having stepped in to help him before. "I'm going to teach you how to hold your own. You'll appreciate it when the other kids decide to single you out for trying to make something of yourself."

"I'm not going to go around busting kneecaps and breaking noses," Sam squawked.

"Yeah. That's right. You're not. Self-defense isn't about that.

What we're going to focus on is how to keep other people from doing that shit to you."

If Sam turned any paler, he'd disappear. "Sure, I guess."

"Then it's settled." Marshall smiled at Fox in a small but pleased way. A jolt of satisfaction shot through Fox, sating a hunger within him he hadn't known existed. It made him want to make Marshall smile for him like that again. "I'm going to go grab my laptop from upstairs and get it set up in the dining room. I figure we'll get to work there. Fox, can you show Sam in?"

"Yeah." When Marshall left, Fox nodded at the door leading from the tower antechamber into the house. "C'mon, kid. Nerd lessons await."

"It's not nerdy to know how to program," Sam mumbled. He followed Fox through the door and into the house. "It's a life skill."

"Right up there with fire starting and navigating by starlight, I'm sure."

"Hey!" Sam jogged to fall into place at Fox's side, his cheeks puffed with anger. "Can it, okay? What are you doing here, anyway?"

"Groundskeeping."

"What?" Sam squinted like he hadn't quite heard. *"Groundskeeping?"*

"Yup." There was a moment of silence, during which they arrived in the dining room. Fox turned to face Sam and let him know they'd arrived in the promised lands to find Sam gawking at him. "What?"

"Groundskeeping," Sam muttered in disbelief. "Marshall really does have his life together."

It took a second for Fox to clue in to what he was inferring. Sam thought he and Marshall were...

"No." Fox narrowed his eyes, but even as he put on his tough guy act, an inexplicable thrill lifted the hairs on his arms and raced through his heart. Adrenaline. Possession. Pride. It was the same feeling Fox had sometimes fed into after besting the guys in his Flight at deadlifting, or when he shaved time off running a mile, and while he couldn't explain why he felt it, he relished it all the same. "It's not like that."

"Hey, you don't need to explain." Sam held up his hands, but there was a shit-eating grin on his face that irked Fox all the same. "It's not my business. I'm sure you do excellent *groundskeeping*. I hear it's honest work, getting dirt—"

Sam stopped abruptly, and soon enough the reason became clear —Marshall had entered the room. He had his laptop tucked under his arm, its power cord around his neck like a boa. His gaze flicked between Fox and Sam. "I feel like I missed something."

"Nope." Sam stepped around the table to help Marshall set up, leaving Fox by the door. "Everything is totally normal. There's absolutely nothing to worry about."

Marshall plugged the charger into the wall. "Why am I not convinced?"

"Just... nothing." Fox shook his head. "You two dorks get to work. I need to go back to what I was doing. Sam, when you're done, meet me outside."

"Sure. See ya later." Sam gave him one last curious look. "And... thank you. I think."

"Yeah, yeah." Fox waved a hand dismissively as he left, but on the inside, he was smiling. Could all of this turn into a shitshow? Undoubtedly. But right now it felt good, and Fox wouldn't let it slip through his fingers because of a few what-ifs. "Later."

On his way out, he heard Sam whisper, "So what's the story? Are you like... you know? Together?"

Fox didn't get to hear Marshall's response, but it didn't matter. Even if Sam spread rumors high and low that he'd witnessed Fox bend Marshall over the kitchen counter and bang his brains out, nothing would change. The town could think what it wanted. What Fox was doing he did for himself, and that was all that mattered.

11

FOX

"Eyes up."

Sam jerked his gaze from his shoes to Fox's face, but his expression lacked the conviction Fox wanted to see. It was closing in on five o'clock, and while the day was still bright, Sam was fading fast. After a fifteen-minute warm-up so light Fox barely thought it counted, his charge looked ready to throw in the towel.

"If you shrink away from your attacker, you've already lost the fight." Fox broadened his stance, modeling proper fighting posture for Sam. "The second they see fear in your eyes or hesitation in your actions, they'll know they have the upper hand. *Never* back down, even if all you're going to be doing is bolting the second you get a chance."

"This is dumb," Sam muttered, but he mimicked Fox's body language regardless. "If someone's going to bully me, they're going to come for me whether I stand like a normal person or if I look like I'm about to pop a squat. If I make eye contact, they're only going to come after me that much faster."

"No, they won't. Not if you don't let them see that they have the upper hand." Fox eyed Sam's attempt to brace himself for combat. It wasn't bad, but it could be better. The kid was lacking stability. To fix his stance, Fox tapped the inside of Sam's shoe with the toe of his work boots. What should have happened was a little shuffling of feet and maybe a few grumbled words, but that wasn't what ended up happening—Sam leapt back and windmilled his arms like Fox's foot was made of cockroaches that might, at any second, take flight.

His stance went from passable to nonexistent.

This whole mentorship thing was off to a great start.

"What the heck was that?" Sam scowled. "You kicked me!"

"I tapped you with the toe of my shoe."

"Foot-to-body action is the definition of a kick. You can't fool me."

Fox's temple twitched, but his temper was short-lived, because in the next second, Sam tore off his hoodie and cast it aside, then resumed his stance. It was improved.

"Next time can you use your words if you're gonna get up in my personal space?" Sam lifted his arms to protect his face, just like Fox had taught him. "I don't like unexpected contact, okay? Even 'taps.' I know you're Mr. Tough Guy and all, but if we're going to be working together, we need to be on the same page."

The "kick" had been so small that if Sam hadn't seen it coming, he likely wouldn't have felt it, but Fox wasn't going to argue. "Sure."

"Good. Thanks. Now, am I doing this right?"

He wasn't, but he could be soon enough. Fox spent the rest of the afternoon guiding the kid through several basic exercises. For now, they'd focus on a few key principles—awareness, confidence, and posture. All three were things Sam could use help with, and it was easy for Fox to point him in the right direction. By the time they were done, Sam was a sweaty mess. Eyeliner had smeared in the corners of his eyes and his t-shirt was stained dark at the pits. He looked several seconds away from falling over. But, despite it all, there was a glimmer of determination in his eyes that hadn't been there before. Fox hoped like hell that it stuck.

"Next time I'm bringing a change of clothes," Sam muttered to himself as he fanned his t-shirt.

"You're gonna want to. Next time we'll be moving on from the basics. You might actually get a workout."

Sam glared. "You're saying this wasn't a workout?"

"Nope. Not by a long shot."

"This isn't boot camp."

"Doesn't need to be. You're training under me. I'm not going to let you step out into the world unprepared."

With a grumble enriched by ample amounts of sarcasm, Sam grabbed his hoodie and slung it over his shoulder. When he was done complaining, he nodded at Fox. "Duly noted. Marshall asked me to come back next week, so I guess I'll see you then."

"Hold up."

Sam froze. "Yeah?"

"Your, uh, makeup." Fox swiped a finger across the corner of his own eye to demonstrate. "It's smudged to shit. You should probably wash it off before you head home."

Sam winced. "God, that would have been a disaster. I almost forgot."

"I figured." With a nod at the house, Fox led the way to the porch and beyond it to the French doors leading into the kitchen. It wasn't like him to pry—lord knew he hated it when people did it to him—but after seeing what he had at the brunch, he felt a sort of duty to ask. "Your dad not know?"

"No," Sam admitted miserably. "I usually only wear it at school or when I'm gonna be out of the house for a while. One time he found a dead sample-sized eyeliner pen I'd buried in the bathroom garbage and it was bad. I think the only reason he didn't fly off the handle was because I was able to convince him that I had a girlfriend, and that she was the one who tossed it in the trash." With a roll of his eyes, Sam opened the door for them. "Like girls are the only ones who wear eyeliner. He doesn't get that times are different than when he was a kid."

Or that Sam was different, Fox mused as they stepped into the kitchen. He let the thought die. None of them were normal.

Normal, he was beginning to think, wasn't an attainable state of being.

When the door was closed, Sam cleaned up as best he could in the sink, then dried his face on a clean dish towel Fox had procured from a nearby drawer. When he was finished, he looked somewhat like a raccoon who needed a good night's sleep, but insomniac raccoon was much less incriminating than spurned-prom-queen-in-the-rain. If Fox had to guess, he'd be fine.

"People don't get that things change," Fox offered by way of explanation while he tossed the used towel in the sink. He'd take care of it later. "More than that, they don't like what isn't like them. It scares them. No matter where you go or what you do, you'll find that 'us versus them' mentality. It's part of the reason why I think even though you hate it, self-defense is a good idea."

Sam wrinkled his nose. "I never said I hated it."

"Your body language did."

"Yeah, about that? I know Shakira said that hips don't lie, but I'm pretty sure that's BS. My body didn't like that it had to do things other than play Fortnite, but I understand why you and Marshall think it's important for me to do this. I don't mind it. I'm going to complain the entire time, but I'm grateful you'd take time out of your day to do something decent for me." Sam tucked himself against the counter, his hands braced on its edge so his fingers curled beneath it. "I wasn't expecting anything like this, to be honest. I didn't even know you and he were, uh, *groundskeeping.*"

Fox rolled his eyes. "We're not."

"Look, I'm not going to say anything. Of all the people in town who could have found out you guys were living together, I'm probably the one who cares the least. I'm not going to spread it anywhere, either. I know what it's like." Sam awkwardly scratched the back of his neck. "I think it's really encouraging that you guys are back in town, you know? I heard rumors that Marshall used to be bullied because he was gay, and when I heard he'd come back, I didn't understand it, but"—Sam glanced shyly at Fox, then looked away—"I think I get it now. People do crazy things for love."

"It's not—"

"I mean *groundskeeping*." The sarcasm was palpable. When Sam was done rolling his eyes, he shook his head. "It's fine. If I could, I'd have a guy groundskeeping for me, too."

What was he supposed to say to something like that? Fox opened his mouth to speak, then closed it again. No one had ever come out to him before. The whole gay thing... it wasn't really his bag. Was he supposed to make a big deal out of it, or not mention it all?

Before he could make a fool of himself, Sam yawned and pushed off the counter in the direction of the front door. "I've gotta get going. It'll start getting dark soon and it's gonna take me a while to walk home."

"You're walking?"

"Yeah."

"I'll drive you."

Sam squinted at him. "You sure? You don't have to. While my legs will probably be jelly tomorrow, they're working okay right now."

"It's fine. I need to haul the weeds I pulled today to the dump before it closes, anyway. I can drop you off on my way."

"You mean you don't burn them illegally like everyone else around here does?" Sam wiggled an eyebrow. "I see you take your *groundskeeping* seriously."

To Fox's relief, the conversation wasn't any more awkward than it had been before. Sam was still Sam—awkward, good-natured, and delightfully strange. "Oh my god."

Sam snickered.

If this was how the mentorship was going to go, it was going to be a *long* summer—but groundskeeping and all, Fox got the feeling it might not be such a bad thing.

It was dark by the time Fox made it home, and the house's large windows were lit up from the inside. One of them had yet to be curtained, revealing Marshall's ridiculously large living room with its plush sectional couch, sleek modern coffee tables, and wall-mounted monster of a television. It was the kind of living room plucked from the pages of a magazine—the crowning achievement of a pearl-clutching Martha Stewart housewife who lorded her superiority over her guests with artfully arranged *amuse-bouche* and *canapés.* Only it belonged to Marshall Lloyd, who was about as likely to host a dinner party as he was an angry, pitchfork-wielding mob.

Somehow, despite how strange it was, it fit Marshall to a T.

Fox was about to leave the truck and head inside when Marshall, wearing fuzzy socks and pajamas, slid dramatically into the living room. He clutched a wine bottle in one hand. As Fox watched, he arched his back and outstretched one arm while using the other to hold the bottle to his mouth like a microphone. Whatever music he was singing along to had to be high energy, because in the next moment he was on the move again. Fox watched in silence as he slid back and forth across the living room, busting out one dorky, outlandish dance move after the next.

Fox would never admit it out loud, but it was kind of cute.

As the show went on and Marshall got into his performance, a smile took root on Fox's face, growing until it was so large his cheeks ached. The way Marshall fanned his arm and worked his hips, wiggling to the beat like a misguided middle schooler trying in all the wrong ways to impress a girl at his first dance, was so heart-felt and true to who he was that Fox couldn't help it. He crossed his arms on top of his steering wheel and rested his chin on them, watching Marshall be a total goof while having the time of his life.

What a difference ten years made.

Or was it just that none of them had ever given Marshall a chance to come out of his shell?

A pang of guilt clenched Fox's heart, but it was quickly super-seded by something far brighter—hope. Hope that Marshall, as damaged as he had been, could continue to rise above his past and shine—and hope that someday, he might be able to do the same.

The show ended a few minutes later. After the last pose had been struck, Marshall secured the bottle between his knees and struggled with the cap. Figuring there wasn't anything left to see, Fox sat up straight and went to open the door when Marshall flailed and landed on his ass. The bottle of wine remained locked between his knees, upright and in one piece. The cap had come off, but it didn't look like a drop had been spilled.

Fox snorted.

Unperturbed by his clumsiness, Marshall rescued the bottle from between his knees, took a quick swig, winced, and bounded to his feet. He disappeared from view.

"Dork," Fox mumbled affectionately. "You really are something else, aren't you?"

Marshall, of course, didn't reply. Not only did a few walls and doors divide them, but he was off on some other adventure—either terrorizing their wine glasses or boogying in the kitchen.

Marshall's wine glasses, Fox realized with a jolt. They didn't belong to him.

Before that little slip could wreak too much havoc on his psyche, Fox left the truck and headed for the house. Missy Elliott—of all artists—was playing when he got inside. Marshall, who was in the hall on his way back from the kitchen, stopped in his tracks and looked at Fox with wide eyes. Then, initial shock bleeding away, he laughed. "You've got great timing. If you'd have come home a minute sooner, you would've caught me butchering early two thousands classics."

"Oh?"

"Luckily I got it out of my system." Marshall wiggled an eyebrow. "For now."

Where there'd once been guilt was now warmth. Fox tucked his hands into his pockets and cocked his head slightly to the side, taking Marshall in. Not only was he still wearing his fuzzy socks, but he was dressed in oversized sweatpants and a threadbare t-shirt with a cracking *Space Jam* graphic. The look wasn't meant to be flattering, but Fox thought he was handsome like that, dressed-down and beaming with happiness.

A moment passed. A tingling sensation joined the warmth in Fox's chest, teasing the hairs down his arms into standing up straight. It was almost like...

Fox smiled.

There was no sense in complicating things. It was what it was. Marshall was a vibrant person, and it was a joy to spend time with him.

That was all.

The song changed. Fox's ears perked. He lifted an eyebrow, put on his best smirk, and said in time with the music, "Music make you lose control?"

Marshall's grin couldn't have been brighter. "Music make me lose control."

"Let's go."

On cue, Marshall darted out of the hall and into the living room, sliding to a stop in the middle. As he danced artlessly, Fox joined him—albeit with more talent and rhythm—and they broke it down in the most outrageous ways they could until Marshall was laughing so hard, he was crying. That night, after their dance party was done, Fox joined Marshall on the couch for a movie instead of shutting himself in his room. For the life of him, Fox couldn't remember what they watched, but he'd always recall the way those few hours had made him feel—the way *Marshall* had made him feel—like he was worthwhile, and that life after the crash wouldn't always be so bad.

MARSHALL

"You're doing it wrong." Fox sighed and nudged Marshall out of the way. They stood in front of the barbecue on the back patio that adjoined the porch, overlooking Marshall's extensive property. Over the last few weeks, Fox had successfully uprooted the creeping ivy and tilled the garden beds both out front and in back. While his primary focus had been making sure the front yard was presentable, the back didn't look bad—and it would look even better once Fox got the vegetable gardens he'd been talking about up and running.

Unfortunately for Fox, not even the promise of fresh-picked produce could save him from the grievous mistake he'd just made. Nope. Marshall was the man with the tongs, and that meant he was King of the Barbecue. When Fox went to commandeer his scepter, Marshall clicked it at him furiously.

Fox laughed. "What? Are you serious?"

Click click!

"Marshall, gimme the tongs."

Click click click!

"C'mon, crabman. You're about five clicks away from eating carbon for dinner."

"They're not going to come out that badly!" Despite his protestations, Marshall surrendered his tongs. "I researched how long to cook them and everything."

"You sure it was tips on cooking steaks?"

"Yes!"

"Not tips on how to perform at-home cremations?"

"Hey!" Marshall elbowed Fox playfully in the ribs. "If you're so confident I'm doing it wrong, why don't you cook them?"

Fox shrugged like it was no big deal, but the hint of a grin in the corners of his lips gave him away. He moved the steaks from the perfectly valid place on the grill Marshall had put them to a different place, like that would help. "My job's planting the gardens, not cooking your dinner."

"*Our* dinner."

"Which is the only reason why I'm stepping in to save it." Fox took a literal step closer to Marshall, his head cocked slightly to the side and the tongs held loosely in his hand. The way he held himself was confident and cocky, and as the distance between them shrank, the tension between them increased. A shiver plunged down Marshall's spine, and his lungs tightened as the air became charged. Excitement rolled over in his gut, stirring his dick enough that Marshall felt guilty.

Straight, he forced himself to think through the haze of utter want. *He's straight. So straight rulers are jealous. He's—*

Fox leaned in close—close enough that he had to hear the pounding of Marshall's pulse. Marshall swallowed nervously and glanced at Fox's lips, then lifted his eyes to meet Fox's gaze. The steaks could turn to ash and he wouldn't care—not when twin rings of blue perfection held him captive like they did.

"I can do all kinds of things, you know," Fox muttered into the scant space between their lips. "But all I'm being paid to do is garden. Guess you'll never know all my secrets, will you?"

In an alternate universe, it was at that very moment that Fox slid a possessive hand around the back of Marshall's head and kissed him until their lips were bruised. Five minutes later he'd drag

Marshall to the wicker couch on the porch, push Marshall onto his knees in front of it, and sit with his legs spread while Marshall greedily sucked his cock. In the dreary cocktease of a universe they actually lived in, Fox lingered near Marshall's lips for another few moments, then stepped back and shoved the dirty plate Marshall had used to transport the steaks from the kitchen into his hands. "You're going to need a clean one so we can bring the steaks inside. Get it for me while I babysit our dinner."

Marshall made a show of rolling his eyes and muttering under his breath about his unfair treatment, but he went about doing what Fox had asked regardless. With the way his heart still raced with notions of what could never be, anything else was impossible.

The steaks turned out medium-rare, which Marshall thought wasn't all that bad considering he knew as much about cooking as he did astrophysics. Marshall served them with green beans and sautéed mushrooms, which he thought turned out great considering that the vast majority of what he'd eaten in California had either come from an app or a microwave. For his first foray into cooking, it was a success.

To his great pleasure, Fox seemed to think the same.

"I'm impressed," Fox admitted as he speared another mushroom. "After the debacle with the steak, I thought for sure your crowning culinary achievement was Lucky Charms straight out of the box."

"I resent that."

Fox raised an eyebrow as he chewed. "Yeah?"

"Yeah." Marshall lifted his chin. "I'll have you know that I can make mac and cheese out of the box at least half the time without burning it."

"I had no idea I was in the presence of a Master Chef."

"It's a lot to process, I know." A grin cracked Marshall's face. "I figured that if I didn't start to teach myself how to cook real food,

I'd get tired of all the processed, readymade meals I've been relying on since coming back to town. I forgot that Postmates isn't a thing here. I used to order out all the time when I lived in California."

"You miss it?"

"The food, the place, or Postmates?"

"Surprise me."

"I miss the food." Marshall pushed a green bean around on his plate, trying to sort through his feelings about having left one life behind to come home to another. "There was this one place near where I lived—Let Us—that served the best salads I've ever had in my life. It was all local organic produce and dressings made in-house. They had this veggie wrap there that was probably laced with crack. It was what I lived on for a good week or two one quarter. God, I would've committed crimes for that thing. And the sushi? Don't even get me started."

Fox scrunched his nose. "Gross."

"*What?*"

"Raw fish." Fox speared his steak and sawed off a piece, like eating cow was any less horrifying than eating tuna. "I can do cooked, but raw? No way. Humans started cooking for a reason."

"Yet you were the one complaining about my charred steaks."

"Hey, beef is different."

"Keep telling yourself that." Marshall took a second to make sure he hadn't pushed Fox too hard, then shrugged. "But you're allowed to not like fish just like you're allowed to be wrong."

Fox almost choked.

Marshall continued on about California without missing a beat. "But when it comes to the place? To be honest, not so much. I liked it well enough and I'm proud of what I accomplished while I was there, but I needed to work on me, so I came home."

In the time it took Fox to clear his throat and recover, the tone of the conversation had changed. Lighthearted banter bled into serious discussion, and Fox acknowledged it by looking Marshall in the eyes. "Not many people who went through what you did would dream of coming back."

"I'm not many people." Marshall smiled. "At least, that's what I like to tell myself."

Silence descended on the table. Fox set down his utensils with care, gentle enough that they didn't clink. He must have felt what Marshall did—that any extraneous sound would burst the moment, deflating it from something taut and powerful into a limp mockery of itself. It made what Fox said next all the more impactful. "You're not."

Imagination was a powerful thing. It had seen Marshall through lonely nights and given him hope for what the future would hold. But, as encouraging as it could be, it wasn't always kind. Right now it tried its best to convince him that Fox meant more by those words than he was willing to let on.

Heat rose up Marshall's neck and crept beneath his jaw. If he wasn't already red-faced, he would be soon.

What was that about rulers, Marshall?

If Fox noticed his new firetruck-esque complexion, he didn't mention it. "Do you feel like it was worth it?"

"Yes." Flustered as he was, Marshall spoke with confidence. "I didn't think it would be, and for a while I was on the fence about coming back at all, but I'm glad I did. I don't think I'll ever forget the bad memories I have of this place... but the good memories I'm making now help take the sting away."

There was a chance that Marshall's heart would beat so hard, it'd leave his chest to start its solo hip-hop career. What he'd wanted to say was that the memories he'd made with Fox stripped his high school nightmare of its power—that bush sitting and hay drinking and their impromptu nineties dance party had made his life so rich, he wasn't sure he'd ever want to leave—but fear kept him from saying it. Instead he looked into Fox's eyes and hoped the emotion translated.

By the way the hairs on Marshall's arms stood on end and his chest tightened with feeling, he thought it might.

Straight. Straight. Straight.

"I, um, I think I'm done eating." Marshall gestured lamely at his plate, vaguely aware that he had to look like a game show model with a killer case of stage fright. "I'm gonna put my leftovers away. Do you want anything?"

"No."

But judging by the look in Fox's eyes, Marshall didn't think that was true.

There was a glimmer there not sated by food or drink—a want that simmered inside of him in a place he couldn't reach. While Marshall didn't know what it was, it was clear that it existed. If Fox wanted it gone, he'd have to figure out what it was and act on it. There wasn't anything Marshall could do to help him with that, but damn if it didn't make his heart race all the same. It was too easy to believe that look in Fox's eyes—that hunger and need—was because of him.

13

FOX

Frothing toothpaste spilled from the corner of Fox's mouth, and he had to jut his neck out to keep a glob of it from landing on his chest. The excess splattered in the sink, where Fox rinsed it away. As it swirled down the drain, he rinsed the trail it had made from his lips and jaw and looked at himself in the mirror.

A hint of stubble. Baggy eyes. And there, beneath his exhaustion, a sparkle of something he hadn't seen in a long time—happiness.

Fox finished off his bedtime routine with some mouthwash, then crossed the hall to his bedroom, where he settled between the sheets and reflected on recent events. If someone had told him three years ago that he'd be living in Marshall Lloyd's creaky old Victorian house and loving it, he wouldn't have believed them. Then again, if someone had told him that Marshall Lloyd had a guilty pleasure for early two thousands hip-hop and was an avid bush sitter, he wouldn't have believed them, either. In a few short weeks Fox's life had been turned upside down, and he couldn't honestly say he wanted it flipped back around.

A few hesitant raindrops struck the roof. Fox closed his eyes and listened to their patter. April through May was stormy season—the time of year when tornadoes were most likely to wreak havoc. The temperature wasn't right for them tonight, but before the season was through, Fox figured he'd find himself bunkered down in Marshall's basement while winds whipped outside. No doubt Marshall had already outfitted the place with Bluetooth speakers so they could jam to something classic while the world crawled to a stop around them. If Fox was lucky, he'd break out the Lucky Charms and they'd pick the marshmallows out together before curling up to sleep, Fox with his arms around Marshall, keeping him safe from the storm.

It didn't have to be gay.

Not really.

Marshall had been through shit in high school, and while he was older now, he still needed protection. Fox had let him down when they were kids—he wouldn't make that mistake again.

That was all.

It wasn't like he was actively pursuing Marshall. Even if he was, what would it have mattered? Marshall was brilliant, hilarious, and quirky. He made Fox smile, which was more than he could say about his family or any of the friends he'd lost since joining the Air Force. It wasn't wrong to like someone who made him feel good. If anyone wanted to make a scene, Fox would shut that shit down. No one would fuck with Marshall. Not ever again. It didn't matter if Marshall liked men—Fox would stand up for him no matter what.

The rain came down faster. Fox listened for a while longer as it pinged and pelted the roof, then rolled onto his side and gazed across his darkened room. No sooner did he than his phone lit up, stripping the darkness from his surroundings. Fox winced, then picked the offending device off the bedside table and narrowed his eyes into slits so he could read the screen. A new text message had arrived.

It was from his mother.

Mom: Honey, I'm sorry

Fox's stomach clenched. What did she think she was doing? It'd been weeks since he'd left home and just as long since they'd last spoken, but even now thinking about what had happened at home pushed Fox toward panic. At the time he'd blamed himself for his inexcusable behavior, but now that he was in a safe space, he'd begun to change his mind. Yes, he'd acted out, but he'd been clear about his boundaries and she had overstepped every one of them. If it hadn't been for Marshall, who'd shown Fox what respect was like, he might not have seen it. It was easier to blame himself than it was to blame his parents, but that wasn't always the right thing to do. It certainly wasn't right when it came to this mess of a situation.

Another text arrived.

Mom: I didn't mean to chase you away. All I wanted was to see you get better. It wasn't healthy living the way you were. I wish you'd understand.

A cold sweat broke across Fox's brow. He shoved his phone back onto the bedside table and closed his eyes, but not even the space behind his eyelids was safe—the darkness lit up red as another text arrived. What was her goal? Nothing had changed. It'd been weeks of silence, and now this? If she'd really been concerned about his safety and wellbeing, she would have said something—anything —before now.

She wouldn't have let him leave.

Familiar dread settled in Fox's bones. He opened his eyes and picked up his phone again, telling himself he wouldn't read what she had to say. All he needed to do was dismiss the text, put his phone on silent, and call it a night. No one was forcing him to reply. When he was rested and had come down from what he was feeling, he'd be able to handle the situation then.

If only life worked that way.

The message preview sat on his lock screen, taunting him, and as dread churned into rage, Fox had no choice but to read it.

Mom: I don't know where you are now, but you need to come home. Pastor Barton says he can get you a job in town if you want. We know you're still here. People have seen you driving around and they've been asking where you are and why. Won't you come home, baby? We can help you.

Fucking *liars*. None of them cared. None of them wanted to help him. The only reason why his mother had reached out was because people were talking, and to admit she'd demanded her veteran son leave her house and not return would reflect poorly on her. Or maybe, Fox thought bitterly, it wasn't a poor reflection—it was a crystal-fucking-clear truth about who she was that she didn't want people to see. If she'd listened to him and respected the fact he was fighting a battle she couldn't see, none of this would have happened, but no one but Marshall had wanted to listen. No one gave enough of a shit to try to be sympathetic. The in-house doctors on the MEB had told her what to expect and she'd *still* managed to fuck it up.

And she was his mother.

His *mother*.

Why should he expect any better from the community?

Why should he give any of them one more second of his time?

The godawful sound of enamel scraping against enamel rang in his skull—he'd started to grind his teeth. Before his stress got the better of him, he needed to calm the fuck down, and the only way that was going to happen was if he disengaged. With a rattling breath, Fox turned his phone screen down and focused on letting go of his emotions. As he did, the storm receded, its patter diminishing to a few wayward plinks followed by silence. No insects chirped. No frogs croaked.

Quiet.

Then, through the thin walls of the old Victorian house, Fox heard Marshall. It was muted and distant at first—a muffled noise barely distinguishable against the nothingness of the night—but it wasn't long before the sound took shape. Marshall was humming along—badly—to one of the songs they'd danced to a few nights back while he headed down the hall. Before his voice faded into nothing, he stopped abruptly and snort-laughed, then took the stairs at a jog. After that, Fox didn't hear him anymore.

Quiet resumed.

After all the shitty things that had happened to him since the incident, one good thing had come along, and its name was Marshall Lloyd. Fox focused on the memory of his voice, the stupidly cute tone-deaf way he'd butchered their dance party playlist, and the way his sunny smile was always a little brighter when it was meant for Fox. After all the darkness he'd been through, Marshall was his guiding light.

This was where he belonged.

Fox blinked away stinging tears and picked up his phone. It was a hard realization to come by, but just because it hurt like hell didn't mean it was wrong. Standing in the flame wouldn't make him immune to fire—it'd only eat him up until there was nothing left. If he ever wanted the pain to stop, he had to distance himself from its source.

> **Fox:** I know you think you're helping, but I'm not ready to try to fix this. One day I will be, but until then, please respect that I need space. I'll come to you. I promise.
> **Mom:** All we want is to see you happy.
> **Fox:** Then all you need to do is respect me. I love you and Dad, but I need to love me, too. When I'm strong enough to work this out, you'll be the first to know.

There was nothing else to say. Proud of himself for not being a total dick, Fox returned his phone to the bedside table and let out a final, grounding breath. Not every day would feel this way. His skin was still blistering, but one day his burns would heal. While he might never fully recover, there'd come a time when he'd be whole enough to try to fix his toxic relationship with his parents. Until then, he had to be patient with himself and with others. If they cared, they would wait for him. The way Marshall treated him proved it.

Marshall.

What was he doing right now, anyway? Fox pulled one of his pillows into his arms and buried his face against it, imagining Marshall rocking a pair of earbuds as he danced solo across the living room floor to the songs of their childhood. With his hair mussed and his mismatched pajamas sitting awkwardly on his frame, he was no Beyoncé, but he didn't need to be. Marshall was attractive because of who he was, not how he looked, and Fox wasn't afraid to admit it. Girls called each other hot all the time, after all. It was normal to appreciate other people. There was nothing weird about that.

Except for the goosebumps.

The chills.

The way Fox smiled a little more when Marshall was in the room.

If Marshall had been a woman, Fox would have said he was crushing hard, but that was ridiculous. Men could be attractive—Fox had eyed a few guys in the showers and during PT—but he'd never actively *felt* for any of them before. Nothing beyond brotherhood, at least.

But there was nothing brotherly about Marshall or the way he made Fox feel. Maybe he did have a crush. It wasn't like it mattered. Whether he liked Marshall or not, who Fox was didn't change.

So what if he liked men?

So fucking what.

That night, as he came down off the stress of distancing himself from his mother, Fox imagined what it might be like to have Marshall there in bed with him, his lean body safe in Fox's strong arms and his lips Fox's to take with one breathtaking kiss after another. It didn't take long for Fox's cock to get in on the fantasy, stiffening and twitching in anticipation of someone it badly wanted.

Fox rewarded it with his fist, jerking off to thoughts of Marshall with his face buried in the pillows and his ass in the air while Fox pumped into him from behind.

It was sexy as hell, and new, and exciting, and Fox couldn't get enough.

He stifled a guttural moan in his pillow and came hard and fast into his hand, but even after, thoughts of Marshall remained. His laughter, his smile, his quirkiness... all of it stuck with Fox even after his dick had had enough and confirmed what he'd thought to be true. He had a crush on Marshall Lloyd. And if, one day, the opportunity presented itself to take things further, Fox didn't think he'd be able to resist. Marshall was the one he wanted, and with so few good things in his life to call his own, Fox would take him, and Marshall would be his.

14

MARSHALL

Late spring flirted with early summer. Marshall occupied his days with trips to his mother's place during which he sipped tea and loved on her orange tabby cat, Pete; mentoring sessions with Sam; and guilty peeks out the back windows while Fox got hot and sweaty in the backyard. Now that the vegetable gardens were planted, Fox had switched gears and started work on revitalizing the neglected koi pond. Over the last few weeks he'd replaced the shoddy liner, installed a filtration system, and cleverly masked the machinery with a rock border that would look timelessly beautiful once he got the whole thing up and running. As if that wasn't enough, he'd taken it upon himself to replace the rotting boards on the bridge spanning the pond and sealed the wood against the elements.

The man was working for his money, which was all kinds of admirable—but all work with no play had, at one point, turned a fictional man into a homicidal maniac, and Marshall wasn't keen on finding out if the same could apply to real life. Since his lessons were already planned for Sam's next visit, the rest of the morning was wide open, and he decided he'd spend it causing trouble—

namely, hanging out with a shirtless Fox by the koi pond and being a distraction.

Fox, who'd been scrutinizing the depths of the recently filled pond, lifted his head as Marshall approached. "Hey. You here to crack the whip on my lazy ass?"

Marshall sneaked a look at the ass in question—which looked hot as hell in Fox's worn work jeans—and cleared his throat. "It depends on if you'd like it."

"Perv."

"You started it."

Fox grinned, which Marshall both found surprising and not that surprising at all. Over the last few weeks there'd been a change in Fox—subtle, but present. Where before he'd been serious and stoic, he'd started to lighten up. Marshall liked to think it was because Fox was finding the pieces of himself that he'd been missing that day in the bush, but it was more likely because they'd started to adjust to living with each other, and Marshall was no longer the stranger he'd once been.

What did surprise Marshall, however, was the way Fox tucked his hands into the back pockets of his jeans, drawing attention to the ass in question. God, was it a sight. The way he cupped himself and pulled the denim tight made it seem like he *wanted* Marshall to look, which was ridiculous.

Hot—*way* hot—but ridiculous all the same.

There was no way the not-gay character in his boy-meets-boy story was flaunting his fine ass for Marshall's viewing pleasure. Marshall was the World's Biggest Perv for even thinking it. Fox's accusation hadn't been all that far off the mark. But god, the way he held himself and the glimmer in his eyes, like he was *daring* Marshall to say something...

No.

Nope. No way.

Marshall steeled himself to Fox's accidentally seductive ways and lifted his chin. He was a man of dignity and honor, and while he'd ogle his hot groundskeeper in secret, he wasn't about to eye-fuck him in the middle of a conversation. To do otherwise would be rude.

Thankfully for boys both gay and not, Fox changed the topic of conversation. "Why don't we pick up this debate some other time? There's something I need your help with. Do you have a second to spare?"

"Um, yeah." Perfect. A distraction. It was about the only thing that would put Marshall's dick back in line when Fox continued to cup himself for reasons unknown to god or man. "What's the problem?"

"It's something you need to see. I'll show you."

Fox led Marshall onto the bridge and dropped to his knees, pointing at something in the water—and by "something," Marshall was pretty sure he meant "nothing." He was no pondsmith, but to his untrained eye, everything looked fine. "Um, okay?"

The eye roll he received would have put Sam to shame. "You've gotta get down on your hands and knees to see it. It's at the very bottom of the pond, and it's not too big. You need to get in close to see it."

What the hell kind of problem could there be that was that small? Marshall shot Fox a wary look, then dropped to his knees and scanned the depths for signs that something was wrong. Was it the liner? The rocks? The pump? Marshall squinted, scrutinizing every inch he could find, but came up short. "Okay, call me crazy, but I'm still not seeing anything. Laser eye surgery might have fixed my vision, but no one's invented a laser to cure obliviousness yet, so you're gonna have to help a guy out. What am I looking for?"

"You don't see it?"

"No."

"Right at the bottom." Fox pointed, his finger hovering right above the surface. "It's right there."

Apparently laser eye surgery had fixed Marshall's vision to the point where he saw a different version of reality, because there was nothing where Fox was pointing. Frustrated, he leaned over the water to get a better look, narrowing his eyes into slits.

"You're still not seeing it?" Fox asked.

"No."

"Oh. I guess that's because it was a trap."

"What?" At least, that was what Marshall tried to say. What he actually managed was, "Whahh!" which was the sound all tech billionaires made when their stupidly hot groundskeepers splashed them in the face with water. Following his graceless serenade, Marshall topped his performance by launching himself backward with such force that he fell on his ass. Stunned to breathlessness, he wilted onto the bridge and stared at the cloudless sky.

Fox had tricked him.

Him.

The one who'd come out here intending to cause trouble.

Water dripped down the sides of Marshall's face and soaked into his hair, and as it did, he barked out a laugh. "Fox, what the hell!"

"Told you my ass was being lazy." There was the sound of splashing water, which prompted Marshall to scramble to his feet. Fox was poised by the edge of the bridge, his hand dipped below the pond's surface. "The lawn's already been cut, the plants have been watered, and I even know what kind of torture I'm gonna put Sam through next time he comes over. What else is a guy to do but start shit? By the way, you have three seconds to find safety before it's all-out war. Three... two..."

Safety?

Please.

Marshall dove for the edge of the bridge as Fox reached "one." He wasn't fast enough to avoid the ensuing splash, but as Fox soaked his side, he fed his hand into the water and retaliated. Glistening drops of warfare clung to Fox's chest and darkened his now reasonably lengthy blond hair. Marshall only had a second to appreciate how fucking gorgeous he looked before Fox cackled with laughter and bolted across the lawn toward the house, leaving the pond and its bridge in his dust.

"What?" Marshall called after him. "You're giving up already? Some fight that was."

"Please." Fox stopped just short of the French doors and stooped down, fishing up the garden hose. "It's only just begun."

"Shit!" A jet of water striped the back of Marshall's calf as he hightailed it across the lawn to the nearest plastic garbage can. He wrenched the lid off in passing, then bolted around and faced Fox with his newfound shield. "Wouldn't you rather go jogging?"

"Why jog when we can have a water fight?" Fox let loose a torrent of water aimed at Marshall's chest, which burst across the surface of the garbage can lid. The spray misted Marshall's arms. "Tell me your heart isn't racing right now."

"It is."

But not for the reasons Fox thought.

The playfulness, the laughter, the light in Fox's eyes…. god, what Marshall wouldn't do to keep it forever.

While Fox inched to the side, looking to strike, Marshall followed him carefully with his shield. They circled each other until Fox changed direction suddenly, and in response, Marshall swept around and forged forward with a battle cry. He deflected one last jet of water, then cast his shield aside and tried to grapple the hose out of Fox's hands. Fox laughed and locked himself in for a fight.

Sleek muscle flexed beneath Fox's sun-kissed skin. Their hands collided, brushed, and met. Water dripped from the handle of the hose, soaking their fingers and slicking their grips, until Fox pulled a little too roughly and the hose went off. Its nozzle was pointed upward between the two of them, but the worst of its icy blast struck Fox. Marshall didn't waste his opportunity—he yanked the hose away and let loose a hollering cry of victory.

Victory didn't last long. A second later, Fox tackled Marshall and pinned him to the ground.

"Wrestle you for it," Fox growled as he grabbed Marshall's hose-carrying hand. Marshall barely noticed. Their faces were way too close—closer than they ever should have been, even with Fox on top of him. All it would take was a single slip for their lips to meet. High-school Marshall had dreamed of this moment, and adult Marshall was so stricken by it that he almost relinquished his grip.

Almost.

It was too bad for Fox that Marshall wouldn't let a set of off-limit lips keep him from water fight supremacy. "Try me."

Fox chuckled darkly and wove their legs together, then used his newfound leverage to hold Marshall in place while he pried his fingers off the hose one by one. Needing to do something—anything—to knock him off, Marshall bucked and squirmed, only realizing his mistake when his cock started to stir.

Judging by the way Fox's eyelids drooped, he wasn't the only one who'd realized what they were doing.

Straight, a breathy voice whispered as it shriveled and died in the back of Marshall's mind. It was too weak to stop him from rolling his hips again, grinding their soaked cocks together. *So straight...*

Straight enough that Marshall could have sworn that Fox bucked back, grinding his cock into Marshall's needy body.

The hose fired again, shooting a stream of water across the lawn. Marshall couldn't have cared less. He pushed into Fox, craving the pressure their bodies created and needing the friction against his aching cock. It was blatant, but Marshall had no shame. Not anymore. If Fox didn't want it, he could climb off.

But Fox didn't move.

With a low, lusty moan, he pushed back.

Straight, the voice in Marshall's head wheezed. *Don't...*

The scrape of stubble against his jaw. The touch of lips on the corner of his mouth. Marshall's heart, pounding to the point of near explosion, took over from the voice in his head and cried, *Kiss him!*

Fox didn't give him the chance. He let Marshall go and grabbed him by the wrists, pinning them over his head. Marshall drew in a breath and closed his eyes, ready for Fox to crush his lips in a fierce kiss, when there came a gasp from across the lawn. *"Marshall?"*

Both Marshall and Fox froze. The hose tumbled from Marshall's hand.

His mother had come to call.

15

MARSHALL

Oh fuck.

Double fuck. My-mom-walked-in-on-me-about-to-bang-the-groundskeeper kind of fuck.

At least, Marshall mused as Fox rolled off him and scrambled to his feet, they both still had their pants on—although with the way the soaking wet fabric clung to the outlines of their erections, it wasn't much better than being nude.

To his mom's credit, she didn't look fazed by their water-fight boners. While Fox helped Marshall to his feet, she held back a laugh and politely averted her gaze. "Um, should I leave you two alone?"

"No!" Marshall cleared his throat and tried to sound less like a teenager who'd been caught mid-act and more like the adult he often pretended to be. "Of course not. It's fine. You remember Fox, right?" Marshall gestured at Fox in the hopes he might provide a distraction, hopefully not of the penile variety. "Frederick Fraser?"

Fox lifted a hand in a quick wave. "Hello, Mrs. Lloyd."

"Hello, Fox." She sounded cheerful enough, but Marshall was sure he heard a note of uncertainty in her voice. "Marshall, hon, are you sure I shouldn't go? It was rude of me to stop in unexpected. I should have realized..."

"No, Mom. You're fine." Marshall scratched the back of his head. "It's not what it looks like. Fox is my, um, sort of like my groundskeeper, I guess. I hired him to care for the property and plant the gardens. And, um, well I mean we're friends, too, but... but not like that."

"Right."

"We both had the day off today, Mrs. Lloyd," Fox offered. "We were just being boys."

Being boys? That was one way to put it. But if boys had acted like that when Marshall had been in high school, he might never have left town.

The amused look on his mom's face suggested she was thinking the same thing. "Please, call me Elizabeth."

Fox stepped forward and shook her hand. "Of course. It's nice to meet you, Elizabeth."

If there was anything hotter than Fox dry-humping him into the ground, it was seeing him be a gentleman to his mom. Marshall hid his approval, figuring it'd blow their "being boys" story out of the water. To distract himself, he focused on the something that would keep his brain out of the gutter—their unexpected visitor. After all the times she'd entertained him since he'd come back to town, it was only fair he do the same.

"Do you want to come in for tea, Mom?" Marshall asked. "Fox and I will need a second to change since we just ended The Great Awkwardly Timed Water Fight of 2019, but after that neither of us have plans. It'd be nice to sit and talk for a while."

"Don't let him give you Yin Zhen Pearls," Fox warned. "If it tastes like anything at all, it'll taste like hay, and then he'll get angry at you for adding milk, like hay is some fantastic flavor profile that you need to savor."

"Jerk." Marshall went to elbow him in the ribs, grinning, but before he could act, Fox linked their arms together. He went on to twist Marshall around, tugging him so Marshall's back was pressed into his chest. Once he'd manhandled Marshall into position, he locked his arm over Marshall's throat, effectively trapping him in a headlock. While Marshall was sure he meant it as further proof that they were just horsing around, the way Fox's cock pushed against his ass told a different story—one that made Marshall's knees weak. If Fox hadn't been holding him up by the neck, he would have dissolved into a puddle of hormones and poor life choices.

"All I'm saying," Fox said in husky tones against the back of Marshall's ear, his stubble prickling the edge of his jaw, "is if I wanted to eat hay, I'd go find a farm. I don't need to drink it in my tea."

Marshall's mom looked curiously between the two of them, her eyes lit up with hesitant hope. Marshall had never brought home a boyfriend before, and Fox… well, try as he might to prove otherwise, Fox was touching him like there was something more between them than they were letting on. It was easy to think they were together when they acted like this. Not that they were. It was all very confusing, and Marshall both looked forward to and dreaded the moment his mom left so he could talk it out with Fox alone.

"Well, there's no need to worry about that, now is there?" His mom fixed him with a tender smile. "You have Earl Grey, right?"

"I do. I even have some without the added hay flavor." Marshall tapped Fox's arm, which was still braced around his neck. "You want any, Hulk Hogan?"

"You know it, brother." Fox coughed, dropping the imitation. "You gonna make fun of me if I add milk?"

"Heathen."

Fox's arm tightened—not enough to hurt, but enough to draw Marshall closer. His cock pushed with greater insistence against Marshall's ass, and Marshall had to bite the inside of his lip to keep from moaning. "That's a bold declaration for someone at my mercy. I'm not against suplexing you if you start getting sassy."

God, was he doing it on purpose? He had to be. There was no way that Fox didn't know he was making Marshall horny as hell.

Was this supposed to be gay chicken? A tactic to win the water fight?

If it was, Marshall was going to win the shit out of it.

"You think this is enough to make me give in?" Marshall angled his head backward as best he could to look at Fox. He couldn't see much, but that didn't matter—what he wanted was to rub his ass in retaliation against Fox's cock, and twisting around so he could get a better look gave him a reason to squirm. "You're going to have to do better than that if you want to wrangle me into submission." A shiver ran through Fox that was anything but innocent. Marshall wanted to push and see how far they could take it, but his sensible brain beat out his libido. His mom was standing right there. It wasn't the time or the place to explore what Fox did and didn't want. "But I'll let you off easy this time. Yes, you can defile your tea with milk. I'll look the other way."

"Good. Then I'm in. As long it's not hay, I'll defile anything."

Defile *anything*?

Don't get your hopes up, Marshall's brain insisted.

His heart, far more prone to excitement, screamed like a fangirl who'd been winked at by Jason Momoa.

"Wonderful." Marshall's mom clapped her hands. "Marshall, do you have your kettle set up in the kitchen? I can brew the tea while you two change."

Tea. Oh yeah. Right. Marshall blinked back into focus and pried Fox's arm from his neck. The sooner he got out of his wet clothes and distanced himself from what had just happened, the better. He could talk to Fox about what was going on later—hopefully at a time when his dick wasn't so eager to jump to conclusions. "Yeah, it's in the kitchen. You'll find my stash of tea in the cabinet right above it. I'm not too picky about what I drink, so feel free to surprise me."

There was a small but delighted smile on his mother's face as she said, "I will."

Morning wore into afternoon, and around two o'clock, his mom said her goodbyes and left. They'd enjoyed the day out on the patio, chatting and sipping tea. Fox had been on his best behavior, and as far as Marshall could tell, it'd thoroughly charmed her.

Not that it mattered.

Maybe.

What had happened continued to confuse him. Despite everything, he clung to the notion that Fox was straight—it was infinitely more plausible than believing he'd switched teams—but even then, doubt quibbled in Marshall's mind. If the situation had been reversed and Marshall had been the one in a heap on the ground on top of his female employer, he wouldn't have gotten hard. Even if he had, it would have been on accident, and he wouldn't have proceeded to rub his crotch all over hers like he wanted something more.

Nor would he have brought their faces so close together, or said the things Fox had said.

As Marshall's mom's car disappeared down the driveway, leaving Fox and Marshall in the front yard alone, Marshall decided to put his doubts to rest when Fox stretched and yawned, cutting him off before he could begin. "Your mom's a nice person. I see a lot of her in you."

Total meltdown.

Nuclear crisis.

Marshall's insides superheated, and the serious conversation he'd been about to start was shunted to the side in favor of making sure he didn't melt into a puddle of goo. "She's great. I mean, really great. I, um, I never told her about what was going on at school, but when it started to take a toll on me in my sophomore year, she took time out of her schedule because she saw me start to withdraw. I think she was working three jobs at that point, but she never complained. If it hadn't been for her being there for me, I don't know what would have happened."

Fox stood still at his side, the wind teasing his shirt. A storm was rolling in—the air was charged not only from the heaviness of the confession, but from the promise of rain. "You never told her what Elijah and his sycophants did to you?"

"No."

"Why not?"

"Why would I want to make her worry?" Marshall watched the space where her car had disappeared, but his focus was on somewhere unseen—the past. While the trees dividing his property from Highway Fifteen bowed gently in the breeze, he saw himself in the living room of his childhood home, curled up on the couch with a mug of tea while zoning out in front of *To Wong Foo, Thanks for Everything! Julie Newmar* with his mom. The scene changed. Marshall shoveled spoonfuls of an Oreo Blizzard into his mouth while looking across one of the lakes in Shawnee National Forest, seated in the passenger seat of his mom's car. When the weather was nice she'd drive him out to one of the parking zones for the boat ramps, where they'd sit for a half hour or two and listen to an audiobook on CD. No matter what, she'd been there to give him the break his brain needed. After everything she'd done for him, he would never burden her if he could help it.

From the corner of his eye, Marshall noticed Fox lower his head. "Because your safety and happiness is worth worrying about."

"I didn't think so back then."

Fox slid his hands into the back pockets of his jeans and was quiet for a minute. The wind rose up to fill the silence, rustling through newly shaped leaves and weaving between neatly cut blades of grass. When he spoke, his words were as weighted as the air, nuanced by a storm that had yet to breach the horizon. "We can't go back. We can't change what's happened. Not for you, and not for me."

"No, we can't."

"But we still have the future." Marshall glanced at Fox, who stood still and stony-faced beside him as he spoke. "You and I... we're still alive."

"Yeah. We are."

"I don't think I'm a good person, Marshall." A chill swept down the back of Marshall's shirt carried by the breeze. It teased the hairs on the back of his neck and sent goosebumps racing down his arms. "I don't think I deserve your compassion, but you've given it to me anyway, and it makes me wonder... you and I... did our stories happen like they did for a reason?"

"I don't know." Marshall took a half-step sideways, minimizing the distance between himself and Fox. "I don't know if we'll ever know. All I can go by is what I feel."

"It's hard for me to know what I feel right now." Fox reached for him, and Marshall thought he'd tug him into a side-hug until Fox's hand found his. He wove their fingers together. "I don't know what's happening to me, or why, or if I'll ever be better. But what I do know is that right now, I feel safe when I should feel terrified. And more than that? Despite every goddamn miserable thing I've done in my life, I feel hope."

A raindrop burst on Marshall's shoulder. Another struck the top ridge of his ear.

"Maybe we should go inside." Fox lifted his chin and looked at the sky. It had darkened since Marshall's mom had said goodbye, but even though a storm was on its way, Marshall didn't want to leave.

"Will you come sit with me on the back porch so we can watch the rain?"

"Yeah." Fox squeezed his hand and kept their fingers laced. "As long as you're there with me."

"I will be," Marshall promised.

For once, his heart and his brain agreed.

16

FOX

The wicker couch out back creaked beneath Fox's weight as he settled, then made no more noise. Marshall sat at his side, and they stayed there, not speaking, as they listened to the beating rain and shared the thick, humid air the storm brought with it. Fat raindrops sank into the koi pond, so heavy and impactive that they seemed to spike its surface. The tinny beat from the rain gutters serenaded them. Their world may have been small, but it was beautiful in ways Fox had never thought to notice before.

"I was an airborne translator." Fox looked out over the backyard as he spoke, watching as the trees along the property line bowed and dripped beneath the weight of the downpour. Since Marshall had shared some of his story, Fox thought it polite to reciprocate. "I joined the Air Force immediately after graduation and went through rigorous training—the kind that either breaks men, or shapes them. I fought to make it with everything I had, and I graduated."

Marshall said nothing. He set his hand palm-down on the empty space between their thighs.

"As part of my training, I studied Middle Eastern languages. Pashto first, then Farsi. Along the way, I learned others. Dialects, mostly. All of it blends into this… this mess in my memory, like it happened decades ago, or like I was never actually there."

Words were hard to come by. Fox stopped and tried to piece together exactly what it was he wanted to say, but doing so proved impossible. He'd never spoken about his experience with anyone— not his parents, not his old high school friends, and not even the therapists and doctors who'd treated him while he was laid up in a CONUS medical facility, praying the PEB wouldn't end his career— but Marshall wasn't just anyone. It wasn't that Fox felt he owed Marshall an explanation, but that he wanted him to know.

When he found the right words, Fox continued. "When I finished my training, they sent me on tour. It was my responsibility to listen to and translate radio transmissions and other broadcasts while my Flight executed flyovers. It was exhilarating like nothing else, and I guess I got addicted. You get hooked on the adrenaline— on knowing there's not anyone else out there who's as good at what you do as you."

Fox tilted his head back. It was the strangest feeling to have one foot planted in the past while the other was rooted in the present, but it was stranger yet to be thinking of the future while he did it. If he told Marshall his story, there was no going back. All the details of his failure would be laid out, and Marshall would see what a waste he really was. There was a chance he'd lose this—the happy place he'd found that was cleaved from the real world by Marshall's perpetual mirth and sunny disposition—but if he kept his past to himself, Marshall would never know who he really was. As much as Fox wanted nothing to do with who he'd become, it was unfair to hide it from the man who'd given him everything. Fox cared about him too much to keep him from the truth.

"Most of the men I worked with went after promotions, ranked up, and got out. The guys in my original Flight all got cushy desk jobs back in the US. They served their time and left as soon as they could. It's not easy being shipped overseas. You don't realize how good you've got it back home until you're thousands of miles away."

Desiccating heat. The whir of F-16 afterburners. The shrill blare of an incoming alarm. Fox remembered it in fragments, sharp, jagged, and poised to slice right through him. Words that were once stuck spilled out now without filter.

"But I was the hotshot. Even after my tour was over I kept signing up for IA service, meaning I stepped in to fill empty positions to augment different units, and they kept sending me out. I was coming up on ten years in service when I went out on my last flight. We were cruising low over hostile territory on a recon mission, searching for signs of IEDs for the ground troops coming up behind us, and it was all on me. Every transmission I picked up was vital to our survival... except this time around, the dialect wasn't one I'd heard before. It was jarring. Some parts I understood, some I didn't."

Fox set his hand down beside Marshall's. A wind whipped by, blowing the rain sideways, but not into their covered alcove.

"When I figured out what they were saying, it was too late— they'd already fired off a lob bomb. The, uh, the media likes to call them 'improvised rocket-assisted mortar,' but fuck that. No one should give such a neat name to something so destructive and ugly. Most of the time, lob bombs are too inaccurate to be effective, but we were flying low and slow enough that we were hit." Fox ran his teeth over his lip as guilt laced his ribs and tightened around his stomach. What little he could remember of that moment—the fear, the frustration, and the crippling concern for the men on his Flight —still made him sick. "The plane went down. I don't remember much after that."

Marshall's fingers crept over his. His touch was tender and sympathetic in a way Fox didn't believe he deserved.

Twisted metal. Anguished screams. Gunfire. Burning flesh and hair. Tremendous heat.

His hand trembled, and as it did, Marshall slotted their fingers together and squeezed.

"I want to go back and tell myself to stop being so arrogant," Fox whispered as the tremble made it to his voice. "I want to tell myself that I need to stop pretending I'm so high and mighty—that the desk jobs the other guys on my Flight aspired to are good enough for me as well. I want to tell myself that if I don't stop, my ineptitude will kill the men I loved like brothers—that I won't even be able to go to their funerals to get to say goodbye." Tears clouded Fox's eyes. "I was the only one who survived, but I was the only one on that Flight who deserved to die. It was my mistake. I killed them all. Every single one of them."

"Fox..."

The tears once clouding Fox's eyes rolled down his cheeks. The world blurred. No matter how many times he blinked, nothing changed.

It never did.

"I'm not a good person, Marshall." Fox followed it up with a heart-wrenching laugh that barely masked a sob. "I stood by while my friends bullied you in high school, and I was the one who killed the men in my Flight. I'm rotten. What happened broke my brain, and the doctors don't know if I'll ever be okay again. The panic, the emotion, the paralysis... all of the evil I've done lives inside of me, and I don't think it'll ever come out. Everything I do is selfish and wrong."

"Fox—"

"So I needed to let you know." Fox swallowed hard, choking out the racking despair trying to overwhelm him. "I needed to let you know who I am, just like you've let me know who you are—I needed you to see the truth in me and know how broken I am—because I like you, Marshall, but I don't want you to think that I'm someone I'm not."

"Being broken doesn't change who you are." Marshall's hand tightened around his. "And it doesn't change how I think of you."

"You haven't seen me at my worst. You don't know what I'm capable of. There's a bomb in my head waiting to go off, and I'm scared you'll get caught in the explosion."

"It hasn't happened yet, has it?" Marshall was looking at him—Fox felt the affection of his gaze, but he couldn't bring himself to see it. "If it happens, we'll take it as it comes. We'll figure things out."

The last of Fox's tears rolled down his cheeks. "I don't know what I'd do if I hurt you."

"You don't have to." There was a smile in Marshall's voice that shook the anguish from Fox's soul. It didn't promise perfection, but that wasn't what Fox wanted. All he needed was someone who would be there—someone who was willing to try. "If it happens, we'll figure it out together. You don't have to face this alone."

Fox blinked the last of the cloudiness from his eyes and looked at the man beside him—the scrawny nerd who'd grown up to be an inspiration. Determination and tenderness softened his face. He'd meant what he'd said. Despite everything, he wouldn't give Fox up.

Fox traced his fingers along Marshall's jaw, then cupped the back of Marshall's neck and kissed him.

Marshall hesitated, then kissed him back.

The rain continued to fall.

17

FOX

Kissing a man was different from what Fox was used to—bolder, rougher, and more sincere. Unlike the pretty girls he'd hooked up with while on leave, Marshall knew what he wanted, and he didn't bother to try and hide it. As their kiss deepened from sweetness to crushing need, he showed Fox the way.

And fuck, what a way it was.

Wicker creaked. Bodies shifted. Marshall straddled Fox's lap and kissed him with everything he had. Rain poured over the sides of the gutters like shimmering drapes, shielding them from the outside world, but Fox didn't care who saw. He slid his hands up Marshall's thighs and grabbed his ass, then pushed him forward so their clothed cocks brushed together.

"Fox," Marshall gasped against his lips. "F-Fuck…"

"Not yet." Fox tightened his grip. "But soon."

Marshall shivered and kissed him hard in selfish, greedy ways that made Fox's balls tighten. He returned the passion just as fiercely and rolled Marshall's hips against his, forcing him to grind. It hadn't been until recently that Fox had thought of being with another man, but now he couldn't get the idea out of his head. Would Marshall drop to his knees, tear his fly open, and suck his cock with the same hunger he put into their kiss? Would he moan and twitch and tremble as Fox stretched his tight ass wide open with his cock?

Fuck yes, he would.

Fox knew it. He felt it. Marshall would do whatever he wanted, and he'd love every goddamn second of it. All he needed now was to see it happen in real life. "Get on your knees."

Marshall shimmied out of his clutches and did as told, then nuzzled Fox's bulge and looked up at him with his fucking beautiful blue eyes. Fox ran a hand through his hair, then pushed gently on the back of Marshall's head to rub his face against his crotch. Marshall moaned and nuzzled, then ran his tongue along the length of Fox's fly while making eye contact. It was the hottest goddamn thing Fox had ever seen, and he had to hold himself back from coming then and there.

"God, you want it, don't you?" Fox stroked Marshall's hair, then rubbed his face against his crotch again. Marshall moaned and kissed him all over, the pressure of his lips a tantalizing peek at what was still to come. "You don't have to wait. Take it. It's yours."

The small, guttural noise Marshall made was all the answer Fox needed.

Marshall opened Fox's fly and smoothed down each side, then tugged down the boxer-briefs beneath while Fox lifted his ass. As they gave way, Fox's cock sprang free. Rigid, thick, and flushed with excitement, it bobbed between his thighs, ready for Marshall's greedy mouth. A drop of precum rolled from its slit over the silken skin of his head, leaving it glossy. It hadn't been the first—before Marshall let his boxer-briefs settle around his thighs, Fox spotted a large dark spot on the front.

He'd leaked all over himself for Marshall.

For his wonderful, needy boy.

"All for you," Fox uttered. He guided Marshall forward by putting pressure on the back of his skull, but Marshall didn't need to be led—he came willingly. With a tilt of his head, he took position by the base of Fox's cock, but didn't devour it like Fox thought he would. Instead, he looked at Fox from beneath his lashes with the fucking sexiest bedroom eyes Fox had ever seen, then slowly ran his tongue from Fox's base to his crown, where he lapped up Fox's precum.

"F-Fuck." Fox closed his eyes and let his head fall back, but the fantasies of Marshall behind his eyelids paled in comparison to what was happening between his legs. Drunk on lust, Fox rolled his head down to watch as Marshall tongued his slit and chased more precum from inside, then kissed it and took him between his lips. Fox wove his fingers through Marshall's hair to get a better grip and push him forward, but Marshall didn't hesitate—he swallowed Fox's cock on the first bob of his head, choking on it like it was what he'd been born to do.

A convulsion pulsed around Fox's shaft, followed quickly by another. Marshall sputtered, but otherwise held his head in place, swallowing again and again around Fox's cock as his body struggled to reject it. Gasping for breath, Fox stroked Marshall's hair and watched his face turn red from the effort. Even as tears leaked from the corners of his eyes, he was fucking beautiful.

"Take it, baby." Fox kept caressing, encouraging Marshall to keep him sunk deep for as long as he could. "You feel so goddamn good."

Marshall whined and pushed until his nose flattened against Fox's pelvis, causing his throat to convulse harder than it had before. Fox groaned and pushed his hips forward, but it proved too much—Marshall launched backward, gasping and sputtering for breath. He looked Fox in the eyes, his own muddied with arousal, then took Fox's tip beneath his lips and kissed it deeply again and again, as if to apologize.

"You don't have to be sorry," Fox promised as tenderly as he could. He wrapped his hand around the back of Marshall's head again and kept it there idly as Marshall kept making out with his cock. Watching his own glistening skin slide in and out of Marshall's lips turned Fox the fuck on, but he wanted—*needed*—

more. "Everything you do feels so good, baby. Every little thing. But I need you to let me back inside. I'm going to fuck your throat until I come, and you're gonna take it all, okay?"

Marshall blinked the tears from his eyes and hummed in agreement, and with nothing more said than that, Fox pushed on the back of his head until his cock was back where it belonged.

Pleasure. It exploded behind the bars of Fox's ribcage like fireworks at night and cascaded into his groin until his whole body was lit up with it. Holding Marshall's head in place, Fox fucked into his throat, stealing more of that feeling for himself while Marshall choked and spluttered.

"I'm gonna come," Fox warned with a growl. He threw his head back, but just like before, he couldn't keep it there for long. He needed to see Marshall, to watch the pleasure pass between them as it grew increasingly intense. "Oh, fuck, baby—you'd better be ready to swallow, cuz I've got so much of it to give you."

The pitch of Marshall's whine begged for it, so Fox didn't hold back—he groaned and shot down Marshall's throat, pulling out enough so some spilled across his tongue, giving him a taste.

Being with a man was different than being with a woman, Fox realized as he pulled free from Marshall with a wet *pop*. A strand of cum escaped Marshall's lips and streaked his chin. Fox brushed it off with his thumb and fed it back to him, and he sucked on it indulgently in a way that made Fox want to fuck his mouth all over again. Being with a man was raw and primal, stripped of fear and drenched in unbridled desire. Fox didn't have to worry that he was stepping out of line or being too rough, not only because he knew that Marshall would tell him if he'd gone too far, but because he knew Marshall could take what he gave him.

And fuck, did he still have so much to give him.

"We're not done yet," Fox said as he kicked off his shoes and socks. When he stood, he stepped out of his pants and underwear and ripped off his shirt, then offered a hand to Marshall, who still knelt in front of him. Marshall clasped it and rose on shaking legs.

Once he was on his feet, Fox tugged him close to keep him stable, then whispered against his lips, "You know who I am now, and you know what I can do. If that hasn't chased you off, nothing will—so I'm going to claim you. I'm going to make the one good thing in my life all mine. This is your last chance to run. Tell me no. Tell me you don't want me and I'll never touch you again."

Marshall didn't reply with words—he kissed Fox instead. It was a crushing, fierce kiss devoid of doubt, and it stole Fox's breath away. With a throaty growl, he pushed Marshall against the French door and ravaged his mouth. Marshall had made his choice. Fox would have him, he would claim him, and from here on out, Marshall would be his.

18

MARSHALL

They stumbled in through the door, all jumbled limbs and bruising lips. Marshall was vaguely aware that Fox kicked the door closed by virtue of the noise it made as the latch clicked into position, but after that the only thing that mattered was Fox, the straight bush-sitting boy who wasn't so straight anymore.

Told you, Marshall's heart crowed as Fox pinned him to the kitchen counter and yanked down his pants.

Marshall's brain was unavailable for comment. It was too busy melting down as Fox grabbed his dick and started to stroke.

Gasping, Marshall wrapped his arms around Fox's neck and bucked desperately into his fist. Fox's hand was toughened from manual labor, and his grip was as firm as it was certain. Not once did he hesitate or reconsider. He wanted Marshall and he made it clear—there were no ifs or buts.

Fox would claim him just like he'd said.

He would make Marshall *his.*

Their kiss, once interrupted by Marshall's gasp of pleasure, picked up in intensity at Fox's insistence. Marshall tried his best to match it, but his focus was divided between Fox's lips and his fist.

The more Fox pumped, the less the split was even, until all Marshall could do was thrust into the tightness surrounding his dick.

With a grunt of frustration, Fox ended their contact and lifted Marshall onto the counter. The nearby utensil holder clattered as it fell over, but as soon as the thought of picking it up crossed Marshall's mind, it was gone—Fox wrenched off his shoes and tugged free his pants and briefs, leaving him nude from the waist down.

"You have twenty seconds to find something to use as lube, or I'm going to take you dry," Fox growled. The sound of those words rolled through Marshall, crushing the last of his composure. The possessive, covetous, dominant side of Fox was hot as hell, and he needed more. "If you run, I *will* catch you, and wherever I do, I'll fuck you right then and there."

Twenty seconds.

Marshall could make a mad dash for the bedroom, but there was a chance Fox would catch him on the stairs. If it hadn't been so long since Marshall had last played with himself, he might not have minded, but the cock he'd sucked such a short while ago was thick, and it would wreck him without some prep work. He couldn't take the chance.

As the timer ticked down, Marshall scrambled to reach the cabinet over the stove and pulled out the bottle of coconut oil. The lid slipped in his grip, but after a brief struggle, came off. Once it did, Marshall poured a thick pool of oil into his hand and reached between them to slick Fox's cock as the oil melted the rest of the way. Fox hadn't gone flaccid after his blowjob, Marshall realized. He was so turned on he'd stayed hard.

"Put it in," Marshall gasped as he finished coating Fox's cock. "Fuck me. I don't need twenty seconds. I—"

Fox grabbed him by the hips and yanked him over the edge of the counter. The position was precarious enough that if Fox dropped him, Marshall would slide all the way off and onto the floor, but Fox's grip was unyielding, and he supported Marshall's weight without batting an eye. Marshall braced his hands on the edge of the counter and hooked a leg over Fox's shoulder, spreading the other to the side so his foot rested on the counter running along the adjacent wall. A second after that, the tip of his fat cock probed Marshall's hole, and with a low grunt, Fox pushed inside. The coconut oil did the trick, but in no way had it prepared Marshall for how thick Fox would feel. A wounded cry of pain and pleasure broke in his throat, and he threw his head back as Fox rocked into him, stretching him all at once on his cock.

"*Fuck*, you feel good, baby." Fox pumped his hips, sliding in and out of Marshall's body without ever fully pulling out. "So fucking tight. You're so fucking *tight* for me."

"All for you," Marshall panted. "Only for you."

It was true.

It was true even though it had come on so quickly, and even though Marshall wasn't sure it would last. There was a chance that after this, Fox would be through with him—that he'd realize men weren't for him, and that he was better off on his own—but the same voice that had been so quick to crow in victory that it had been right about Fox corrected him. No straight man would do the things Fox had done, say the things he had, or touch Marshall like he was someone special.

What they had was real.

The boy Marshall had wanted in high school had grown up to want him, too.

Marshall internalized that thought and let it feed his desire. Positioned like he was, there wasn't much he could do but let Fox fuck him, so he wiggled his hips and closed his eyes, losing himself in fantasy. There was a cock inside of him—a cock he'd wanted for years, but that he'd thought he'd never have. Now it was laying claims on him, stuffing him, *owning* him, and all Marshall could do was let it.

"I'm so fucking close," Fox rasped. He'd picked up the pace and started to slam into Marshall, each movement more deliberate than the last. "I'm negative, baby, so tell me where you want it and I'll give it all to you."

"Come inside me," Marshall begged as the fantasy tightened his balls and pushed him closer to the edge. *"Come inside me."*

Close.

He was so *close.*

The position they were in meant that with every thrust, Fox drove upward into him, striking Marshall's prostate before sliding deeper inside. What had started as grunts of pleasure turned into moans, then screams. Marshall's toes curled and his balls tensed, tingling pleasure sweeping through his gut as he let go.

He was coming.

"Yes. Yes. Fuck *yes,*" Fox rasped as he pumped into Marshall's body. "Come on my cock. Fucking come all over it, Marshall."

Spend striped Marshall's chest and stomach. His body tensed all over, and he clenched around Fox's cock as orgasm took control.

"Come in me," he begged again. "Come in me, Fox. Come in my fucking ass."

With a roar, Fox bucked into him one last time. His cock twitched and pulsed, and Marshall felt it—the rush of heat as Fox flooded his body. Pleasure ripped through Marshall a second time, and as he silently screamed in ecstasy, he came again, draining his balls entirely. When he was done, he went to wilt onto the counter, too exhausted to move, but Fox was having none of it. He slid out of Marshall and held him to his chest, then did the unexpected—he kissed Marshall slowly and sweetly, and he did it again, and again, until Marshall thought they might never stop.

"Will you come to bed with me?" Marshall murmured as the kiss continued. "Don't wanna have to stop."

"Yeah." Fox kissed him one last time, then swept Marshall into his arms and carried him upstairs. Apart from a surprised laugh, Marshall didn't protest. Fox had left him boneless.

They spent the afternoon cuddled in Marshall's bed while rain struck the roof and the wind whipped by, only getting up to eat before finding their way back between the sheets. Fox slept in Marshall's bed that night, spooning Marshall from behind while warming his flaccid cock in Marshall's ass, and there they stayed until late morning, when they were woken abruptly by someone incessantly ringing the doorbell.

19

FOX

Fox jolted awake and rolled away from Marshall, heart in his throat. Panic rose to fill the place it had left behind, dragging Fox beneath its surface like a cruel riptide. Touch, sight, sound—it robbed him of everything. Nothing was meaningful where light couldn't shine. Safety was a social construct. The darkness was out there, and it was coming for him.

A siren.

A scream.

The vile stench of burning.

Then a hand on his shoulder. Fox thrashed in its direction, ready to strike it down, and blinked back into focus a second before he wrapped his hand around Marshall's throat. Marshall, wide-eyed, stared at him from where Fox had pinned him on the mattress. The ringing continued.

The doorbell.

It was just the doorbell.

"Fox?" Marshall asked. He cupped Fox's cheek like he hadn't just been in danger, his expression mellowing from surprise to concern. "Are you okay?"

"Yeah." Technically, it wasn't a lie—Fox's racing heart wasn't going to kill him even though it felt like it would. To put Marshall at ease, he combed his fingers through Marshall's hair and kissed him sweetly. "You stay here. I'll go get the door."

"What time is it?"

"Fuck if I know. Just stay here, okay?" Fox rolled out of bed, tugged on his jeans from yesterday, and padded across the room. "I'll tell them to come back later. I'm not done with you yet."

After a brief struggle with the lock, Fox yanked the front door open, ready to tell whoever the hell was there to leave them the fuck alone. He didn't anticipate their visitor would shut him down with a judgmental, eyeliner-darkened stare.

"Let me guess." Sam crossed his arms loosely over his chest and eyed Fox's bare torso. "You've been hard at work 'groundskeeping,' haven't you?"

Fox let that little dig roll off, too surprised by the teen on his doorstep to think of trying to deny what Sam already knew. "Sam?"

"Uh, yup." Sam patted down his chest and sides. "Last time I checked, at least. Sure feels like me. The beanie might be throwing you off"—he gestured at the gray and blue striped woven beanie pinning down his swooping black hair—"but despite my *haute couture*, rest assured I'm still the same guy who can't do a chin-up to save my life."

Haute *what?*

Fox narrowed his eyes in confusion. "What are you doing here?"

Sam answered the question not with words, but with a look— one eyebrow hitched and one eye narrowed. A silent, incredulous "Really?" hovered on his lips. Sam was due over around eleven that morning, but...

Fox turned his attention skyward. Last night's storm had rolled out and now there wasn't a cloud to be seen. Unfortunately, that meant the sun was in plain view directly overhead. It was almost noon, and he was supposed to have picked Sam up an hour ago. "*Shit.* Why didn't you text us?"

"I did." Sam waved his phone in Fox's direction. "Both you and Marshall. Several times. When I didn't hear from you, I figured one of two things happened—either you'd both moved to California without me to take advantage of Marshall's pool of rubber ducks, or you were both busy doing something here. At the same time. *Together.*"

Fuck.

"I didn't realize how late it was." Fox stepped away from the door, letting Sam in. "That's my bad."

"It's cool." Sam waved a hand and came inside, heading directly into the main house. "Tons of people lose track of time while 'groundskeeping.' It's no big. I'm gonna go grab a glass of water and set up in the dining room while Marshall gets ready. I figure he'll need a hot minute to shower, right? Tell him that I'm okay working on coding stuff for our side-scroller, so he doesn't have to rush."

Maybe it was the result of marathon sex scrambling his brain, but Fox was having a hard time processing. "What?"

"Look…" Sam sighed and turned around, tucking his hands into the pockets of his hoodie. "I'm not thirteen. Total shock, I know, but I'm going to be eighteen soon, and I've been around the block long enough to know when… *you know.*"

"No, you don't."

"Fox." Sam laughed. "I've been coming around for almost two months now. What am I supposed to think when you don't come to pick me up, then answer the door in nothing but jeans, and uh, well…" He tapped the space where his collarbone met his neck with two fingers. "If that's an injury from actual groundskeeping, I don't want to know what kind of kinky weeds Marshall has growing out back."

What the hell? Fox slapped a hand over the spot Sam had pointed out, mortified. Marshall had given him a *hickey?* The sex had been worth it, but Fox hadn't been counting on wearing it around like a badge of honor—especially not in front of a kid.

Sam waved a hand dismissively. "You're fine. It's not that bad. Besides, I know how to cover up a bruise. With a little concealer, no one's gonna know."

Fuck.

Fuck.

No doubt Marshall was laughing his ass off upstairs. If he wasn't, he should have been, because Fox was going to get him back for it big time.

"I'll go get him," Fox said, choosing not to acknowledge the hickey at all. Sam rolled his eyes like a true teenager and headed for the dining room, leaving Fox to relay news of his arrival. He didn't have to go far. Marshall was on his way down the stairs, his hair dripping from a quick shower. He'd pulled on a pair of tan cargo shorts and a heather-gray graphic tee with a NERV logo Fox didn't recognize, but that he was sure was steeped in geek culture. Despite the heinous and unusually cruel things Marshall had done to his neck, Fox brightened when he saw him. The way he was glowing after their night together was cute as hell. "Hey."

"Hey." Marshall stopped a few stairs from the landing. "It was Sam, wasn't it?"

"Yep."

"I can't believe we slept in so late."

"You and me both." Fox nodded in the direction of the dining room. "He said he'd meet you at the table."

"Mm." Marshall yawned, stole a look toward where Fox had gestured, then hopped down the remaining few steps and slid his arms around Fox's waist. Thoughts of revenge fled—all Fox wanted to do was kiss the shit out of his sweet lips and bring him back to bed. Unable to do both, he settled for a kiss, which ended when Marshall pulled away to rest his head on Fox's shoulder. "Guess we're gonna have to postpone that whole 'I'm not done with you yet' thing, huh?"

"Guess so."

"That's okay." Marshall's hands roamed down Fox's back, settling over his ass. "You can come back to sleep in my bedroom tonight. Until then... mmm, what do you say we do something fun? I'm not feeling desk work today. How would you feel about taking Sam on a field trip?"

Fox had been so wrapped up in Marshall's touch that he'd almost missed the question. "A field trip?"

"Yeah. I don't know where. It just seems like it'd be good for all of us to get out of the house and have fun for a while. It's the start of his summer break, after all. We should celebrate."

"Is that so?" Fox grinned and nipped the ridge of Marshall's ear. "Are you sure it's the end of school you're celebrating, and not something else?"

Marshall made an indecipherable noise of pleasure and kissed Fox again, but was interrupted by a yelp from the kitchen.

Marshall winced. "Oh no."

"Oh no?"

"Sam, he's—"

"*MARSHALL!*" Sam squawked. "There are *SEX PANTS* in here. And what the hell is on the counter?! Oh my god. *Oh my god!*"

"So." Marshall grinned sheepishly. "About that field trip..."

Fox had just the place in mind.

20

FOX

Tucked away off a seldom traveled stretch of state highway twenty minutes south of Bulrush was an unnamed dirt road. It continued on for a few miles, leading through a segment of forest kept pruned by unknown volunteers, then ended on the shore of a small, clear lake. There'd been a summer before Fox had left town when he'd come here almost every day, sometimes with friends, sometimes alone, but always with a purpose. Whether it was paddling out to the middle in a canoe with a case of illicitly obtained beer or afternoons swimming laps from shore to shore, hoping like hell he wouldn't bump into any water moccasin burrows, it'd been the escape from real life that he'd needed. With sex pants on the kitchen floor and questionable stains on the counter, it was exactly what they all needed.

Well, everyone except for Sam, who wilted against one of the truck's back doors and pushed his nose into the gap made by the open window. He made a noise reminiscent of a wounded buffalo and sucked in a greedy lungful of fresh air. "I'm going to be sick."

Fox glanced at him through the rearview mirror, one brow playfully raised. "You'd better not. No puking in the car."

"Believe me, if I could stop myself, I would." Sam stuck out his tongue and squeezed his eyes shut like he was playing dead, then tugged his beanie down over his face. "I'm not gonna take the blame if I hurl all over your upholstery. When you said we were going on a field trip, I thought we'd head a town or two over and go for a picnic or chill out at the mall. I didn't realize I was signing up for a nonstop mechanical bull ride hurlfest of *pain* and *suffering*."

"It's not that bad." The truck struck another dip in the road and bounced. Sam groaned. "I admit that my suspension is a little shot, but it's not the worst it's been."

"*This isn't the worst?*" Sam groaned. "God, Fox, is this how adults get their kicks? Driving around in the grown-up equivalent of a bounce castle? Someone stop time—I need to get off. I didn't sign up for this."

Marshall, who sat up front to Fox's right, snickered. "Good luck. The ride operator is an asshole. There's a strict 'all passengers must remain on the ride at all times' rule, and I haven't seen anyone get around it yet." He twisted around in his seat to look back at Sam. "But in all seriousness, are you okay? We can pull over."

There was the shuffle of fabric—likely Sam pulling his beanie off his face—and another wounded buffalo wail. "I think I'll be fine. As long as we don't hit any more huge bumps, I can deal."

Fox drove around a bump in the road that would have sent Sam over the edge. "We're almost there."

"Great." Sam's sarcasm was so thick, it was about to go Instagram famous. "And I'm almost ready to heave. Which'll happen first? Find out on this episode of *Teens Gone Mild: Don't Rock the Boat Baby—Like Seriously, Don't Rock It. Do You* Want *Vomit All Over Your Back Seat?*"

Fox choked back a laugh. "That's some title."

"Yeah. Fans tend to just call it *Vomit*, but studies have shown it leaves an unpleasant taste in the mouth of the target demographic."

An unavoidable bump ended Sam's comedy career. There was the sound of skin slapping skin—likely Sam clamping a hand over his mouth to keep from hurling—then a muffled cry of distress.

"Fox, pull over." Marshall swiveled around frantically, like it would make Fox stop any sooner. It was almost as bad as the time he'd gasped dramatically after spotting a rabbit off to the side of the road. "He's going to be sick."

"No need. We're here."

The line of trees on either side of the road ended, and they emerged in a small clearing worn by human use over a long period of time. Tall grass speckled with towering purple wildflowers fenced off the area to the left and right, while the shore of the lake cut them off ahead. As the truck rolled to a stop, Sam flung open the door and sprang from the still-moving vehicle, bolting for the nearest patch of tall grass. Several birds took flight as he barreled through the foliage, no doubt on their way to complain to the HOA about the teenager puking on their lawn.

"Do you think he'll be okay?" Marshall asked as Sam bent at the waist and disappeared into bird city.

"He'll be fine."

"I hope you're right."

"I am." Fox unbuckled as he spoke, letting the seat belt spool back into its retractor. "I wouldn't push him to do something he isn't capable of. I know too well what it feels like to be on that side."

Marshall gave him a meaningful look, then left the truck to stand vigil by Sam's last known whereabouts. Fox watched him for a second, then left the vehicle to haul their supplies out of the cargo bed. Sam wasn't entirely off the hook. Self-defense lessons may have taken a backseat to fun, but there was still a thing or two Fox could teach him about life. Today, that thing would be fishing.

While Fox hauled the tackle box and the night crawlers they'd picked up at the gas station to the shore, Sam emerged from the grass. He wiped his mouth with the back of his hand and trudged back into the clearing. "Do you guys have water? Emergency toothpaste? The thing from *Men in Black* that makes you forget what you've seen and done?"

Fox headed back to the truck. "Fresh out."

"Ugh, really?" Sam groaned. "What did you guys even buy at the gas station? I knew I should have come in to supervise. Neither of you can be trusted. Can I rinse my mouth out with lake water, or am I going to get that brain-eating bacteria you hear about in all those mystery disease shows?"

"I meant the memory thing from *Men in Black*, dork. We've got water." The fishing rods could wait—Fox tugged the back door open and grabbed a bottle of water out of the bag of goods he and Marshall had picked up at the gas station. Condensation stuck to the plastic and made the glossy label slippery. He tossed it at Sam. "Wash up."

Sam cracked the lid and took a swig, making a show of rinsing his mouth and spitting. While he did, Marshall folded his hands over his forehead like a visor and turned his attention to the lake. Fox followed his gaze, eager to share the experience. The reservoir was as serene as the last time Fox had been to visit, its waters still and sparkling. Aquatic plants floated on the surface near the shore, interrupted by the occasional log where the forests encroached upon the water. A family of turtles sunbathed on one, blissfully unconcerned with their presence. The great blue heron across the lake was more wary—he lifted his head and peered at the trio before resuming his hunt.

"What do you think?" Fox asked as he came to stand beside Marshall.

"Honestly?" Marshall looked at Fox from the corner of his eye. As small as the attention was, it thrilled Fox to know that he was looking. After yesterday, just the sight of Marshall was enough to get him riled. To think that he was looking back? If they hadn't been chaperoning, the lake would be seeing a different kind of action today. "I'm a little worried that we're trespassing. Are you sure we won't be shot?"

"Yup. Everything's aboveboard." In an attempt to mitigate his excitement, Fox looked out over the water instead of at Marshall. The heron on the other side of the lake struck the surface with his beak and came back with a fish. "I consider this one of the only good things to come out of my friendship with Elijah. He brought a big group of us here one time for a party."

"And you trusted him?"

"No." Fox snorted. "I looked this place up with the power of the internet to make sure I wasn't going to end up with a record. Believe it or not, I kept my nose clean the last year of high school so I didn't end up on the wrong side of the law. I was paranoid about fucking up and ruining my chances at getting out of here."

There was a moment of contemplative silence before Marshall spoke. "You wanted to get out?"

"Hell yeah." Fox chuckled. "I didn't have it as bad as you, but what kid who grows up in a small town wants to stay there? I can't think of many. Some of us get trapped by circumstance and pretend it's what we want, but when you get to the heart of it, small towns are for people who've already seen the world. Bulrush is a place for settling down after you've found yourself—not for discovering who you are as a person. I couldn't be who I wanted to be while here, so I left. I know I'm not the only one."

A feeling sparked in the air. Marshall crossed his arms over his chest like he felt it, too, but said nothing. He leaned into Fox instead.

"Big mood," Sam agreed. He'd come to stand beside them, mercifully vomit-free. "So, I'm done rinsing the gross out of my mouth. Do you two need some time to do some groundskeeping, or are we gonna… uh… what are we doing here, exactly? You don't want me to go swimming, do you? I'll probably get leeches *and* brain-eating bacteria, and it'll just be a bad time all around. We don't swim in the UmK."

"The *what?*" Fox narrowed his eyes suspiciously at Sam.

"The UmK," Sam repeated, although this time a little more slowly, like the problem was that Fox hadn't heard and not that he was speaking gibberish. "As a nation, we generally take a water-repellent stance."

"Marshall, I need a translation."

"The UmK is the Umbrella Kingdom, and they don't tend to like water there," Marshall explained, although what he said really wasn't much more illuminating. "Sam is Umbrella nobility."

"And this is the part of the conversation where I go put together the fishing rods." Fox left Marshall's side to head for the cargo bed. While he collected the rods, Marshall came to get the folding chairs they'd thankfully had the foresight to grab before hitting the road. Sam tagged along beside him, eying the rods with trepidation.

"So, about the whole fishing thing..." Sam frowned. "Are we, um, are we gonna throw the fish back after we catch them?"

"No." Fox finished wrangling his gear and carried it over to where he'd left the tackle box. Sam followed him. "If we're lucky, we'll catch something for dinner tonight. If we catch more than that, I'll freeze them for another night."

"Yeah, so, uh, that's gonna be a problem." Sam scuffed his heel. "I'll sit with you guys in the sun and be sociable and everything, but I'm not a fish murderer."

Fox stopped what he was doing. "A fish... murderer?"

"I mean, that's what it is, when you get down to it." Sam pinched his shoulders to his neck, clearly uncomfortable. "It's kind of like in alien movies when people get sucked into the tractor beam. Like imagine you're doing your own thing, totally cool with life, and then the next minute you're yanked out of your universe by extraterrestrial beings and being spit-roasted." There was a pause, then he hastened to add, "And I mean literally spit-roasted, not the groundskeeping version."

Marshall snickered.

"So I can't fish," Sam concluded. "Not unless we throw them all back."

Fox spent a long, incredulous moment studying Sam. "So you watched me load the truck with fishing gear, let us drive all the way out here, and didn't think it'd be a good idea to mention the whole I-can't-fish thing along the way?"

"Hey! It kinda goes two ways here. You didn't tell me that you wanted me to commit murder."

"Oh my god." Fox dragged a hand down his face. "Marshall?"

"What do you want me to do?" Marshall asked. He'd finished setting up the chairs and now lounged in one of them. At some point he'd stripped down to his swim trunks.

If there hadn't been a teenager in the vicinity whose mission of the day was to push all of Fox's buttons, he might've let his gaze linger to soak in Marshall's lean physique, but there were more important fish to fry. Metaphorically speaking, because apparently there wasn't going to be any fish murder today. "Talk to him! He listens to you."

"Uh, pretty sure I'm standing right here, and also that I'm old enough to make my own decisions." Sam rolled his eyes, which was annoying as hell. "I'm not stopping *you* from fishing. If you want to, that's fine. I just don't wanna be responsible for ending a poor fish's life. That's all."

Fox pinched the bridge of his nose and squeezed his eyes shut to keep from saying something he'd regret. Was this what it was like to be a parent? Fuck. "Sure. That's fine. You and Marshall can... sit. I guess. Sit and watch. If you change your mind and decide you'd rather participate, I can get you set up."

"Awesome." Sam grinned, and his happiness almost made up for the fact that Fox was one eye roll away from committing fish genocide. "And don't worry about the whole watching thing—Let's Plays are popular on YouTube for a reason. Just don't show me the fish and I'll be fine."

"Sure." Fox finished slotting his pole together, strung it, and got set up to wade out. While he went back to the truck and pulled on his wading boots, Sam plopped onto the lounger next to Marshall, hoodie and all. It was strange, Fox thought as he made his way into the lake, that Sam wouldn't take it off on such a hot day, but then again, he'd worn a beanie today, too. Fox cast his line and let the thought go. Teenagers were not to be reasoned with. If they were, the whole fish-murder debacle never would have happened.

21

MARSHALL

Fox sloshed into the lake, disrupting a family of nearby turtles, three of whom glared at him. The fourth tumbled off his log and disappeared into the water, likely to go teenage mutant on his ass. If need be, Marshall would talk him down with the promise of pizza, but he had a feeling Fox could take care of it on his own. Even with his knee-high waders impeding his movement, he was capable. After how he'd proved his strength during their kitchen encounter yesterday, Marshall was pretty sure Fox could handle a vengeful turtle or two.

Marshall's gaze wandered down Fox's back, tracing a line from his strong shoulders to his fantastic ass. Bush-sitting, turtle-thwarting, and a body that wouldn't quit. What a catch.

Before he could get too wrapped up in fantasies, a hoodie-clad Sam rolled onto his side and peeped at Marshall from his lounger. Marshall averted his gaze from the vision in the lake to give his protégé his full attention. "Yes?"

Sam grinned nervously. "Hi."

"Hi."

"So I can't help but see that you're not a fish murderer, either." From the lake there came a grumble of dissension. "But, um, anyway, since you're not out a'murderin', I was wondering if we could talk. I was going to talk to you today anyway when we sat down with the side-scroller project, but I don't think we'll get a lot of progress done today, huh?"

"Probably not."

"So I'll just bring it up here, then, if that's okay."

"Yeah, of course." Marshall stretched out and made himself comfortable. The hint of uncertainty in Sam's voice led him to believe this was going to be a difficult conversation, and the glimmer of fear he saw in his eyes did nothing to convince him to the contrary. "I didn't really have plans for today, so if you want to talk, I'm all ears."

"That's such a weird saying," Sam mumbled. He rolled onto his back and spent a long moment staring at the sky, then said awkwardly, "So. Groundskeeping."

Oh.

Oh.

Marshall opened his mouth, then closed it again. What was he supposed to do? Sam was a smart kid and Marshall adored him, but he was still a kid. There was no way in hell Marshall was going to talk to him about his sex life. It was bad enough that Sam had walked in on yesterday's pants.

Sam, who'd seemingly arrived at the same conclusion, sighed. "C'mon, Marshall, I'm not gonna make it weird. It's just... I kind of want to talk about groundskeeping in general with you, because you're probably the only one here apart from me who likes to have his grounds kept the way you do. Well, you and Fox, but I get the impression he might still be in the shed."

Marshall arched a brow. "The shed?"

"It's like the closet, but for groundskeeping."

"Hey!" Fox called from the lake. "I can hear you, you know."

"Shh. You're scaring off all the fish you're trying to murder," Sam called back. When Fox didn't reply, Sam turned his attention back to Marshall. "I'll keep it PG-13. Promise."

PG-13 was doable. Marshall nodded, which prompted Sam to pluck the beanie from his head and nervously stretch and release the fabric. "I'm just... really confused right now, and I don't know what I should do." Sam sighed. "It feels gross to pretend I'm someone I'm not just so I can fit in, but if I stand out, then... I don't know what's gonna happen. It could get bad really fast. My senior year is coming up and I shouldn't have to worry about any of this, but I feel more anxious than ever. For the most part the other kids in my class are fine with it, but it..." Sam trailed off and set his beanie on his chest. The emotion bled from his face. "It's just not a good situation."

"Do you have a group of friends you can turn to for support?"

"Yeah. Sort of. We're friends at school, but we don't hang out otherwise. Most of my real friends are online."

"The guys you play Fortnite with?"

"Yeah." Sam scratched his cheek, then dropped his arm dramatically over his chest. "I shouldn't have brought it up. I'm sorry. You're doing me a favor by teaching me as much as you can about how to be you, and here I am spilling my guts like you're my therapist." With a huff of a laugh, Sam locked his arms over his face. "Ugh. I'm pathetic. Ignore me. Being Umbrella nobility apparently doesn't stop me from being royally stupid. I didn't mean to bother you."

"You're not bothering me at all."

"Nah. But it was still dumb of me to bring it up." Sam waved a hand dismissively, but there was a little too much frantic energy behind it to be sincere. "It's just a year, right? I can totally survive that long. You're doing your part by giving me the skills I'll need to get into a top-notch university, and if I just keep focusing on that, I won't need to worry again." There was a momentary pause. A hint of poorly masked sorrow flashed through Sam's eyes, and when he spoke next, it crept into his voice. "Even though I complain about everything, I really am thankful to you and Fox for taking me on. Without you, I don't know if the future I want would be possible. You're making my dreams come true, and you're doing it out of the kindness of your own hearts. It really means a lot to me."

"Any time." Marshall smiled, but like Sam, what he really felt remained beneath the surface. Memories of a time long past crashed back to the forefront of his mind. It felt, in a way, that he and Sam were one and the same. Sure, Sam was better adjusted, truer to himself, and more charismatic than Marshall had been at his age, but his struggles were ones Marshall resonated with. It was hard to be other in a place where being normal was revered. Marshall had been targeted for being too quiet, too feminine, too nerdy, and too gay, and once he'd been stuck with those labels, they had never gone away completely. No matter how he scrubbed, the adhesive never came clean. "And just FYI? If you do want to talk about it, I'm here. I don't think it's dumb at all."

"Thanks." Sam yawned, badly feigning disinterest. "It's cool, though. Everything's good. I think I get caught up in my own head sometimes. All I need to do is wait a year to graduate. It feels bleak, but it's not really that bad."

"And we're here for you," Marshall added. "Well, I am. I can't speak for Fox. If anyone's giving you a hard time, you come to me and we'll figure out what to do about it."

Sam hitched an eyebrow, grinning. "Too bad it's not fish telling me they wish I'd just die already. Fox could stomp over in his stupid boots and hook 'em."

The casual mention of death threats caught Marshall by surprise, and he found himself too stunned to speak. By the time he'd collected his wits, a sloshing noise from the lake distracted them both, ending the conversation. Fox was on his way back to the shore with nothing to show for the brief time he'd spent attempting fish murder. The sun caught in his hair like golden fire, and there was light in his eyes that had nothing to do with any kind of astral body.

It was happiness.

Actual happiness.

And when Fox met Marshall's gaze, that happiness grew.

Heat spanned Marshall's cheeks. Reality put his teenage fantasies to shame. Sex was good, and the hot, primal, possessive way Fox liked to touch him was even better, but to see the man he'd wanted for years light up at the sight of him beat porn any day of the week.

"What's wrong?" Sam asked as Fox emerged. "Tired of waiting for the victims to come to you?"

"Nah." Fox headed for the truck. "I decided it wouldn't be fair to stand out there for hours honing my skills while you two dorks make targets of yourselves."

"Well, that's—" Sam stopped abruptly and narrowed his eyes, spinning around in his chair to face Fox. *"Targets?"*

Fox reached the back of his truck and began to disassemble his fishing rod. "Yup."

Oh, this was going to be good. What was he planning? There was something going on in that brain of his, and Marshall was determined to figure it out.

Sam was a little less tactful in his quest for enlightenment. "What do you mean by targets? I overheard you telling Marshall that the land is public property. No one's gonna come shoot us for trespassing."

"Yup. That's not what the threat is." Fox finished with his fishing rod and removed his boots.

"Uh, then what are you talking about?"

"Sitting out by the shore like you are makes you perfect targets for snipes." Fox pitched his waders into the cargo bed and stretched. "Since I don't want you two dying a horrible, bloody death, we're gonna call it a day. I'll come out fishing some other time."

"What's a snipe?" Sam sat up a little straighter and wiggled as he took his phone from his back pocket. He spent a second unlocking the screen, then held it over his head and groaned. "You're full of bullshit, aren't you? I've lived here my whole life and I've never heard of a snipe. Brown recluses? Sure. Cottonmouths? Yup. Feral hogs? I mean, I routinely fend off thirty to fifty within three to five minutes of me going outside. But snipes?"

Fox shrugged and went to grab his tackle box. "I'm not bull-shitting."

He was—Marshall *knew* he was—but it seemed like poor Sam had never been snipe hunting before. With his aversion to murder, it made sense.

"You so are," Sam grumbled. "I don't have reception out here or else I'd look it up and call you out on it. Why wouldn't anyone have told me to look out for snipes before? Mrs. Warren taught a wilderness survival unit as part of her biology class, you know. She would have mentioned if there was some kind of forest... lake... *creature.*"

"She didn't warn you about bears, did she?" Fox secured the tackle box in the cargo bed and lifted the tailgate. "Or wild dogs, or turkeys?"

"Turkeys?" Sam couldn't have sounded less impressed if he tried, and Marshall had to fight to hold back a laugh. "Are you being serious right now? You want me to be afraid of a *turkey?*"

"You ever seen one up close?" Fox tugged open the back door to pitch an unopened bottle of water inside. "If you had, you wouldn't be laughing. They're like dinosaurs. Huge, unpredictable, and prone to violence. They'll rip you open with their raptor-like claws and peck out your eyes. But because they're not venomous, no one talks about them."

Fox was selling it, and Marshall was living for his performance. A little humor would do them all good.

"So what?" Sam got up and folded his chair. "Is a snipe like a turkey? Are you saying that sitting out by the lake makes me a target for a killer bird?"

"Yeah. I am." Fox took the chair from him and leaned it against the side of the truck. "Thanks for waiting until I put the tailgate up to bring me your chair, by the way."

Sam bowed. "You're welcome."

Fox's story, as good as it was, wouldn't hit the bestseller list without someone endorsing it. Marshall yawned, trying his best to look totally casual while he added, "Fox is telling the truth, you know. Snipes were a problem in this area when we were kids, and I've been hearing reports on NPR that their population is starting to recover after the mass hunt of '99. I'm not surprised you haven't heard of them. After the incident in Alabama, they were pretty much wiped out."

"Wait, what?" Sam spun around and wrinkled his nose at Marshall. "What incident in Alabama? What happened?"

"Oh, fuck, I forgot about that." Fox shook his head and whistled low and mournfully. "That was the one where a snipe killed a group of teenagers who were out celebrating prom, right? I heard they were pulling that airy netting stuff that puffs up under prom dresses out of trees for months. That's when the Feds put a bounty on snipe beaks and people pretty much drove them to extinction."

Sam puckered his lips like he'd bitten into something sour. "You don't expect me to believe that, do you?"

It was hard to keep a straight face, but Marshall persevered. He shrugged. "I'm not asking you to believe anything. All I'm saying is that I think Fox has a right to be concerned. If you don't agree, that's fine."

The color drained from Sam's face. "So... snipes. What are they, exactly?"

"Birds." Fox lowered his tailgate and tucked the chair into place. "It's kind of like what I was saying before about turkeys, but bigger. The females are smaller than the males, but they have better camouflage, and after their chicks hatch they get fiercely territorial."

"It is that time of year, isn't it?" Marshall mused. It was killing him not to laugh and blow their cover. "Most of this year's chicks should be old enough that they're attempting to strike out on their own. It's a stressful time to be a mama snipe. It wouldn't take much to send one over the edge."

Doubt narrowed Sam's eyes, but it was quickly losing out to paranoia. When he spoke again, there was a hint of a telltale quiver to his voice that hadn't been there before. "So why are they called snipes?"

"Because the best way to hunt them is to snipe at them from the trees, where they can't get you." Fox strolled by Sam on his way to Marshall's side. The second his back was to Sam, he dropped his serious expression to smirk at Marshall, who was having the time of his life as Fox's partner in crime. "We should go snipe hunting sometime. You've been doing good with your self-defense training, so I'm sure you could handle yourself if things got out of hand. You wanna come, Marshall?"

Not grinning back required superhuman levels of self-restraint. "Absolutely not. A snipe bit my mom once. She almost lost her leg."

Sam's mouth fell open. "Were you there to see it?"

"Yeah. It was awful. We got a flat on our way to St. Louis one day, and when she got out to change it, it came at her out of nowhere. She had to beat it to death with a hubcap."

"Oh my god." The birds that had flown away when Sam had stormed the tall grass returned. They rustled the vegetation as they settled and chirped as birds were wont to do. Sam locked onto the source of the disturbance, crossed his arms as if to hold himself, and shivered. "Are we even safe here?"

It was Marshall's turn to wave him off. "Oh, Fox was in the Air Force. He'll keep us safe."

"Plus, snipes hate water." Fox gestured at the shoreline. "They love preying on animals that come to the lake to drink, but they hate getting wet. They won't even step into the shallows. If you see one, all you have to do is run in and you'll be fine."

The brush continued to rustle ominously. Sam glanced over his shoulder at the truck and took a small step toward it, but didn't turn his back on the location of the could-be snipe. "That's messed up."

"Yup." Fox's lips trembled, but no hint of a laugh broke through his serious facade. "Marshall, what was that thing you were telling me about a few days ago? That, uh, that one really dangerous thing that was even worse than a snipe?"

"Oh, drop bears." It was the lie that could make or break their game of King of Bullshit Mountain, but Marshall went for it anyway. Worst-case scenario, Sam would already know about them and the gig would be up. Best case, he was totally oblivious and they could milk it for a little longer. If Sam got too upset he'd shut the story down, but until then, seeing Sam forget his troubles was worth it. "Yeah, I'd say drop bears are worse. Snipes stick to the forests and are ground-bound, but from what I hear, drop bears are being driven out of their natural habitat and heading into cities."

"*Drop bears?*" Sam squeaked.

"Yeah. From Australia." Fox offered Marshall his hand—which Marshall took—and pulled him to his feet. The spark in his eyes suggested that holding hands wasn't all Fox wanted to do, but with Sam there, it was as far as either of them were willing to go. "They look like koalas, but they're predators. Right, Marshall?"

"Yeah." Goosebumps spread down Marshall's arms, a product of the thrill he got from the seamless way they naturally built off one another. "They live in trees and drop onto unsuspecting creatures that pass by. While they don't go out of their way to hunt humans, they can and will attack if one is in range. Since they land on your head or shoulder, all it takes is a slice or two from their razor-sharp curved claws to sever your jugular, and once you bleed out, they feed. They're terrorizing Sydney, and I heard Melbourne is reporting sightings for the first time in fifty years."

"Why is Australia cursed?" Sam took another step toward the truck. "Being outside isn't worth the vitamin D. How did any of our ancestors survive? All of us are just squishy, meaty, anxious balls of awkward. You can't tell me that everyone back then was some kind of Rambo."

"I don't know what to tell you." Fox broke eye contact with Marshall and reeled in his expression so he could turn and face Sam. "It was a different time. All I know is that in this day and age, with Marshall and me here to look after you, you'll be fine."

The ominous patch of grass twittered at them. Sam paled. "Okay, but what do they *sound* like? The snipes, I mean. Not the drop bears. What do I need to look out for?"

"That's easy. They sound like"—Fox coughed hard into his hand —"*bullshit.*"

"What?"

"Like"—another cough—"*bullshit.*"

Come this time next week, even Chris Evans would be jealous of Marshall's abs—containing his laughter had started to hurt.

"*Fox,* you need to stop *coughing,*" Sam barked, outraged. "Tell me what a snipe sounds like so I don't get clawed to death."

Marshall couldn't help it—the seal broke, and he snickered. Triggered by his reaction, Fox burst out laughing, and Marshall gave up trying to hold back and joined him. Through his laughter, Fox managed to say, "Kid, snipes aren't real. We're messing with you."

"Marshall!" Sam cried. He rushed across the clearing and smacked Marshall on the arm.

"What?" Marshall jumped back, still laughing. "Why are you hitting me?"

"I wouldn't have believed him if you hadn't gone along with it!"

"Okay. So maybe I deserve it." Marshall stuck out his tongue, and Sam smacked him on the arm again. "But you have to admit, it was kind of funny."

Sam stopped lashing out and pushed his lips to the side like he was giving it a hard think. At last, he sighed. "Yeah, okay, fine. It *was.* You guys got me good."

"Take your time and plan some payback." Fox worked himself down from full-out laughter to an occasional snicker. Once he had himself more or less under control, he packed up the last of their belongings. "See if you can't pull one over on us in return. That's your homework for today."

"It's summer," Sam grumbled. "We're supposed to be celebrating another school year done, not piling on the homework."

"Because pranking us is work?"

"Ugh."

"Don't ugh me, kid."

"I'll ugh who I want, plebe. I'll have you know that you should feel *blessed* that Umbrella nobility has deigned to give you an ugh."

The snark went on, but Marshall tuned it out. All the joking, poking fun, laughing, squabbling… he'd come back to Bulrush hoping to find a way to move on, and instead he'd found his own tiny family. Unable to stop smiling, Marshall ushered Sam into the truck and made eyes at Fox that told him in no uncertain terms what he wanted to do with him after they dropped Sam off. The hole within him was finally under repair. For what felt like the first time ever, Marshall was truly home.

22

MARSHALL

After dinner that night—pizza, since Marshall hadn't needed to use it as a bargaining chip for a vengeful turtle—Fox left to drive Sam home. While he was gone, Marshall folded their empty pizza box, stuffed it in the garbage, and changed into his pajamas. Thoughts of scouring his wardrobe for something sexy to slip into before Fox got back crossed his mind, but fled just as quickly. The fact that a purportedly straight man was interested in sleeping with him was miraculous by Marshall's standards, and pushing the envelope even further by throwing sexy panties into the mix was taking it a step too far.

All good things would come in time.

Well, if Fox was into it.

In the absence of sexy panties, Marshall pulled on his favorite pair of boxer-briefs—the maroon ones that did his dick justice—and covered them up with a respectable pair of gray sweatpants. They weren't his top choice, but the chances of getting laid in his Poké Ball pajama pants were scientifically proven to be lower, so boring it would be.

While Marshall tugged an old graphic tee over his head, his phone vibrated with an incoming call. He grabbed it, popped his head free of its cotton prison, and answered without looking at the screen. It would either be Fox checking in to see if he wanted anything from town or his mom, although she tended to text. "Hey, wannabe fish murderer. You rang?"

There was silence. Marshall furrowed his brow and started to take the phone from his ear to double-check the call had connected when an unfamiliar man's voice stopped him. "Hello? Is this Marshall Lloyd?"

Oh, shit-sticks.

It wasn't Fox, and it definitely wasn't his mom.

Marshall coughed. There was next to no chance it would convince the caller he hadn't meant to call him a murderer, but it was the best Marshall could do on short notice. "This is he. May I ask who's calling?"

"It's Josh. Joshua Kingsbury. Do you remember me?"

Marshall's eyes widened. How could he forget? Joshua Kingsbury, CEO of Syndicate Tech, was one of the biggest names in platform-based services. Marshall had met him a few years back at Google's Cloud Next developer's conference, where Josh had impressed him with a breakout presentation that had inspired Marshall to take a few more risks as far as his infrastructure was concerned. While he hadn't kept in close touch with Josh after the conference, they emailed from time to time, and their conversations had always been pleasant enough, but Josh had never called him before. There had to be something going on. "Of course I do! It's good to hear from you. It's been a long time."

"Too long." Josh paused. "Long enough that I only just heard that you'd stepped down from Luminous. I'm sorry to hear it."

"Oh." Marshall winced. Why did he have to be so awkward at phone calls? Small talk wasn't his thing, but business talk disguised as small talk was even worse. "It's, um, it's not forever, maybe."

"Maybe?"

"It was supposed to be the equivalent of a yearlong vacation." Marshall's mouth went dry. Why was he so unsure about that? He'd set aside a year to sort out his personal life, after which he'd had every intention of returning to work, but now that plan felt flimsy, like it was a suggestion rather than an edict. "I guess word's started to spread."

"Did you think it wouldn't? Not having a mind like yours pioneering advancements makes the future a lesser place." Oh, he was smooth. Marshall squirmed. He had an idea of where the conversation was going to go, and it was making him uncomfortable. Josh wouldn't have tracked down his personal cell without a good reason. "It's why I wanted to touch base. Syndicate Tech has been expanding in unprecedented ways over the last two years, but I think we could still do better. If you need space from Luminous, come develop for me. I know PaaS isn't your strong suit, but under my tutelage I have no doubt you'd catch up quickly."

"Josh…"

"Let me fly you into Denver," Josh insisted, smooth as ever. "You can tour the campus and get a feel for the environment. I'd be delighted to have you stay with me as my guest for the duration of your visit—let's say next weekend?"

As far as business went, Marshall should have been on his feet and packing his bags right that second. The passive income he received from Luminous was enough that he'd never have to work another day in his life, even after stepping down. Aligning himself with another giant would mean another influx of money and, if he played his cards right and signed the right contracts, one day another stream of passive income that would further inflate his assets. But Marshall hadn't left the industry to think like a businessman—he'd left it to feel like himself. "That's a generous offer, and I'm flattered—I really am—but I can't. I'm sorry."

"If someone else got to you first, I can promise you that whatever they offered, I can exceed it."

"No, that's not it. I'd have turned them down, too." Marshall grabbed a nearby pillow and tugged it to his chest, only realizing after he had that it smelled like Fox. He closed his eyes and breathed it in. It wasn't wrong to turn down a great opportunity for personal reasons. No matter how much Marshall's head told him that it was a mistake to turn down the offer, his heart promised that what he'd gain by staying was worth it. "I made a choice and I'm going to stick with it. I hope you can understand."

"Of course." There was finality there that Marshall appreciated. Josh knew better than to push. There'd undoubtedly be a few follow-up emails and perhaps a text or two, but negotiations were more or less over. Marshall had made his choice. "If you change your mind, get in touch."

"I will."

They said their goodbyes, which were blissfully short, then ended the call. In the quiet that followed, the reality of the situation sank in. He'd just turned down a multi-million-dollar deal.

For Bulrush.

For Fox.

For himself.

Marshall let out several panicked breaths, then wiggled his way off the bed and headed downstairs to drown out his racing thoughts with some Netflix. *The Great British Baking Show* wasn't helping him learn how to barbecue steaks, but woe be unto he who challenged Marshall to bake a Génoise.

When Fox came back, Marshall was sprawled on the couch with a box of Lucky Charms on his lap, muttering about cherry filling. It wasn't the seductive welcome home he'd envisioned, but it didn't stop Fox from straddling his lap, casting the box of marshmallow-devoid disappointment aside, and kissing him until Marshall didn't care whether the moisture of fresh fruit would ruin a sponge cake or not. With his arms wrapped around Fox's neck and his carefully selected maroon boxer-briefs shunted down around his thighs, Marshall discarded thoughts of Denver for good and cashed in on the wealth he'd found right in his backyard.

Fox didn't sleep in his room anymore. Every night he followed Marshall to bed, and once they were between the sheets, he showed Marshall just how not-straight he could be. It was a fairy tale come to life, only in this case, magic wands weren't waved as much as they were inserted. Repeatedly. Nevertheless, the results were the same— every night Marshall's dreams came true.

One night several weeks after their fishing adventure, exhausted from a strenuous round of wish fulfillment, Marshall yawned and snuggled closer to Fox. They lay spooned in bed, Marshall's back to Fox's chest while Fox's softening dick warmed itself inside of him. Rain beat on the roof, its pattern a familiar song that Marshall had come to love. Rainy days meant Fox spent his time inside, and more often than not, without work to do, he'd find Marshall, pin him wherever he happened to be, and keep them both busy for an hour or two. It was perfection in a way Marshall had never known perfect could be, which cast doubt on the whole "one boy wasn't" narrative. All this time, had Marshall had it wrong?

On a quest for the truth, Marshall hummed sleepily and started a conversation. "Fox?"

"Mm?"

"This isn't your first time, is it?"

"What?" Fox kissed the back of Marshall's neck in a drowsy, mellow way, like they'd been lovers their whole lives.

"*This.*" Marshall pushed his ass against Fox's groin, causing Fox to moan and leisurely pump into him a few times. "Being with a guy. I got the impression in high school that you were straight. You dated your way through almost all of the girls in our graduating class, didn't you?"

"Yeah." Fox kept thrusting, working his spent cock in ways that made Marshall moan. "All of this is new to me, but fuck if I can't get enough of you."

Marshall closed his eyes and ground against Fox, chasing all the pleasure he could while he tried to stay on topic. "Why?"

"Why not?" Fox hooked an arm around Marshall's stomach,

holding him in place as he drove himself deeper. "So what if you're a guy? You're smart, funny, and goddamn good for me. You make me feel like I deserve happiness. I can't think of anyone else who's made me feel that way. Of course I'm going to want you."

"There's such a thing as friendship."

Fox nipped his ear and bucked into him in retaliation. "Fuck that."

"You already did."

"Mmm, and I think I might do it again." Fox's cock twitched and hardened, and Marshall had to choke back a moan so loud, they would have heard it back in town. "But in all seriousness, I don't know if I can give you an answer. I don't consider myself gay. Hell, I don't consider myself bi. Until now, I've only dated women, and I never had thoughts about"—Fox's hand slid from Marshall's stomach to stroke his hardening cock—"this, but with you it feels so fucking right."

There had to be a fairy godmother somewhere working a little magic, because what Fox said was too good to be real. Marshall bit his lip and bore into Fox's hand, then pushed against him to work his shaft deeper. Euphoria. Relief. Bliss. Marshall sucked in a breath and writhed, desperate for more of Fox's touch, and was rewarded for his efforts. Fox lifted him, adjusting their positions to better the angle of penetration. It wasn't long before he pushed against Marshall's prostate with each thrust, robbing Marshall of all sensible thought.

"I love being with you, baby." Each sultry note caressed the ridge of Marshall's ear. "I fucking love it. I don't care if it makes me gay. I want you. I want to *be* with you. If you think I'm going to pass that up because I can't accept the fact that you've got a dick, you're out of your mind. You and me, we work. We work so fucking good."

It was true. God, was it true. Marshall whimpered and squirmed, wanting more, but too high from Fox's touch to know how to ask for it. He didn't need to. As Fox stroked him toward orgasm and pumped into his ass, he kissed Marshall's shoulder, prompting him to turn his head. Once he did, Fox captured his lips in a crushing kiss that continued even as Fox claimed him.

Starved for breath and on the brink of letting go, Marshall tried to turn his head forward again, but Fox wasn't ready to give him up. The kiss darkened and grew more possessive, and Marshall gave himself to it completely. "Please," he gasped against Fox's lips. "Want it. Want it so bad."

"Want it, too." Fox silenced them both with redoubled passion, fucking Marshall in the hard, frantic way they both needed. "Wanna feel you come on my dick and know you're mine. Always mine. Wanna hear you moan my name when I push you over the edge."

Yes.

Yes.

So close. All he needed was a little more—just a little more—and he would be Fox's forever.

Like he knew he would, Fox pushed him the rest of the way. "Let me come in you, baby. Want you to take it all."

"*Yes.*" Marshall's breath hitched, and he went rigid with pleasure. "Come inside me. Want it. Want you. Want you so fucking bad."

"Here it is." Fox groaned, but as he thrust deep into Marshall, it turned into a growl. "Take it. Take it all. Love you. Love you so fucking much."

"Love you," Marshall echoed. Tears squeezed from between his closed eyelids, leaking from the corners of his eyes. "God, I love you, Fox."

Fox shuddered. There was a new rush of warmth in Marshall's ass, then nothing. They lay with each other, panting for breath and sharing the fairy tale they'd made together as a storm brewed on the horizon.

23

FOX

Darkness.

Oppressive. Restrictive. Stifling.

It wrapped around Fox like rope, coiling and abrasive, tightening until it crushed his ribs and choked the air from his lungs.

Groaning, twisting metal. The shriek of scattershot bolts exploding from their holes. Crackling fire.

The stench of burning hair.

Sick to his stomach, Fox opened his eyes. Unnatural red light turned the familiar into a nightmare. The C-130 was down—the AC generator had kicked on, and it was starting to fail.

The aircraft was on fire.

Fox wrenched at the straps holding him to his seat, but they were locked in place. The buckle wouldn't budge. A new noise joined the hideous cacophony of warping metal and failing hardware—voices.

Nearby voices.

Muddled words with intermittent meaning.

A thought flashed through his head ad nauseam until it was his sole focus: *enemy.*

Enemy.

Enemy.

Fox struggled with his buckle, but no matter what he did, it wouldn't work. There was no button, no latch, no flap—just smooth, unyielding metal. A frustrated bellow of anguish ripped itself free from his chest, but emerged as a garbled wail. He needed to get out. He couldn't die here. Not now. Not like this.

Voices, closer this time.

Indistinct.

Frantic.

Fox's pulse spiked. He gritted his teeth and put his whole body into struggling against his restraints, but it was no use. Shadows shifted through the red light. Hands grabbed his shoulders. Fox's brain turned off. He grabbed through the dark, seized the threat by the neck, and squeezed.

24

MARSHALL

The whimper that woke Marshall turned into a sob, then a heart-breaking, close-lipped cry. It came from Fox, who'd rolled onto his back to occupy the empty space on the other side of the bed. While they'd been sleeping the storm had gained force, and the patter of rain on the roof had evolved into an angry onslaught interspersed with the *clink* of hail. Thunder rumbled in the distance, followed by an eerie flash of light that washed over the room.

Fox cried out again and squirmed, and once more Marshall was faced with indecision. Should he wake him? Last time Fox had woken up on his own and sealed himself inside the bathroom in a fugue state, but the way he'd stumbled and sprinted gave Marshall the impression he'd been terrified. If Marshall could help him by waking him up...

"Fox?" Marshall hazarded. "You're screaming in your sleep. Wake up. It's gonna be okay."

Nothing.

A sob broke in Fox's throat, followed by an eerie howl of agony that was too much to bear. Wanting it to end, Marshall put a hand on Fox's shoulder and shook it gently. "Fox? You're having a night-mare. It's okay. It's—"

A crack of thunder rattled the windowpanes. Too-bright lightning lit the room just long enough that Marshall saw Fox's eyes pop open.

He never saw Fox's hand reach through the darkness.

Never saw it close around his throat.

But he felt it squeeze.

Marshall gasped and tried to scramble back, but Fox's grip tightened, joined by a second hand. His thumbs dug inward without mercy. Marshall couldn't breathe.

If Fox didn't let go, he would die.

A tingling sensation—much like the tactile manifestation of static on a television screen—prickled its way across the inside of Marshall's skull. Dizziness set in. In a blind panic he clawed Fox's chest, but his fingernails were too short to do damage. Even had they been longer, he didn't think it would matter—the longer he went without breathing, the heavier his arms became. Holding them up took monumental effort, never mind trying to use them.

Fox's hold tightened. Black dots bloomed before his eyes. Marshall tried one last time to pry his hands away, but it was no use —Fox was stronger than he was when he was at his best. At his worst, Marshall had no chance.

The black dots swelled. Marshall's head throbbed. His dizziness grew. Another crack of thunder shook the room, and then—

Fox let go.

Marshall fell back on the bed, gasping for breath. He clutched his neck and squeezed his eyes shut, praying that it was over. The mattress dipped. The bedspring creaked. Fox leaned over Marshall, his eyes wide with fear. Marshall expected him to speak—to apologize, or comfort, or even just to ask Marshall if he was okay—but instead Fox's expression shattered, and he let out a warbling sob that broke Marshall's heart.

Lost.

It sounded lost.

Lost, alone, and afraid.

Silent tears rolled down Marshall's cheeks. It hurt too much to sit up, so from where he lay he set a hand softly on Fox's thigh and stroked it as if to say he understood. This was the darkness Fox had warned him about—the part of himself that he hated, but lived with all the same. It had isolated him, stolen his confidence, and convinced him that he was something he wasn't, but Marshall knew better than that. What had just happened hadn't been Fox's fault. Now that he knew what he was up against, Fox didn't have to face it alone.

They could fight the darkness together.

It was going to be okay.

"I'm sorry," Fox rasped through a sob. He laid his hand hesitantly over Marshall's, then pulled it away as if the touch had burned him. Even in the dark, Marshall could see that he was shaking. "I'm so fucking sorry."

"It's okay." Marshall's voice was raw and gritty, and each word scraped his throat like gravel, but Fox needed to know that he understood. It wasn't Fox who'd hurt him—the enemy came from a deep, dark place inside of him, a place Marshall knew, and had come home to try to fix. Fox's darkness was bigger and more painful, but while its shade was different, its color was the same. While it might never go away, it could be diminished over time. It didn't have to be a losing fight. "It'll be okay. I'm here. I'm fine."

"It's not okay," Fox murmured. He backed across the mattress and stumbled off the bed, uneasy on his feet. "None of this is fucking okay, Marshall. You almost died. I—I—" Fox shook his head and took a few shuffling steps toward the door. "Fuck. *Fuck!*"

"Fox—" Marshall sat up, but before he could do anything else, Fox bolted from the room. The guest bedroom door slammed shut. After that there was silence, save for the plink of rain on the roof and the rush of Marshall's pulse as it thudded in his ears. For a long while Marshall sat there and listened, the blankets pooled over his thighs and the bed still warm from where Fox had been. Thunder rumbled in the distance, and while the worst of the storm had passed, an anguished scream from elsewhere in the house rattled the walls. Defeated, Marshall settled into bed and closed his eyes, then let loose with a rattling sob of his own. When he had no more tears left to cry, he rose on trembling legs, crossed the room, and flipped the deadbolt on the doorknob.

That night, for the first time in weeks, Marshall slept alone. He kept his door locked.

2 5

FOX

Sleep was an impossibility. Each crash of thunder brought Fox back to the same dark place.

The panic. The fear. The desperation.

The stench in the air and the groan of warping metal.

The certainty that he was going to die.

All of it had been so vivid. If he hadn't snapped out of it...

No. Fox squeezed his eyes shut and bared his teeth, clawing at his face as the memory flashed in his mind's eye. A strained cry of agony escaped from between his clenched teeth. He wouldn't give thoughts like those room in his head. If he did, they'd never leave. It was bad enough that his disjointed recollections of the crash controlled him like they did, swelling fat with his suffering and insecurities like bloated ticks on a dog. What had happened to Marshall was undeniably his fault, but Marshall had survived. Rather than obsess over what could have happened, he needed to take action to make sure it never happened again.

Nude, Fox curled up in his blankets and stared at the wall while the shadows gave way to the first wedge of morning light. It streamed through the gap in his curtains, golden and hopeful, chasing night from the distant corners of the room and Fox from his bed. Eyes dry from lack of sleep, he rose, dressed, and left his self-imposed place of exile. Marshall's bedroom door was closed. Fox passed it by without trying to open it, heading downstairs and out the front door instead.

Ten years ago he'd stood by and watched while Marshall suffered. He would never do the same again.

Williamson County hospital was small and understaffed. When Fox arrived the ER was open, but the general clinic was closed. He parked, tucked his keys into his pocket, then sat by the front door on a raised stone garden bed until gentle footsteps redirected his attention. A nurse in floral print scrubs was on her way across the parking lot, a coffee in hand. When she spotted him, she changed course to approach where he was sitting and stopped an arm's length away. "You've still got an hour before the clinic opens, honey. Are you okay waiting out here? If it's something urgent, you can visit the ER."

"No." Fox dropped his gaze, unable to look her in the face. While she was a few pounds heavier and a few years older, her almond eyes and blonde hair reminded him too much of his mother. Thinking of her made it too tempting to doubt what he knew to be true—that he was sick, and that he needed help. "I'll wait."

"Well, okay then." It sounded like she was smiling, but Fox didn't risk checking to find out. "We'll see you in a little bit, okay?"

"Sure."

God, what was he doing? It wasn't like he was physically unwell. The doctor would take one look at him, internally roll his eyes, and brush Fox off the same as his parents had. All the guilt, all the fear, and all the pain was in Fox's head. No medical professional was going to be able to wave a magic wand and make it better. Not even Marshall, who made Fox feel more human than he ever had, could reverse the damage done.

The nurse let herself into the clinic, leaving Fox on his own.

Maybe that was what he needed—to be on his own. It was what he'd been planning before Marshall had stepped into his bush and made him reconsider. Maybe—

Fox's phone buzzed, startling him.

It was Marshall.

Fox raked his teeth over his lip and studied the profile picture attached to Marshall's contact info. It hadn't been there before. Sometime over the last few weeks, Marshall had stolen his phone and snapped a goofy picture of himself while he lounged in bed, his eyes alight with laughter and his hair pushed out at all angles from sleep, or sex, or some combination thereof. He'd done his best to put on the ugliest face he could, but had failed. As long as he was laughing, he was radiant. Fucking gorgeous. A goddamn vision.

Fox couldn't run.

He couldn't steal that smile away from a man he'd grown to love.

No matter what his parents thought, the problems he was facing were real. If the doctors here didn't take him seriously, then Fox would find ones who would. There had to be someone out there who could help. As long as he kept fighting, there was still hope. He didn't have to face this alone.

Fox didn't answer the call—he didn't think he could handle talking after what he'd done—but he sent Marshall a text to let him know he was safe.

Fox: I'm okay, I promise. I'm not going to try anything stupid. I'll be back later, okay?
Marshall: Okay.
Marshall: I love you, Fox.

Fox's hands trembled. He closed his eyes and focused on his breathing to keep himself from breaking down.

Marshall loved him. It wasn't something he'd said in the heat of the moment, so corrupted by pleasure that he'd do or say anything to get more. Fox had nothing of value to offer him but his body, but Marshall—quirky, clever, lovable Marshall—wanted him all the same.

Fox: I love you, too, baby. I'll come home soon. When I do, we'll figure this out together.

An hour later when the clinic opened for business, Fox was still seated on the edge of the flower bed. He was the first to check in that day. There might never be a fix for what was wrong with him, but he'd be damned if he didn't try. He deserved it. *Marshall* deserved it. Fox would fight for them both.

26

MARSHALL

Of all the pitiable things in the universe, few of them consumed marshmallows at as alarming a rate as Marshall Lloyd. With one box of Lucky Charms reduced to nothing but disappointment oats and another partially picked over, Marshall showed no signs of stopping. S'mores everywhere were coming up with contingency plans, and the nation of Peeps had declared a state of emergency— not that Marshall would ever resort to sugary infidelity. There was a third box of Lucky Charms stashed in a hard-to-access cabinet over the fridge in case the worst happened, and since last night the worst *had* been happening. Watching Fox's taillights disappear between the trees had broken him in ways he didn't care to say.

"He'll be fine," Marshall muttered to himself as he dug through his current cereal box in pursuit of what appeared to be a misshapen clover. "He's an adult. He told you everything was going to be okay. You don't need to freak out. All you need to do is trust him."

Which was fine in theory, but a few steps short of full-out torture in practice. As much as Marshall trusted Fox, he didn't trust the dark place Fox had lost himself to. It whispered too many lies.

Marshall wrinkled his nose and flicked a few toasted oats aside.

Nothing was ever straightforward. The small blips of pleasure on the radar that was life were always torpedoed by circumstance, and if they somehow managed to escape, it was only because they'd wandered into shark-infested waters. As a kid, Marshall had imagined that money would fix all his problems. With a fat stack of hundred-dollar bills, he'd been certain he could buy his way to happiness—or at least numb himself enough to the outside world to not care about anything at all—but that hadn't been the case. The problems he'd had as an impoverished kid from a single-parent household in rural Illinois had gone, but the difficulties he'd faced as an individual—as Marshall—hadn't gone anywhere. Money couldn't buy him peace of mind any more than it could Fox.

Fox…

God, the whole situation was fucked up. Marshall scrunched his face, let out a decompressing whine, and searched for another marshmallow. The sound hurt his throat, which was bruised and tender from Fox's outburst. If Fox did come home, then what? Would they pretend he hadn't almost choked Marshall to death? Marshall could hide the bruises with concealer and foundation, but he couldn't cover up the memory. The longer they danced around the issue, the worse it would become. Marshall had come back to town to confront his past, and if they were going to make it as a couple, Fox would need to do the same.

Depleted from worrying, Marshall groped for his phone. It'd tumbled out of his pocket and gotten wedged in the gap between the cushions. In his current emotional state, a phone call would end in disaster, so he did what he always tended to do when life kicked him in the balls—he texted his mom.

Marshall: How's the garden going?
Momzilla: Good!!!
Momzilla: you should come see it. Do you want to come for dinner?
Marshall: Not tonight. How about this weekend?

Momzilla: okay

Momzilla: Can I talk you into coming over in the afternoon so you can look at my computer?

Marshall: What's it doing now?

Momzilla: I think it's possessed

Momzilla: and not by a friendly ghost, either

Marshall: I'll come over and bust it for you

Marshall: Do you think we could work in a viewing of *To Wong Foo, Thanks for Everything! Julie Newmar* somewhere in there?

There was no reply, but a second after the text was marked as read, she tried to call. Marshall winced and declined. His throat already felt tight, and he didn't want to break down and make her worry.

Momzilla: baby, what's going on??

Momzilla: are you okay?

Marshall: I'm okay, Mom. I promise.

As soon as he realized what he'd written, his stomach churned. Empty words. Placation. When Fox had tried to reassure him with exactly the same message, had he meant it?

Marshall: I'm sad. That's all.

Momzilla: what happened?

Marshall: Fox is gone, and I don't know if he's ever coming back

Momzilla: baby...

Momzilla: Come over. I'll make tea

The offer was tempting, but Marshall couldn't accept it. He could explain away the bruises as hickeys, but the thought of leaving the house made him too sad. Even if he sent Fox a text to let him know what was going on, he was worried it'd sound like an easy out —an excuse to leave and never come back. Before he went anywhere, they needed to have a conversation. Besides, in light of the whole worst-day-ever thing, Marshall didn't feel much like peopling.

Marshall: I love you, but I can't
Marshall: I need to be a lump on the couch for a while until I get things figured out
Momzilla: I understand
Momzilla: are we still on for this weekend at least??
Marshall: Of course
Momzilla: even when I make you cast out the demons in my computer?
Marshall: Even then.
Momzilla: Good
Momzilla: I'll cook you something really nice to make up for it
Momzilla: will you keep me updated about Fox?
Marshall: Yeah, I will
Momzilla: Love you honey

Marshall had just replied, telling her the same, when the front door opened and Fox came home.

27

FOX

It was cruel the way Marshall always looked like he'd been plucked from a dream. Eyes wide, lips slightly parted, and hair mussed from sleep, he was the picture of a lazy Saturday morning in fall—the kind best spent falling in love under a thick duvet while the wind whipped crisp leaves past the bedroom window. If it weren't for the shadow of uncertainty on his face and the dark bruises on his neck, Fox would've been tempted to bring the fantasy to life, but not every dream was meant to be. Sometimes, as ugly as it was, reality was necessary.

Now was one of those times.

"Hey." Fox lifted his chin, trying his best to keep the emotion out of his voice, but only partially succeeding. A telltale tremble cracked his confidence. "I'm back."

"Fox?" In a mad rush of limbs, Marshall scrambled off the couch and launched himself across the room. A box of Lucky Charms was ejected into free fall somewhere along the way, its contents spilling across the floor. Marshall didn't bat an eye—he dodged the notedly marshmallow-free mess and sprinted for Fox, managing to slip on his stupid hamburger-print socks at the last second. With a gasp, he flailed and latched onto Fox's neck.

Unwilling to let him fall, Fox caught him by the waist and held him close. When he'd imagined what it would be like to face Marshall after what he'd done, he'd expected anger, bitterness, or fear, but Marshall was as vibrant as ever—the same goofball Fox adored.

One heaving lungful at a time, Marshall caught his breath. "I didn't… I didn't think…"

"You didn't think I'd come back."

Marshall dropped his gaze. The excitement drained from his face.

"I wouldn't have believed me, either." While Fox kept one arm looped loosely around Marshall's waist, the other went north. He smoothed Marshall's neglected hair. "I'm so fucking sorry I made you worry, and I'm even more sorry for what I did." Fox's knuckles trailed downward, caressing Marshall's cheek before dipping lower to run tenderly over his bruises. "I swear to god, I didn't mean to."

Marshall flinched, and just like that, Fox's hope shattered. The man he loved and respected was afraid that Fox would hurt him.

No, that's not right, sneered a voice in Fox's head. *He's not afraid you'll hurt him—he's afraid you'll hurt him **again**.*

The voice was joined by a second, then a third. They built off each other, dug into the meat of his brain, and multiplied.

Worthless.

Failure.

Monster.

Useless waste of air.

Weak fucking excuse for a man.

The onslaught didn't stop. At one point it would've been enough to shut Fox down, but that was when he'd been alone.

He wasn't anymore.

Marshall might have been afraid, but he hadn't run. Fox took comfort in his touch and focused on the scent of his skin—Irish Spring, dried tea leaves, and something sugary sweet. It was okay to be afraid. The world was overwhelming at the best of times, and

Fox hadn't been operating at full capacity for a while now. What mattered was that he didn't let the fear win.

"Fox?" Marshall asked. As small as his voice was, it cut through the chatter in Fox's head and gave him something different to focus on.

"I'm here."

"What's going on?"

Fox chuckled dryly. "I wish I could tell you. If I knew, we wouldn't be here, would we?" The question was met by silence, so Fox continued. "I'm dealing with a lot of shit right now, Marshall. It's not easy to unpack."

"I understand." Marshall rested his head on Fox's shoulder. He kept his arms looped around Fox's neck. "I don't expect you to have answers. All I really want to know is if you're going to be okay."

"I don't know if I can make you that promise." Fox kissed the top of Marshall's head and spoke into his hair. "I'm trying. I swear to god, I'm trying. It's why I left."

The hum of central AC and the shrill cry of cicadas filled the space the conversation had vacated. Fox held Marshall loosely, worried he'd feel trapped if he held him too tight. By rights, Marshall should have already left. The problems Fox was facing were the kind that broke men—that chipped away at their resolve until all that was left was frustration and hopelessness. Marshall didn't deserve a future shackled to a man like that. If he was going to stay, he needed to know the full truth. "I'm sick, Marshall." Fox closed his eyes, focusing on the way Marshall's hair brushed against his lips and the thrill he always got when they touched. "I have been for a long time. I thought I could beat it if I manned the fuck up, but that hasn't done me any good, has it? Last night was a wake-up call that almost came too late. I can't fight this thing on my own. The longer I pretend that nothing's wrong, the harder it's going to be. I need to accept it for what it is and fill you in on what the hell is going on with me so I never hurt you again." Admitting it felt like an admission of weakness, but when it came to Marshall, Fox would rather be weak than proud. "I was let go from the Air Force because of my PTSD."

Since his discharge, Fox had carried the diagnosis inside of him like a grenade with a loose pin. It was something he was hyperaware of, something that he knew was dangerous, and something he'd been terrified to release into the world. The consequences of being careless with it were explosive. At least, that's what he'd believed. Now he knew differently.

Cicadas continued to buzz. The dishwasher beeped. The AC clicked off. Marshall made a small, sympathetic sound and held himself that much closer.

Fox tightened his hold in turn.

If this was Marshall's choice, he wouldn't push him away.

"It doesn't always feel the same," Fox murmured. He wasn't sure if Marshall could hear him, but at this point, it almost didn't matter. He'd kept it all inside for so long that he needed to get it out. "Sometimes I dissociate. Sometimes I panic. Sometimes I get so fucking angry over nothing that I can't control myself and I black out. Sometimes I have nightmares. Sometimes it's my survivor's guilt that kicks in and convinces me that I'm a monster. It was so bad after they recovered me from the wreckage that the PEB ordered a medical discharge—they saw that I was unfit for duty, and they sent me back home with a plan. Therapy, medication... I thought it was so much bullshit. All I wanted was to get back in the air. My career was all I had, and the idea that I was losing it because sometimes I'd wake up screaming..."

Fox shook his head. More denial. It hadn't just been screaming, had it? There'd been times when he'd been sent into a blind panic by unexpected noises and moments when he'd been so angry that he'd ripped out his IV in the hopes he'd hurt himself. There'd been other incidents, too—ones he didn't remember, and ones he wanted to forget—yet through it all he'd told himself that he was fine.

"But I know better now." Fox's lips brushed Marshall's scalp, each word a fleeting kiss. "I'm so goddamn sick of running from the truth. It's like I'm stuck in a downward spiral that never ends, always circling the same central point, but never getting any closer to it no matter how far I fall. I don't want to live like this. I don't want to feel like broken goods, and I don't want to be the bad guy. Thinking about what I did... about everything... I can't take it. I can't take who I've become. So that's where I went when I disappeared this morning—to find help. I couldn't wait for an opening with the VA, so I went to a local clinic and started to gather resources. They're going to start me on an MAOI to see if we can get some of my panic attacks under control, and I was referred to a therapist who'll start to see me next week. I don't know if I'll ever be one hundred percent okay, but I'm trying. God, I'm trying. Even if it's too late for us and you decide you don't want me here, I'm going to stick with it. I'm going to get better. You showed me that I still have something to live for, and I'm not going to ever forget it."

Marshall shivered and tucked his head closer to Fox's neck. "I don't want you to leave."

"Even after what I did?"

"Yes. And before your brain tries to twist things around and convince you otherwise, it's not because I'm afraid you'll do something to me if I don't tell you what you want to hear. I'm not the timid kid I was in high school. If I thought you weren't serious about getting better, I'd ask you to leave. But that's not the case. You're serious." Marshall pressed a small kiss against the underside of Fox's jaw. "We're going to figure this out. We'll find a way to make this work for us. I don't want to give up just yet."

Fox didn't either. Not ever. Marshall was too special to let go. He rested his chin on top of Marshall's head and let out a slow, steady breath. They were going to work this out. Everything was going to be okay. "Thank you."

"You're welcome."

"You know if I could turn back time, I'd tell you everything."

"Then let's start again." Marshall pulled back from Fox, looked him in the eyes, and smiled like he meant it—like everything would be all right. "Hey. I'm Marshall. Remember me from high school? I'm that nerd your friends used to bully—the one you stood up for when we were in senior year. You're pretty hot. Do you want to drink some liquid hay and fall in love?"

Fox laughed until he cried.

Yeah, he did.

Of course he did.

Liquid hay and all.

28

MARSHALL

In the end, starting over proved to be less about drinking liquid hay and more about adapting to a new normal. While Fox adjusted to his medication and started visiting a therapist, Marshall took it upon himself to learn how best to support military veterans suffering from PTSD. For safety's sake, they slept in separate beds. It was only a temporary measure, but as much as Marshall hated it, he understood that it was necessary. Fox's mental state was delicate, and until it improved, there was always a chance he could act out other nightmares. Neither of them wanted to take that risk.

Safety, however, didn't keep Fox from Marshall's bed entirely. On weekend mornings, Fox stole between his sheets and woke him with hot kisses that always led to sex. On one such morning, while the August sun beat through the windows and cum leaked down Marshall's thighs, Fox yawned, stretched in an exaggerated way, and gave Marshall a look that spelled trouble. "Tell me a secret."

"What?"

"Tell me a secret."

Marshall rolled onto his stomach and narrowed his eyes at Fox, who was ridiculously handsome when stretched out on the bed all naked and sweaty like he was. One of them—Marshall blamed himself—had kicked the sheets down while they'd been mid-coitus. It'd been a smart move. In the glow of post-orgasmic bliss, Fox had only bothered to pull them partially back into place, covering his legs and part of his groin, but nothing else. The cut of his abs and the definition of his pecs lured Marshall into overlooking how odd the question was, and the sliver of dick he glimpsed beneath the poorly placed sheets did him in the rest of the way—if the question was a trick, the view made Marshall willing to fall for it.

"You're not usually the type to go digging." Marshall arched a brow. "Are you developing a taste for tea?"

"What?"

"Oh, yeah. I forgot you're not that gay yet." Marshall snorted and cuddled up to Fox's side, grinning like the goof he was. "That's okay. Ignore me. I have many years on you, young Padawan. Don't be tempted by the knowledge of a master before you, yourself, have mastered, uh... knowledge."

"Are you even speaking English?" Fox pushed Marshall's hair back from his forehead. Adoration glimmered in his eyes. "I'm not convinced you are."

"I'm probably not."

"Figured. What I do know is that you're definitely trying to change the topic."

"Am not!" Marshall draped an arm over Fox's chest, lamenting that it blocked his view of side-dick.

Side-dick, he decided, needed to become a fashion trend. If side-boob could be a thing, side-dick could be, too.

Fox, who wasn't distracted by the fact that he was about to revolutionize the fashion industry, redirected the conversation. "Then tell me a secret."

"This is so weird." Marshall yawned and made a nest from the nearest pillow and Fox's chest. "*You're* so weird. What kind of secrets are you after? Is this something Eileen is putting you up to, or are you just looking to start trouble?"

Eileen Summers, Fox's therapist, had been helping him work

through a few CBT techniques that had begun to reframe how Fox approached life and the people he shared it with. While progress was slow, Marshall had begun to notice a few changes. Fox's mood was more stable than it had been since they'd met, he was smiling more than ever, and now when he laughed, it sounded like he meant it. But therapy hadn't, and wouldn't, change the fact that Fox was still a private person who didn't tend to pry into other people's lives. Either Eileen was putting him up to this, or Fox was up to something.

Fox shrugged. "Eileen's not responsible for this one. I'm curious. Sue me."

There were plenty of things Marshall would rather do to Fox than financially obliterate him, so he decided to play nice. "Do you remember how in senior year Elijah's car started to smell like a garbage fire?"

"Uh, yeah?"

"I did that."

"You *what?*" Fox grinned and rolled them over to pin Marshall to the mattress. Marshall laughed and swatted at his chest, but Fox didn't yield. "Tell me more, oh purveyor of putrid stench."

"Oh, I like that fancy mouth of yours." Marshall cupped his chin and passed his thumb over Fox's lips, hoping to goad Fox into more. "Sam gets Lord of Umbrellas, I get Purveyor of Putrid Stench... now we need something for you."

"No we don't."

"Oh yeah we do." Marshall clicked his tongue. "How about Marquess of Manliness?"

"Forget it."

"Dane of Excellent Dongs."

"Never say that again."

"Sultan of Sex."

"No."

"Sultan of Sodomy?"

"That's even worse."

"I've got it." Marshall laughed before he even spat it out. "Prince of the Penis."

"Oh my god." Fox clamped a hand over Marshall's mouth, likely in an attempt to get him to stop, but only managed to obstruct his hysterical bouts of laughter. "I regret deciding to play this game with you. I should have just sucked your cock without trying to be coy about it."

Marshall stopped laughing. His eyes widened. Despite the presence of Fox's palm, he attempted speech. "*Wheu?*"

"Your cock." Fox glanced down Marshall's body, as if Marshall might have forgotten where it was. "In my mouth."

Unsurprisingly, that wasn't the part of the concept Marshall was struggling with. He turned his head to the side to free his mouth from Fox's hand-muzzle and attempted to find the right words. In the end, he settled on the wrong ones. "Are you serious?"

"Yes."

"You wanna..." Marshall gestured at himself.

"Yes, I wanna..." Fox gestured at Marshall in the same disbelieving way Marshall had gestured at himself, then hitched an eyebrow. "Unless you don't want me to."

"*No!*"

"Okay. I'll go get breakfast started."

Fox made a move to roll off the bed, which Marshall was pretty sure qualified as tactical warfare. Desperate to keep him there, Marshall launched across the bed like an ungainly torpedo and snagged Fox around the waist. "Stop! I meant no, I want you to do it."

"What?"

"My cock." Marshall found himself suddenly flustered. "I, um, I want you to, um, suck... it."

"Well, now you're speaking my language." Fox smirked, and before Marshall's heart had time to start racing, Fox had pinned him to the bed. He captured Marshall in a scorching kiss that chased all notions of embarrassment from Marshall's mind. When it broke, his cheeks were hot and his dick was rock hard. The dominant glint in Fox's eyes and the low, husky tone of his voice only fanned the flames further. "A secret for a secret. It's only fair, isn't it?" One more brief, needy kiss punctuated the question before Fox butted his way beneath Marshall's jaw, where he nipped, then kissed before making his way down Marshall's chest. "So here's something else to keep your mind occupied." Fox tugged Marshall's nipple between his teeth and ran his tongue over its rounded tip. Marshall gasped and closed his eyes, anchoring a hand on the back of Fox's head to keep him there while pleasure sparked and popped inside him. "I wanna know what it feels like to have you inside me."

Marshall opened his mouth, but no sound came out. A whine of pleasure built and burst inside of him. Fox had never been comfortable enough with his sexuality to explore Marshall with his mouth, and he'd never, *ever* expressed interest in bottoming. It hadn't mattered much to Marshall, who loved taking Fox's cock as much as he adored bucking into his clenched fist, but to know Fox wanted him this badly turned him the hell on.

He'd top for Fox.

Fuck yes, he would.

He'd own that tight, muscular ass and spread those solid thighs, then watch as his cock slid home between them. He'd grip Fox's sturdy hips and pump himself to orgasm in his tight heat, then unload into Fox in the same way Fox unloaded into him— deep, raw, and primal. He'd stroke Fox to orgasm while inside of him, feel what it was like to have a man come on his dick, then do it all over again as Fox's cheeks became slick with lube and sex. If Fox hadn't been pinning him to the bed, Marshall would have rolled them over and introduced Fox to what it felt like to be stretched—but Fox had other plans. He kissed his way down Marshall's stomach and arrived at the base of his cock, which he kissed without hesitation before working his way up Marshall's shaft, where he ran his tongue over his cockhead. The pleasure Marshall had felt when Fox had toyed with his nipples exploded, and he let loose with a throaty gasp that betrayed how much he wanted it.

Fox chuckled darkly, then drew Marshall into his mouth and took him all the way. The straight boy from Marshall's imaginary narrative wasn't so straight anymore.

"*God,*" Marshall breathed. The sheathlike wetness of Fox's mouth made him want to buck, but Fox was too new to take advantage of, so Marshall fought his instincts and tried to go slow. It was an agonizing battle. As unskilled as Fox was, each time Marshall saw his shaft slide between his lips, he almost came undone. Orgasm clenched inside of him, and knowing he wouldn't be able to hold it back, Marshall had to pull away. "I can't. I'm gonna…"

Fox kissed the inside of his thigh. "Already?"

"Can you blame me?"

"I mean, I'm hot as fuck, but I didn't think I was *that* hot." Fox grinned. "Do you think if I got you to finish in my mouth, I could coax you into getting hard again so you can fuck my ass?"

If Fox wasn't careful, Marshall wouldn't last long enough to come anywhere except all over himself. He pushed a hiss of pleasure between his teeth, then looked down his body at Fox, who'd decided to angelically rest his head on Marshall's thigh. Somehow Marshall didn't buy his innocent act. "Even if I could, it wouldn't be a good idea."

"Why?"

"Because I don't want to hurt you. I'm not huge, but you've never… *you know.*"

"Taken cock before?" Fox ran a solitary finger up Marshall's length, then circled his slit. "I can handle it."

"You don't know that. If you don't know how to relax, then you're not gonna enjoy it. I don't want your first time to be a bad experience. I—"

"How do you know I don't know?" Fox took his finger away and introduced his tongue instead, collecting the precum Marshall had made for him. Marshall tried to compose a reply, but every time he went to speak, his words fizzled into nothing. Fox felt too good. At last, Fox stopped toying with him and met Marshall's eyes again. "I want you to fuck me."

"You're not ready."

"Fuck that."

"I'm not willing to hurt you."

"Marshall." Fox crawled up Marshall's body so they were nose to nose. He sank onto one elbow and gripped Marshall's hair with one hand. Marshall thought it would stop there, but Fox surprised him by grabbing his wrist. He brought Marshall's hand to his ass. "I'll. Be. Fine."

There, nestled between Fox's cheeks, was something hard and flat—something Marshall hadn't expected. "*Fox?*"

"You think I wouldn't notice that you've been making an effort to support me?" Fox let go of Marshall's hand, then rolled his hips downward so his rapidly hardening cock brushed Marshall's. "You didn't have to do shit after finding out about my condition, but you went out of your way to make me feel comfortable. I decided that since you were going to such great lengths for me, I might as well make an effort to do something you'd appreciate, too."

The scenarios that came to mind when Marshall considered the word "appreciate" included surprise cups of tea delivered to his office desk, kisses planted on the top of his head in passing, and dishes that magically cleaned themselves. Discovering that his boyfriend had been training his virgin hole with butt plugs for an undisclosed amount of time took the concept of appreciation and blew it into the stratosphere. He gaped at Fox, unsure of what to say.

Fox chuckled and kissed the corner of Marshall's mouth. "You haven't noticed, have you? How I've been squirming when we're watching TV? How I've been more wild than ever when we fuck? I'm ready for you, baby. Stretch me one final time. I want it to be your cock that finishes the job."

29

FOX

Marshall was lean, but to his credit, he was powerful. Once he regained his wits, he grabbed Fox by the shoulders, rolled them over, and ran his fingers over the flat end of Fox's plug. "How long?"

"I put it in before I came to bed this morning."

"I mean how long have you been doing this?"

"Two weeks, give or take." Inserting it had been uncomfortable at first, but Fox had suffered worse. After a while the discomfort had gone away, and when he'd next sized up, he'd found he liked it. "Long enough that I've started to get off on how it rubs inside me when I'm thrusting into you. Long enough to know I want more."

"God…" Marshall shivered, then kissed Fox fiercely. His confidence was hot as hell. Even if Fox hadn't been into the idea of bottoming, seeing Marshall take control would have sold him on it alone. Fortunately for both of them, Fox *did* enjoy the idea of having Marshall inside him. The fact it kicked Marshall's aggressiveness into overdrive only made it better.

Then Marshall pulled on the plug, and nothing else mattered.

Pleasure pulsed through Fox's body, and he squeezed down around the silicone with a cry muffled by Marshall's mouth. When he tried to relax, Marshall moved the plug again, keeping Fox captive in an endless loop of pleasure.

"Marshall," Fox begged through breaks in their kiss. "F-Fuck..."

"You want more?"

"Please."

"Soon, baby." He pulled with increased force, but only moved the plug enough so the swollen end stretched Fox's hole. Fox groaned and lifted his hips, simultaneously never wanting it to leave and wishing it was already gone so Marshall could take its place. To show his lover how willing he was, Fox fucked himself on the plug as Marshall held it in place. The bulb caressed him from the inside, and Fox whined as his ring stretched and tightened around it. Fuck, was it good. So fucking *good.*

And then, just like that, it was over.

Marshall had removed the plug.

Empty, Fox arched his hips and whimpered, but Marshall didn't keep him waiting long. His cockhead nudged into the space the plug had left behind, only venturing far enough to impale Fox on its tip. There were no words. Fox panted and gasped, lifting his hips in the hopes that if he presented his ass to Marshall's liking, Marshall would fuck it and stretch him fully.

His wordless plea was heard.

"Here it comes," Marshall murmured as he worked his tip back and forth. "You want it, baby? You ready?"

"Fuck yes."

"Then it's yours."

Marshall slid into Fox, filling the aching need inside of him with pressure and girth and heat. There was a moment of discomfort as Fox's body adjusted to its new conqueror, but ended the second Marshall started to pump his hips. Each inward thrust struck a spot inside of Fox he'd been searching for, but hadn't known how to find—one that made him feel like Marshall was pushing the cum out of his balls. Pleasure exploded in bursts behind his eyes and robbed him of higher thought. All Fox could do was moan and lock his arms around Marshall's neck as he met each of his thrusts.

It was different being on bottom—not better or worse, but uniquely extreme. As a top, Fox knew what it was like to fuck like an animal, but as a bottom he had no semblance of control. While he could squirm and roll his hips, Marshall was the one who gifted him with pleasure, and whether Fox was ready for it or not, he had to take it. He had to take it all.

One thrust. Another. Marshall was never unkind, but he didn't hold back. They fucked hard, panting, gasping, and moaning. While they did, Marshall palmed Fox's dick and pumped him in time to his fervent thrusts. Fox thought he might come then and there.

"You want it inside?" Marshall panted. "Can't hold on. Gonna..."

"Keep it inside." The words spilled forth, but even if they hadn't, it was what Fox wanted. Fuck condoms. They'd never used them anyway. What sense did it make to start now? "Wanna feel you. Wanna—"

Another thrust. Another pulse of pleasure driving his cum from his balls. Fox's voice broke, and he came with a truncated cry. Seed striped his stomach, but it wasn't what Fox focused on—as he shot, he tightened around Marshall's cock, milking it so Marshall could come, too. With a few more wild thrusts, Marshall groaned and bottomed out, then moved with slow, superficial strokes as his cock pulsed, and he came.

Warmth. Wetness. Fox moaned and worked himself on Marshall's shaft, never wanting it to end. When he slowed, Marshall settled on his chest like a cat draped over a railing, too happy to dream of moving. Fox dropped his legs and spaced out, too lost in bliss to speak.

Minutes passed. Fox regained his breath, then melted into the sheets. Fox gathered Marshall in his arms and kissed him slowly and sweetly, but was promptly cockblocked by Rihanna.

Marshall's phone was ringing.

"Shit," Marshall muttered, breaking away from the kiss. "It's

Sam. How much do you wanna bet we lost track of time and he's waiting for pickup?"

"After what we just did, I wouldn't doubt it."

"Mm. Worth it, though." Marshall kissed him one last time, then reached for his phone. "Darn it, I missed him. Lemme just—" Marshall's phone beeped with a new text. "Oh, he beat me to it. That was fast. He has to cancel today's session."

"Again?"

"Yeah. Again." Marshall yawned, dropped his phone on the bed, and sank back onto Fox's chest. "I figured he might want to skip a day or two come summer break, but I didn't think he'd be missing this many sessions. I wonder if he found a boyfriend."

Fox snorted. "In Bulrush?"

"You're right." Marshall kissed him, then rolled off and lay on the bed beside him. "I guess being part of the ruling class of the Umbrella nation has been tying him up more than he anticipated, but it'll be fine. He knows his stuff. By the time he graduates, he's going to know more than I did when I was his age."

"Speaking of being Sam's age…" Fox turned his head and looked Marshall over, from the blush of his cheeks to the taper of his waist, then back up again. Goddamn, was he gorgeous. If he was going to glow like that every time after topping, Fox would be getting to know the pillows *very* well. "What did you do to Elijah's car that made it reek like that?"

"Oh." Marshall buried his face in his hands and laughed. "Yeah, I kind of left you hanging, didn't I? He used to crack his windows to vent it on hotter days, so for a few weeks I sneaked into the parking lot during lunch and pushed a glob of tuna salad in through the passenger side window. I always managed to get it to fall between the door and the seat, so it was hard to see. Guess he never discovered what was going on."

Fox almost choked from laughing so hard. Marshall was right—Elijah had never figured out the source of the smell, and it'd pissed him off their entire senior year. It wasn't quite justice, but it was something, and Fox was glad Marshall had had the chance to see it through.

When he'd composed himself enough to speak without losing it, Fox cleared his throat and narrowed his eyes suspiciously. "Wait... tuna salad? Are you telling me you're a fish murderer?"

Marshall opened his hands like barn doors, revealing his devilish grin. "The statute of limitations suggests otherwise."

"There's no statute of limitations on murder, you dork."

It seemed there wasn't one on running, either. Marshall bolted out of bed and sprinted across the room, laughing hard. "You'll never catch me alive!"

Fox's heart filled to bursting for his goofy, crazy, spontaneous lover. As long as Marshall was around, laughter was never far away.

Fox sprang out of bed to give chase. At least, he tried. Running, it turned out, was complicated when his knees had developed the consistency of Jell-O. If it hadn't been for the support of the bed, he would have fallen on his face.

Being dicked down apparently meant losing partial leg function. Good to know.

By the time his legs had gotten their act together, Marshall had already escaped downstairs. Fox apprehended him in the kitchen, where he delivered justice for fish everywhere by busying Marshall's lips with something that wasn't murder. Too distracted by each other's bodies to bother with cooking, they took a box of Lucky Charms to the couch, where Fox ate all the "boring oaty bits" and fed Marshall sad-looking hunks of dehydrated marshmallow. Even without milk, he had a good time. When he was cuddled up with Marshall like this, it was impossible to have anything less.

"So what's with your Lucky Charms obsession, anyway?" Fox asked as he selected a shooting star and placed it on the tip of Marshall's tongue. "I'm beginning to think I might need to stage an intervention."

"Nah." Marshall sucked on the marshmallow for a second, chewed, and swallowed. It wasn't right that something so normal could be so goddamn cute, but Marshall managed it. "When I was growing up, we didn't have much money. I told you Mom worked a bunch of jobs to pay rent and keep food on the table, right?"

"Yeah."

"Well, sometimes when things were tough or when her hours got cut, we'd have to skimp on things. We ate a lot of rice and beans when I was a kid. I never went hungry, but I didn't always get the things other kids did, you know? I never got to bring Capri Sun or Lunchables or Dunk-a-Roos. We were more of a peanut butter sandwich kind of family." Marshall snorted. "Sometimes a little light on the peanut butter. But when there was a little extra money to go around, Mom would bring home treats. My favorite was Lucky Charms. She used to buy me my own box on my birthday, and I'd sit there and eat all the marshmallows out of it like it was the best thing in the world. I guess, at the time, it kind of was." Marshall's face fell, but his cheerfulness returned a second later, lighting up his eyes. "By high school, Mom was still working multiple jobs, but they were paying a little better, and we were able to afford the occasional trip for ice cream or fast food. Even then, Lucky Charms was my favorite by far, and now that I can afford anything I want, I still go back to it. It's the Marshall Lloyd version of comfort food."

"But not the boring oaty bits?" Fox popped a few of them into his mouth.

"Nah. Well, kind of?" Marshall wrinkled his nose. "If we're going to rank them, they come second to the marshmallows, but I'll still eat them if they're all that's left. That said, if you're willing to be my boring oaty bits garbage disposal, then I'm not going to stop you."

"Maybe. With milk." Fox crunched another handful. The marshmallow bits were getting hard to come by. "I'm eating them dry out of desperation. The milk is too far away. I don't think I'd survive a trip back to the kitchen without one of us caving and dragging the other back to the couch for, uh, what does Sam call it?"

"Groundskeeping."

"Yeah." Fox smiled. "Groundskeeping."

"Mmm." Marshall poked through the oats. "Domestic bliss at its finest."

Fox kissed the side of Marshall's head and closed his eyes, lost in the beauty of that thought. This was their reality. Marshall was his and he was Marshall's. Not only had they made a life together, but they were actively working to iron out the kinks. Things would only get better from here.

"I love you, Marshall," Fox said. The words were familiar now. Like Marshall took comfort in Lucky Charms, Fox took comfort in them. "I love you so fucking much."

"Love you, too, oat-eater." Marshall kissed the corner of his mouth, and they were all over each other again. The box fell to the floor, followed by Marshall's phone not all that long after. It ended up nudged under the couch where it was promptly forgotten. Eventually, Fox took Marshall back upstairs, where they celebrated their newfound roles as oat and marshmallow eater. Neither of them remembered to bring Marshall's phone, which, an hour or so later, lit up and buzzed while Rihanna sang to no one about stormy weather.

30

FOX

The sun set. Shadows crept across the bedsheets, chasing out the dreary orange glow of day. Fox pushed a kiss to Marshall's shoulder and was set to do the impossible—leave his side to make dinner—when the doorbell rang.

Panic.

It spiked his pulse and made rational thought impossible. Fox sucked a strained breath through his teeth and closed his eyes, trying his best to ground himself, but it was a struggle. Touch, taste, sight, and sound deserted him, leaving nothing but darkness. In a last attempt to fight it, Fox wrapped his arms around himself and tracked the rise and fall of his chest as he breathed.

In, then out. In, then out.

One by one, sensations returned.

The warmth and slight stickiness of his skin after a day spent in Marshall's arms.

The caress of Marshall's stupidly expensive cotton sheets.

The smell of sweat, and sex, and Irish Spring.

The rustle of shifting sheets and the sound of weight redistributing across the mattress.

Footsteps crossed on the wood floor, followed by the swish of a drawer as it was tugged along its track. Fox opened his eyes to find Marshall partially dressed, hopping toward the door as he tugged on a pair of Poké Ball pajama pants. "I'll get it," he said. A t-shirt hung around his neck like a cowl. "It's probably... well, actually, I don't know. But whoever it is, I'll tell them to go away. Do you know what time it is? I think I left my phone downstairs."

"No clue." Fox swung his legs over the edge of the mattress and took a steadying breath. His phone was also MIA, either in his bedroom or jammed between the couch cushions. "Late enough that I should have already started dinner."

"No rush. If you're not feeling up to leaving bed, I can make dinner, too." Marshall hopped through the door, finally slotting his foot into the leg hole. "I'll be right back, okay?"

Despite the lingering traces of panic and the way it throbbed behind his skull, Fox smirked. "I'm not sure leaving you in charge of cooking is in my best interest."

"Hey!" Marshall had just made it past the doorframe, but he stuck his head back into sight to stick his tongue out at Fox. "I'll have you know that I can do all kinds of culinary things... like make salad, and boil water."

"Uh-huh."

The doorbell rang three times in rapid succession. Fox closed his eyes and inhaled slowly and steadily. The noise hadn't come as a total surprise this time around, but it had still jarred him enough to rattle his composure.

"Gotta go!" Marshall called from farther down the hall. "I'll be right back, I promise."

His footsteps thudded down the stairs. As they did, Fox emptied his lungs, opened his eyes, and eased off the bed. Marshall might have been willing to answer the door, but if it was someone unsavory, Fox wanted to be around to step in should something happen. He had no reason to suspect it would. His parents had been quiet since he'd asked his mom to give him space, and while he sometimes got curious looks when he ventured into town, no one had been rude or aggressive toward him even though word had gotten around that Fox was living with Marshall. Fox still wasn't sure how it'd happened, but he assumed it had something to do with Sam's dad, Kevin, who'd been waiting outside the front door one day when Fox drove Sam home. They hadn't spoken, but there'd been a look in Kevin's eyes like he was starting to put the pieces together.

Fox was in the middle of dressing when the front door slammed. He jumped, heart racing, and before he knew what he was doing, he was already on the move.

Marshall.

What had happened to Marshall?

Fox flew down the stairs and emerged into the hallway facing the antechamber. He would've gone all the way to the front door if it hadn't been for the fact that Marshall was on his way into the house, his arm tucked under the shoulders of a scrawny, black-hoodie-shrouded young man.

Sam.

"What's going on?" Fox cleared the distance between himself and Marshall, falling into place at Sam's side. Without waiting for an answer, Fox supported Sam from the other side and helped Marshall carry him into the living room. Once he was seated in the nearest armchair to the door—the one by the big front windows through which Fox had once watched Marshall bust a move—Fox turned to Marshall for answers, but Marshall's face was pale, and it didn't look like he was willing to speak.

Without a clear-cut answer, Fox went to the source. Despite the sweltering August heat, Sam was bundled up. The Black Veil Brides hoodie he loved to wear was zipped all the way to his neck, and he'd pulled his hood over his head so it obscured his face. Fox squatted in front of him to try to catch Sam's eye and immediately wished he hadn't. Sam's lips and chin were streaked with drying blood.

"Holy shit," Fox breathed. "Sam, what the fuck happened to you?"

"I don't wanna talk about it," Sam murmured. He crossed his arms protectively over his stomach and looked away.

Marshall clapped a hand on Fox's shoulder. "You don't have to tell us anything. Not until you're ready."

What kind of bullshit reasoning was that? Infuriated, Fox glanced up at Marshall, but Marshall's attention was zeroed in on Sam. Did he not see what Fox saw? The blood? The pain? The suffering? Someone had beaten the shit out of Sam—broken his nose, if the crooked way it was situated on his face said anything—yet Marshall was talking like everything was fine.

"Fuck that," Fox grumbled. "Sam, who did this to you?"

Sam pinned his chin to his chest and didn't answer.

"Who did this to you?" Fox balled his fists. "Tell me who the fuck is responsible and I swear to god, I'll—"

"Calm down." Marshall squeezed Fox's shoulder, his voice oddly stoic and firm. It was a jarring enough departure from his normal state of being that Fox snapped out of it. "Violence isn't going to get us anywhere. If we want to help, we need to approach this rationally."

"You don't even need to do that," Sam mumbled. "It was me. I was dumb. I shouldn't have—"

There was no universe in which Sam was the one responsible for someone else having broken his nose, and there was no version of Fox in any of them that would stand by and let Sam take the blame. "No. Stop. I don't care what you did—no one has a right to touch you like that."

Sam lowered his chin and wiped the corner of his eye with the cuff of his hoodie. It killed Fox to see him that way, but until Sam started talking, there wasn't anything he could do. Hoping for guidance, he looked Marshall's way, but Marshall was still laser-focused on Sam.

"Fox is right," he said. "He may be coming across a little strong, but it's the truth. Neither of us are playing King of Bullshit Mountain, Sam. Not this time."

Sam tugged the drawstrings of his hoodie, scrunching the hood until the opening was only large enough to reveal his eyes and broken nose. Fox flashed back to a time when Marshall had been the one in Sam's place, withdrawn and hurting. At the time, Marshall hadn't told his mother because he hadn't wanted to burden her. It was possible Sam felt the same way. "Kid?" Sam looked at him from the corner of his eye. It was bloodshot and puffy, but as much as it gutted Fox to see it, it only strengthened his resolve. He'd let Marshall down once—he wouldn't let Sam down, too. "We're here for you. You're not a burden. Besides, you came to us for a reason, right? It's a long walk from town. Something in your brain convinced you coming all the way here would be worth it. Don't let the bastard who did this stop you from feeling safe. Marshall's here, and I'm here, and we can make it right if you only let us in."

Sam took a shuddering breath that almost turned into a sob, hid the last visible section of his face behind his hands, and admitted in a trembling voice, "It was my dad."

MARSHALL

"I didn't mean for it to happen. It wasn't... it wasn't supposed to go like this." Sam gestured at his nose, then cawed a sad and despondent laugh. "He's never hurt me so bad before. If I'd known to expect it, I could've probably stopped it, but he caught me off guard."

"What else has the fucker done to you?" Fox growled. If he were a dog, his hackles would have been raised. "How long has this been going on?"

In an effort to soothe him, Marshall ran his hand from Fox's shoulder to rub his back. "Fox, give him some space. He'll tell us in his own time."

"He's been abused, Marshall," Fox shot back. "Do you think we should just stand by while Sam suffers?"

"No, but I do think we need to think before we act. Pushing him too far too soon isn't going to help anyone. Our first priority is Sam's safety and wellbeing, both physical and mental. Justice comes after."

Fox swore under his breath, and Marshall went to correct him when Sam waved him off.

"Marshall, it's okay." Sam opened his hood, then let it down.

After a brief struggle with his zipper, he undid his hoodie and set it aside. Blood hadn't shown on it, but it did on the white t-shirt Sam wore beneath. It was drying now, but at one point it'd been drenched. "He's not pushing me. I'm just... I'm struggling to process it, I think. It must be shock or something. I feel really numb."

"You want me to get you a glass of water?" Fox asked.

Sam shook his head. "No. I know I'm thirsty, but I just... need to sit for a second and think. My brain feels like it's a couple steps behind my body, which is kind of like how I imagine getting drunk would feel like. Am I off base?"

"Not so much." Fox sat on the floor by his feet, his legs crossed. Once he was settled, he met Marshall's eyes. There was a promise in his gaze, steely and serious but sincere—despite his frustration at the situation, Fox would do what he was asked. For as long as Sam needed, he'd be there to protect him. "Why don't you take a second to get your head on straight before we continue? It'll give Marshall some time to come up with a plan."

"Right." Marshall nodded, holding Fox's gaze for a second longer before looking away. If he wasn't careful, he'd get swept up in those eyes and lose track of what he was thinking. "I'm going to take care of a few things while you take a second to catch your breath. I'll be right back, okay?"

Sam nodded and slumped into the armchair. Without his hoodie to hide behind, he looked younger and more vulnerable, and Fox, who remained loyally by his side, looked even tougher by contrast. Marshall left them where they were and gathered a change of clothes for Sam and a glass of ice water from the kitchen, then detoured by the couch to grab his phone. There were five missed calls and a single text, all from Sam.

"Don't feel bad," Sam said in a tired voice. He'd draped his legs over the arm of the chair and had his head rested on the opposite arm, giving him a perfect view of the couch. "Even if you had picked up, it wasn't like you could have stopped it from happening. The damage was already done."

Marshall dismissed the notifications and shoved the phone into his pocket. Guilt hit him hard, but he pushed past it. Right now the focus needed to be on Sam, not himself. There'd be time to wallow in what-ifs after Sam was safe and the first steps toward justice had been taken. "You're right."

"I know I am. It's a perk of being aristocracy." Sam closed his eyes. The skin around them had started to bruise. "What are we gonna do now?"

Marshall took his spoils and deposited them on the table beside Sam, then sat cross-legged on the floor on the opposite side of the chair as Fox and rested his elbows on his thighs. "In a perfect world?"

"Sure."

"We take you to the hospital where they'll run tests and document the abuse you've been through. You'll tell them everything, and when they call the police, you'll tell them everything, too. They'll take your dad into custody and make sure you never have to endure the suffering he put you through again."

"Then what?" It broke Marshall's heart how nervous and empty Sam sounded. "I don't have any other family. I won't have anywhere to go."

"They'd take you into foster care." Marshall studied the doorframe, following the grain of the wood endlessly to try to distract himself from how hollow he felt at the prospect. "You're almost eighteen. You'd age out soon enough."

"I'd have to change schools."

"I know."

"The guys I talk to online... would I be able to tell them?" Panic broke Sam's voice. "I don't want them to think... I can't... I need to be able to tell them I'm okay. I can't disappear. I can't let them think I'm hurt, or dead, or—"

"It'll be okay," Marshall promised, even though he wasn't sure. "There's going to be internet there, and even if there's not, I can help. I'll tell your friends that you're okay. I just need to know how to get in touch."

"No." There was a frantic shuffling of limbs from behind Marshall as Sam sat up. Marshall had the feeling that if he and Fox hadn't been sitting in front of the armchair, Sam would have bolted out of it. "It needs to come from me."

"Do they know what he's been doing to you?" Fox asked.

Sam didn't reply. Awkward silence settled between them. Marshall remembered what it had been like when he was Sam's age, caught between doing what he knew was right, and doing what his heart wanted. It wasn't easy. In Marshall's case, friends hadn't factored into the equation, but he thought of the choices he'd made that had been destructive to his own wellbeing, but that had kept his mom comfortable and uninvolved. What Sam was struggling with had to feel similar.

"Can you text any of them?" Marshall asked. "Maybe you can ask someone to spread the word that you're okay, but that you'll be going dark for a while."

Sam sniffled, then yelped in pain. Broken noses didn't heal that fast.

"All of this is so fucked up," Sam said once he'd recovered from his mistake. "I don't wanna have to go to foster care, and I don't wanna have to talk to the police. All I want to do is be here. Away. With you and Fox, where things don't suck all the goddamn time."

"You're starting to sound like me, kid." From the corner of his eye, Marshall watched Fox turn his head to look at Sam. "I know things suck right now, and that it may feel like they won't ever get better, but they will. Even if it feels impossible, they will."

"I'm going to be homeless, Fox." Sam's voice warbled. He sounded close to tears. "They're going to take me to somewhere I've never been where I know no one. I'm not gonna be able to finish school, or go to college, or—" Sam choked up and couldn't continue, but Marshall thought he knew what he'd meant to say—Sam wouldn't be able to escape. With his senior year in shambles while he adjusted to being in the custody of the state, his plans for college were likely to go up in smoke. The stability and support he needed to file college applications, write entrance essays, and court the caliber of schools he was after would be gone, and then, after aging out, he'd be trapped in Bulrush with his broken dreams and limited opportunities.

If he told the truth, he'd suffer for it.

The gravity of the situation settled on all of them, silencing Fox and Marshall. Sam wept softly and hopelessly until he was too starved of breath to make any noise at all. Once he'd reached that point, he sucked in tiny, quivering puffs of air until he'd recovered enough to say, "And it's all my fault. You tried to teach me how to defend myself, but I was too fucking dumb to learn."

"No." Fox pushed himself onto his knees and turned to face Sam, his expression so tight his lips trembled. "No, Sam. That thought can fuck right off. Even experienced fighters get hurt. You did the best you could with the tools you had, and no one can fault you for that. You're not a failure. As long as you're breathing, you've never failed."

Marshall watched the exchange in silence, his heart bleeding for the boy on the armchair and beating for the man who knelt in front of him. Sam would never know the vulnerability behind Fox's words, but Marshall did.

"Life isn't black and white," Fox continued, holding Sam's gaze while emotion flickered in his eyes. "You're gonna feel like the biggest fuck-up of all time every now and then, but you know what? Everyone does. It doesn't mean you're not worthy. It doesn't mean you didn't try."

Marshall blinked back tears, but knew better than to speak. Fox needed this. *Sam* needed this.

"So be easy on yourself." Fox attempted a smile. It was stiff, and it wobbled, but it shone like it needed to, and that was all that mattered. "Don't give up hope. You kept fighting by coming here, and now that we know what you're going through, you can bet your ass we're gonna help. We're your backup now. We're your team. And you know what teams do? They don't leave anyone behind."

For a long moment nothing was said. Time stretched thin, growing so taut Marshall thought it would snap. Sam's composure broke instead. With a warbling sob, he launched himself off the armchair and dropped onto the floor between them, dragging Fox into a bear hug while he wept. Fox looked over his shoulder at Marshall, his arms spread as wide as his eyes, like he had no idea what to do. Marshall gestured vaguely at Sam and nodded, prompting Fox to hug him back. The anger and tension bled from Fox's body, and he closed his eyes as he tucked Sam to his chest like a father might hold his son.

32

MARSHALL

Half an hour later, Marshall stood by the side of the driveway and watched Fox's taillights disappear behind the tree line. Sam had agreed to go to the ER. It had been decided that Fox would drive him there and stay until everything was taken care of to his satisfaction while Marshall stayed home to start work on their next few steps, which was Marshall speak for making phone calls he didn't want Sam or Fox to know about in case things didn't work out.

Once Fox's truck was gone, Marshall shut himself in his home office and got to it. As much as he hated speaking to anyone on the phone, there was no one else who could do what he needed done. The mandated reporters at the hospital would set the ball in motion, and it'd be up to Marshall to make sure he kept up.

After almost an hour spent gathering information and hammering out details, Marshall hung up for the final time and reclined as much as his office chair would let him. If he didn't take a brain break, gray matter might start oozing from his ears. As a general rule, speaking to people was exhausting, but speaking to people whose default language was legalese was a whole new level of tired that not even mainlining caffeine could fix.

Bzzzt.

Marshall looked down his nose at his cell phone, which he'd left, screen down, on his desk.

Bzzzt. Bzzzt, the phone repeated in rapid succession.

Marshall scowled at it, but not even a healthy dose of shame was enough to convince it to drop the call. It looked like his brain break was going to be a short one. Legal jargon, like a clingy ex-boyfriend, just wasn't willing to give him up.

Marshall scooped the phone up with a resigned sigh only to be met by Fox's ridiculously handsome display picture. Unfortunately, rugged good looks weren't enough to keep Marshall from instantly worrying that something had gone wrong. He picked up immediately and answered with an apprehensive, "Fox? What's going on?"

"Hey." Fox sounded equal parts pissed-off and defeated. "They're in the middle of running the assessment now, but some things are already clear. The bastard has hurt Sam before. There are bruises all over his body and old burn mark scars on his hips from cigarettes. They took him in for X-rays to check for broken bones and... I don't know. Whatever else shows up when you X-ray someone. I'm sitting here in the waiting room sick to my stomach thinking about it."

Burn marks? Bruises? Marshall squeezed his eyes shut and tried not to think about it, but it was impossible. Was that why Sam had always worn his hoodies so religiously? Why hadn't he picked up on it before? Guilt hit him hard, worse than when he'd found Sam's missed calls. If he'd noticed sooner, Sam wouldn't have had to suffer for so long.

"Marshall?"

"I'm still here." Marshall lifted his head and occupied himself with a paper clip he found on his desk, running his thumb over the loops. "It makes me feel sick, too, but we're doing the best we can. Is he doing okay? Do you know?"

"I think so. The nurses won't let me back there to see him, but one of them is sweet on me, and she keeps me updated with what's happening even though I don't think she's supposed to. She mentioned that he keeps making them laugh."

"That's a good sign."

"I guess." Fox sighed. "It's eating at me thinking that this was going on under our noses. I thought the whole hoodie thing was part of his edgy teenage sense of style, not a technique for hiding bruises and burns. The one time he took it off while we were training I didn't see a thing, and it's making me feel guilty as fuck. I keep wondering if it was his way of calling out for help and I didn't see it. If I'd have paid more attention—"

"You couldn't have known." The paper clip gleamed as it caught the overhead light. The sun had long ago set, and the world outside Marshall's office window was plunged in darkness. "I was just blaming myself for the same thing, but it's not either of our faults. I don't think that one time was a cry for help. Sam didn't want us to know."

"Why the hell wouldn't he?"

"For the same reason you didn't want to tell me about your PTSD." Marshall ran his thumb over the rounded bottom of the clip. "And the same reason I never told my mom that I was being bullied. When trauma like that happens to us, we blame ourselves. We don't talk about it to other people because we trick ourselves into believing we deserve it."

"It's stupid."

"I know." Marshall tossed the paper clip onto his desk. It skittered across with a series of bright, crisp *clicks* before coming to a stop against the curved wood handle of his rubber duck umbrella. "How much longer do you think the assessment is going to take?"

"I don't know. I don't know if they'll even tell me when it's done. I've been waiting for the cops to show up to file a report, but I guess they're going to wait until Sam's assessment is finished so they have a clear idea of all the fucked-up shit he went through. I figure they'll come through the waiting room, right? Or is there some back door they'll use?" Fox sighed in frustration. "I don't know how any of this works. I'm not gonna leave until I know there's a clear plan for Sam's wellbeing, but unless that one nurse comes to tell me, I have a feeling I'm going to be waiting here a long fucking time."

"It's just for now." Marshall followed the length of the umbrella, from its sturdy handle to its metal tines to its charming rubber duck print canopy. He'd meant to hang it on the wall like a piece of art, but the project had fallen by the wayside. "I'm working on making sure we have better control over his care in the future."

Fox laughed dryly. "You looking to seduce a nurse?"

"No." Marshall laughed, too, but for none of the same reasons. He smiled at the umbrella, then tilted his head back and closed his eyes. "I'm figuring out what it would take to adopt him."

The next few days were a flurry of activity. Marshall spent them traveling, both by ground and by air, to have a background check and medical exam done. Adoption, it turned out, would be too complicated with the complexity of Sam's case and for how little time there was before he turned eighteen and aged out of the system, but the family law attorneys Marshall had consulted suggested he fast-track through the process of becoming a foster parent and elect to take care of Sam until he turned eighteen. After that they could discuss adult adoption, but for now they'd take it a step at a time.

For someone working a nine-to-five, the process of being a foster parent was daunting, especially for residents of Bulrush, whose nearest social services were in St. Louis—a two-and-a-half-hour drive. For Marshall, who had money and time at his disposal, they weren't much of an obstacle. While his legal team filled out his paperwork, he took care of everything else. If he met his targets, he'd be certified as a foster parent in less than three months.

One night, exhausted after a trip to St. Louis for fingerprinting, Marshall was spaced out on the couch listening to Fox cook dinner when his phone buzzed. It was Sam, whose group home had allowed him to keep his cell phone. He'd been one hundred percent on board with Marshall's plan, and kept him updated with the growing pains that entailed adjusting to a new life far away.

Lord of Umbrellas: The beds here suck
Lord of Umbrellas: I hate them
Lord of Umbrellas: I'm so tempted to yeet straight to California
Marshall: First of all, no
Marshall: Second of all, I can't believe you used 'yeet' in a sentence
Marshall: Third of all, why California? You'll need to stop by my place to pick up the keys if you want to use my pool
Lord of Umbrellas: It's where my groundskeeper is going to school
Marshall: You have a groundskeeper?
Lord of Umbrellas: Yeah
Lord of Umbrellas: He told me I could come out and that he'd take care of me while I finished high school

Nope. Nope. A big old bag full of nope. Marshall set down his phone and scrubbed his face. That was mighty fine stranger danger right there. It was a damn good thing he was working as hard as he was to gain custody of Sam, because there was no way he was going to let him traipse off to California to be some internet troll's love slave.

Not that he'd say that to a lovestruck teenager, of course. Marshall didn't need to take parenting classes to know that forbidding a seventeen-year-old from doing something was a guaranteed way to get him to do it. Rather than set boundaries he had no right to issue, he decided to fish for information.

Marshall: Who is he?

Lord of Umbrellas: His name is Emilio. He's 19 and he's going to start at Cal State this semester

All right. Good start. Emilio didn't *feel* like the name a creepazoid would use while attempting to lure damaged teens into his basement dungeon.

Marshall: How did you meet?

Lord of Umbrellas: omg

Lord of Umbrellas: are you... are you momming me?

Marshall: I am not momming you

Lord of Umbrellas: You're totally momming me!

Lord of Umbrellas: all I can picture is you peeping out the living room window while my date comes to pick me up while Fox sits on the porch polishing a shotgun

Lord of Umbrellas: you KNOW Fox would do it, too

Marshall had to hook his arm over his mouth to keep from laughing. Yeah, that was something Fox would do, and he'd do it while giving his best death glare until the car rolled out of sight.

Fox, adorably, had instantly taken to the idea of being an unofficial step-foster dad. Marshall hadn't had the guts to bust out the lacy panties just yet, but he was starting to think it wouldn't be such a big deal if he did—Fox was spicing up the bedroom just fine every time he called Marshall "Daddy."

Marshall: He would

Lord of Umbrellas: he'd be the kind of guy who'd stare my boyfriends down when I bring them home

Lord of Umbrellas: like, not ever verbally threaten them or lay a hand on them, but GLARE

Lord of Umbrellas: never ending disapproval

Lord of Umbrellas: Luckily Emilio is the best guy ever and there's a zero percent chance that either of you will hate him

Marshall perked up.

Marshall: You want us to meet him?

Lord of Umbrellas: Well, yeah

Lord of Umbrellas: chances of stealing my dad's car are slim to nil now that he's in police custody, and if I steal one of your cars, Fox'll go all Liam Neeson on me and track me to the end of the earth to get it back, so I guess that means you guys are stuck coming with me to the land of sunshine and rubber ducks

Marshall: We'd be honored

Lord of Umbrellas: Good. I really wasn't looking forward to having Fox hunt me down :P

The sound of clattering plates distracted Marshall from the conversation. It seemed like Fox was finished with dinner.

Marshall: I've gotta go. Try to get some sleep

Lord of Umbrellas: On these cement blocks they call beds, that's a tall order

With the conversation wrapped up, Marshall tucked his phone into his pocket and padded on bare feet into the kitchen to see if Fox needed help. It didn't look like it. Fox was stationed next to their favorite counter, dishing broccoli out of a microwaveable bag while trying not to steam his fingers off. Ever alert, Fox perked his head when Marshall entered the room. "Ah, the pitter-patter of hungry footsteps."

"I'll have you know I didn't just come to take advantage of your superior culinary skills—I came to see if you needed help." Marshall slotted into place beside Fox to survey the plates, onto which had been portioned a seasoned chicken breast and a serving of store-bought mushroom risotto. "But it looks like you've got things under control."

"Yup." Fox finished with the broccoli and tossed the bag in the sink. Broccoli water gushed out of the opening. "I was going to bring your dinner directly to the couch, but now that you're up, would you rather eat in the dining room?"

"Not picky." Marshall eyed Fox, who he'd also eat anywhere given the opportunity, and decided that maybe he did have a preference—finishing his meal and immediately snuggling up to Fox sounded better than having to deal with dishes and transition from the dining room to the living room. They could do the whole adulting thing some other day, preferably when Marshall wasn't so tired. "Well, actually, maybe the couch. You wanna watch something while we eat? I think I need to turn my brain off."

"GBBS?"

"Oh my god, is it bread week? Please tell me it's bread week."

Fox picked up a plate and handed it to Marshall, then took the second and herded him into the living room while Marshall enthused about yeast. Sadly it wasn't bread week, but the GBBS bakers *were* tasked with making kouign-amann, which was almost as good.

When the competition had one fewer baker and nothing remained on Marshall's plate but a sad little puddle of broccoli water, he slid his dish onto the table and curled up on Fox's lap. Fox, entranced by the montage of glazed desserts that opened every episode of the GBBS, absentmindedly stroked his hair. "I don't know how you do it, you know."

"Burn water?" Marshall's eyelids drooped. There was a chance that Fox had drugged his dinner, but it was more likely that being snuggled up with him had taken away his stress to the point where he could genuinely relax. "It's not hard when you've got a million different things going on in your head all at once."

"No, you goof." Fox smoothed the hair back from Marshall's forehead. "I mean everything with Sam. I was ready to go ballistic, but as soon as shit hit the fan, you were able to come up with a plan and see it through. I don't think I'd even know where to start."

"That's why we make a good team." Basking in Fox's attention, Marshall went boneless, melting onto the couch. "Everyone has their strengths, and ours happen to be opposites. It means that when we're together, we're pretty much unstoppable."

"We are, aren't we?" Fox's fingertips explored Marshall's scalp, then ghosted their way down his neck. "You and me. I never would have thought."

"I did," Marshall admitted while Fox stroked the soft hair on the nape of his neck. He didn't even notice when his favorite baker forgot to preheat his oven. "This is seriously cringey, but I'm going to admit it anyway—I used to daydream about you in high school."

"No shit?"

"No shit." Marshall snorted. "I mean, I was a horny teenage boy, so I wasn't imagining you making me dinner or stroking my hair while we watched baking shows on Netflix, but I used to think about what it might be like if you wanted me like I wanted you. I was crushing on you so hard after you stepped in to save me."

"It's funny how things change." There was a smile behind Fox's words, and hearing it made Marshall fall in love with him a little more. When Fox spoke again, the sound of his smile had sweetened with humor. "And it's even funnier how they don't. Do you really expect me to believe you're less horny now than you were as a teenager?"

Marshall rolled onto his back and glared at him playfully. "Hey!"

Fox raised an eyebrow. "You sure this is the hill you want to die on?"

"Well, I mean… fine. Okay, I'll admit I'm not much better now." Marshall laughed. "But can you blame me? I'm living with the guy I used to have wet dreams about, and not only does he like me back, but we're together. Together-together. As in not only does he like touching my dick, but he also likes touching other, harder to see parts."

"Like your prostate?"

"Like my—oh my god, *Fox!*" Marshall burst into laughter and picked himself up from Fox's lap, sitting with his back to the television screen so he could look him in the eyes. "I meant my heart, you pervert."

Fox grinned, then gave Marshall a not-so-sly once-over. "Can you blame me?"

"I guess it depends on what you're willing to do to make up for it."

"Oh. Is that how you want to play?" Fox's lips twitched. The light from the television played across his eyes, making the blue in them sparkle that much more. "Well, Mr. Lloyd, I'd be happy to show you everything I have to offer, but I don't think the living room is the place to do it. Why don't we meet in your office in ten minutes?"

It was Marshall's turn to arch his brow. "My office?"

"It's business, isn't it?"

Marshall doubted it, but it didn't matter. For Fox he'd sit in man-eating bushes, brave snipe-infested wilds, and even tolerate the criminality that was adding milk to tea. In comparison, conducting a little not-business after hours was nothing.

Feeling lighter than air, Marshall leaned forward and kissed the tip of Fox's nose. "Of course it is. I'll meet you there."

33

FOX

Ten minutes after parting ways, a business-ready Fox knocked on Marshall's office door. There was a moment's pause during which the wheels of an office chair rolled across the floor, then the door opened and there stood Marshall in a pair of white lace panties and nothing else.

Marshall looked at Fox. Fox looked at Marshall.

"Well." Marshall cleared his throat awkwardly and gestured at Fox's suit. "I think it's safe to say that we have two very different definitions of 'business.'"

Fox didn't answer. Struck by the vision before him, he stepped forward, fisted a handful of Marshall's hair, and kissed him fiercely. Marshall moaned and wrapped his arms around Fox's neck, and in seconds they were stumbling blindly across the room while Fox hunted for somewhere—anywhere—he could pin Marshall to show him exactly what he had to offer.

In the end that somewhere ended up being Marshall's desk. A second after Marshall bumped into it, Fox breathlessly broke the kiss and flipped Marshall around and bent him over it. White lace stretched taut over Marshall's cheeks, teasing Fox with glimpses of the most goddamn beautiful skin he'd ever seen. Unable to resist, he ran his hands over the curves of Marshall's ass, savoring the way the lace felt beneath his fingers and imagining how much better it would feel once it was on the floor.

"You're so goddamn fucking beautiful." Fox gripped where the lace wasn't, effectively tugging the back of the panties into a gentle V that revealed more of Marshall's skin. "I can't get enough."

"I thought we were here for business." Marshall glanced over his shoulder, the desire in his eyes no more masked than it was in his voice. "You mentioned something about making it up to me..."

"And I will." Fox guided the panties lower. How the fuck had he never realized how hot a man's body could be? Marshall was no hourglass, but the way his narrow hips met a supple ass supported by lean yet sturdy thighs was the stuff of wet dreams. Fox drew the panties lower, wanting more, and he got it—Marshall's balls, full and heavy, hung between his legs. In what had to be the crowning achievement of expert-level time management, they were totally shaved.

Fox's pulse skyrocketed. He pushed the panties the rest of the way down and leaned over Marshall so his chest was to Marshall's back. While he did, he reached around and discovered Marshall's hairless skin, tracing his way from his groin to his balls, which he cupped in his hand and delicately squeezed. "I thought I was the one making it up to you."

"I don't know what you're talking abou—*ahh!*" Marshall's plea of innocence devolved into a desperate, gasping moan as Fox traced the ridge between his balls. "Don't stop. *Don't stop.* Fox, *please!*"

"I'm not stopping, baby." Fox nipped the back of Marshall's neck. "Never gonna stop. You're mine now. Gonna make you feel good forever."

While Fox fondled, squeezed, and stroked, he worked his hips teasingly, rocking his clothed cock against Marshall's bare ass. The friction was addictive, but knowing what was still to come buzzed Fox like nothing else. Gripping heat. Winded moans. Tension. Pleasure. Release. And in the end, the sight of Marshall with his eyes partially lidded and his lips slightly parted, glowing from what Fox had done.

He wanted it. Fuck, did he want it.

And he wasn't the only one—when he finally tugged open his belt and unzipped, Marshall groaned with relief.

Fox pulled his cock through the slit of his boxers and guided it between Marshall's cheeks, discovering along the way that Marshall was already prepped. Glossy lube slicked his hole and coated Fox's shaft as he teased, readying himself to push inside. "Is this what you want?" Fox growled. He circled Marshall's hole. "You want me inside of you?"

"*Yes.*"

"Then take it."

No more holding back. No more playing nice. Fox pushed inside, burying himself to the hilt as Marshall gasped and groaned. Tight, clenching heat gripped him, and he thrust into it over and over while stroking Marshall toward climax. While he did, Marshall bucked back into him feverishly, meeting Fox's abundant excitement with his own. They fucked hard, Marshall gasping and panting Fox's name while Fox nipped the back of his neck. He pleasured Marshall in all the ways he knew Marshall liked to be touched, but still it wasn't enough. At last Fox's stamina wore out, and with a strained cry he pushed deep into Marshall and came. Marshall, greedy for it, ground his ass against Fox and tightened around him as if to ask for more.

"I fucking love you," Fox whispered against Marshall's shoulder, driving his cock into him in small, shallow strokes as he shot a few last times. "I'm gonna pull out, baby, and then I need you to hop onto the desk, okay?"

"Don't pull out," Marshall pleaded. "Can't... need you too much. Need you to stay."

"I promise it'll be worth it." Fox peppered his skin with kisses. "Okay, baby?"

Marshall whined in agreement, so Fox pulled out and helped

turn him around, then lifted him onto the desk. The pretty lace panties he'd been wearing had fallen around his ankles, and as Marshall settled, they slipped off to dangle from a single foot. It worked to Fox's advantage. He sank to his knees and occupied the empty space between Marshall's legs, then took Marshall's cock into his mouth. While he sucked, he looked up to watch as pleasure shut Marshall's eyes and widened his mouth in a silent scream. Did he even know how fucking gorgeous he was? How unapologetically sexy? How loved?

Fox took him as deep as he could, spluttering sometimes when his confidence and inexperience clashed, but impressing himself at others. The more pleasure consumed Marshall's face, the easier it became. God, what a trip it was to see him like that, all rosy cheeked and addled with need. Each twitch of his hips, each arch of his back, and tender noise that curled on the back of his tongue only made Fox want more.

When Marshall finally came, Fox kept him inside and swallowed every last drop. When there was nothing left, he kissed the inside of Marshall's thigh, then stood, took Marshall by the chin, and lifted his head to kiss him all over again.

"Does that make up for it?" Fox asked against Marshall's lips through kiss after kiss.

Marshall moaned. "What were we... what were you making up for again?"

"I don't remember."

"I don't, either." Marshall slid off the desk, disturbing the rubber duck print umbrella on it as he did. It didn't fall, so Fox let it be, holding Marshall around the waist while Marshall wrapped his arms around Fox's neck. Marshall's semi brushed against his own. "I've still got some office work to do tonight to get ready for the home study, but... mmm... do you think taking this to the bedroom will help us figure out what we forgot?"

Honestly, Fox didn't, but at that point it didn't matter. Whatever it was he'd done, he'd more than make up for it once he got Marshall between the sheets.

Creaking metal. Crackling fire. Shattering glass.

Oppressive darkness cornered Fox from all sides, putting so much pressure on his lungs he thought he might never breathe again.

Distant voices. Creaking wood. A scream.

Marshall.

Fox woke up with a start. Memories of his nightmare clung to him like static, but surprisingly, they weren't the source of his fear. The shattering glass, creaking wood, and panicked scream hadn't come from his subconscious—they'd been real.

Fox was out of bed and down the hall before his brain could catch up with his body. Marshall's office door was open, but while the overhead light was on, the room was empty. Marshall must have heard the crash of shattering glass and run downstairs to investigate.

Heart in his throat, Fox sprinted down the stairs into the dark. There was a clatter accompanied by a muffled bellow of rage—Marshall. It'd come from the living room near the front window. Fox bolted in the direction of the sound, dodging furniture by memory only to slip on something that shouldn't have been there right in front of the living room door. It was as long as a baseball bat, but thinner and more cylindrical, and covered in tarp-like material with interior supports that crunched beneath his foot. Whatever it was knocked Fox off balance, and he went down, catching himself on his palms before he hit the floor. A second later he sprang back up onto his feet, the item in hand. One end was sturdy and solid, and it had a metal core, which meant he could use it as an impromptu club.

With his weapon in hand, Fox scrambled through the doorway.

It was too dark to make out many details, but Fox recognized the shape of Marshall's body. What he didn't recognize was the larger shadow—the one that had Marshall by the neck as he thrashed and struggled to escape.

No.

No.

Rage blinded Fox to the world, and with a roar he rushed forward and smashed his club against the back of the stranger's head.

No one touched Marshall.

No one.

The fucker would pay for what he'd done.

Snarling, Fox hit him again, then again. On the third hit, he let go of Marshall, who stumbled forward and coughed hard, like he was struggling for air. One more strike brought the shit stain to his knees, and with a thud he fell onto his side, out cold. Fox raised his arms for the finishing blow when Marshall stopped him in his tracks with a single croaked word. *"Don't."*

Fox gritted his teeth. "Give me one reason why I shouldn't."

"He's down." Marshall's voice popped and cracked. It sounded painful, but he kept on speaking. "It's over. Killing him won't make it better. We need to call the police."

"*Fuck. That.* He tried to kill you, Marshall. He broke into our house and tried to *kill* you."

"And if you killed him, would that make you any better?"

Fox tightened his grip on the club, but said nothing.

"I'm gonna call the cops." Marshall's voice quivered, but it didn't break. "It's gonna be okay."

With a breathy hiss, Fox let go of the remnants of his rage and lowered the club. As much as he wanted to do the fucker in, he and Marshall were a team now, and he wouldn't let Marshall down. While Marshall rushed to find his phone and make the call, Fox flipped the living room light on so he could see who they were about to put in jail. Kevin Acton—Sam's sorry excuse for a father—

was passed out on their living room floor. Forbidden from ending the bastard's life, Fox nudged his face with the object he'd found in the hall, pushing Kevin's lip back in uncomfortable and unflattering ways. It was only then that a flash of yellow caught Fox's eye. The thing he'd found in the hallway—the weapon that had taken Kevin out—was Sam's rubber duck umbrella, undoubtedly grabbed from Marshall's office in self-defense when he'd run down to investigate the broken window.

MARSHALL

The last of the cop cars disappeared down the long lane leading from the house to the highway, but Marshall stayed seated with his back to the front door, watching the sky turn dreamy shades of red and orange as the sun crested the horizon. Kevin had been apprehended and would face punishment for his crimes. According to the police, he'd posted bail the day before and been released under the assumption that with Sam removed from the household, no further incidents would take place. Unfortunately, it seemed like Kevin had figured out who'd blown the whistle on him, likely due to the time Sam had spent with Marshall and Fox that summer. While it was a relief knowing that he'd serve time for what he'd done, justice didn't feel as good as Marshall had thought it would. What had been going through Kevin's mind to get him to come all the way out here, on foot, no less? How could a man rationalize doing what he'd done, not only to Marshall, but to his own son?

Marshall rested his head on the door and closed his eyes. There were no easy answers. All he could do was take comfort in knowing that Kevin was gone, and that this time he wouldn't be coming back.

The old doorknob turned, giving Marshall a heads-up that the door was about to open. After a brief struggle with the lock it swung back on its hinges and out stepped Fox, who carried two large duffel bags—one in each hand. He put the bags down and sat beside Marshall, giving him silence for a prolonged moment before asking, "Are you gonna be okay?"

"Yeah."

"I'm not going to let him hurt you. I won't let *anyone* hurt you."

"I know."

Marshall placed his hand in the space between their bodies. Fox laid his on top, loosely lacing their fingers together. A comfortable silence settled between them, and for a long while Marshall let it soothe him. The chirp of crickets and the melody of early morning songbirds made up for their lack of conversation, reminding Marshall that even when life came to a standstill, the world didn't stop moving.

In time, everything would be okay.

Fox gently squeezed his hand and kissed the side of his head. "Are you ready to go?"

Marshall nodded.

"I'll get the bags loaded in the truck. You wanna pull up the directions to the B and B while I do?"

"Sure."

Fox eased onto his feet and collected their bags. While he packed them in the truck, Marshall pulled up directions to the bed and breakfast that would act as their temporary home. Until the front window was replaced and Marshall had a security system installed, they wouldn't be coming back.

"Everything's loaded," Fox said upon returning to the door. He held his hand out to Marshall. "I packed you an emergency box of Lucky Charms to tide you over until we can get out to buy some groceries. Is there anything else you'd like me to go grab before we leave?"

Marshall clasped his hand and stood. "Nope. We should be good."

"You didn't even check what I packed for you."

"It doesn't matter." Marshall managed a tiny smile. "I've got you, right? What more do I need?"

"Mm, let's see..." Fox led Marshall toward the truck, never letting go of his hand. "Netflix, or at least some way to watch the GBBS, especially if it's bread week. Your computer, comfy socks, and enough tea that you might not have any more room for clothes, half of which has to taste like hay."

"My clothes taste like cotton and regret, thank you very much." Marshall stopped them in front of the passenger side door to look into Fox's eyes. "All kidding aside, I appreciate what you've done for me. I don't know what I'd do without you."

Fox's face softened. "Funny," he murmured a moment before claiming Marshall's lips in the sweetest kiss of all, "I think the same thing every day."

While life did come to more or less of a standstill those next few days, the world kept on turning. The window was replaced, the broken glass was swept away, and a security system was installed. When Marshall and Fox returned home the house looked better than ever, and by the time the home inspector from the DCFS arrived to inspect the premises, nothing was out of line. Marshall's application was approved, and it wasn't long after that until Sam came home for good.

"You know, the kids in the group home were telling me that foster parents don't get to pick what kid they want," Sam remarked casually while he and Marshall tinkered with their latest side-scroller project one Saturday afternoon. "How did you swing it so that I'd end up here?"

"It was half narrowing down my specifications for the kind of foster child I wanted and half legal mumbo jumbo." Marshall pointed at the screen where Sam had made a mistake with the Java-Script. "Remember that JavaScript doesn't create a new scope for each block of code. Variable 'i' is going to remain in scope even after the 'for' loop has completed. You're gonna have to use a 'let' keyword if you want to do it that way."

"Ugh." Sam rolled his eyes. "It's so stupid. Why can't JavaScript be like all the other programming languages?"

"Dunno. That's just how it is."

"Emilio says that C++ is worse." Sam fixed the error, then folded onto the desk with an exasperated sigh. "Am I really going to be able to learn all this before the end of the year? If I'm not accepted to Cal State, I will literally die."

"No college is going to need you to be an expert at programming languages to admit you as a student." Marshall hid a yawn behind his hand, then stretched to chase away his fatigue. His mom had taken them out last night to celebrate Sam's return to Bulrush and his new place within their family, and it had run late. While Fox and Sam were fine with sleeping in, Marshall hadn't been so lucky. Even though Kevin was back in police custody without the option to post bail, Marshall doubted he'd stop worrying until after the trial, when Kevin would finally serve time behind bars. "But if you're ahead of the game, it'll put you at an advantage, so let's give it our best shot."

Sam looked up at him from where he'd collapsed on the desk. "You really think I can?"

"Yeah, I do. But the only way you'll learn is by doing, so let's get back to work. We've still got lots to do."

The shimmer of confidence in Sam's eyes was worth every hour spent pointing out every memory leak and incorrect reference. What Fox had said held true. They were a team now, and Marshall would always be on Sam's side no matter where life took them.

It didn't snow much in Bulrush that year. Come February, just in time for Valentine's Day, three inches fell overnight and melted just as quickly. It had been years since Marshall had lived somewhere

where snow was a possibility, but he found the storm underwhelming. Three inches just couldn't cut it when he routinely took eight every night.

Blissed out from too many marshmallow bits and feeling lazy after a round of lovemaking with Fox, Marshall hummed sleepily and snuggled up to Fox's side. Over the last few months, Fox had been working on exposure therapy under the supervision of his therapist, and he'd been making strides. There was no cure for the psychological damage he'd sustained, but between his sessions with Eileen and the medication he took, its symptoms could be managed. In light of his progress, he and Fox had made the decision to move Fox back into Marshall's bedroom, and as a gift to each other, they'd timed the move to coincide with the day of the year celebrating romance, love, and waxy chocolate.

"You doing okay, baby?" Fox asked as Marshall curled up around him. "You looked like you were gonna pass out a couple minutes ago."

"I got my second wind."

"I won't complain." Fox rolled onto his side and pulled Marshall into his arms. "I'm having a hard time sleeping, anyway. You ever notice how bright falling snow makes the night? It weirds me out."

"I think it has something to do with refraction."

"Refraction?"

"Like in physics," Marshall explained, although he was only half convinced he knew what he was talking about. "It has to do with the way light interacts when it passes through different, um... things."

Fox smoothed Marshall's hair back from his forehead as he seemed to like to do, a glint of trouble in his eyes. "So I take it refractory periods are unrelated."

"Refrac—" Marshall cut himself off mid-sentence when he realized what Fox had said. *"Oh my god."*

Fox smirked. "Well? Is it?"

"No. I'm sorry to say snow redirecting light will have absolutely no effect on your dick, Fox. I know the news must be very sad for you, so if your dick needs a private place to mourn, let me know. I think I know just the spot."

Fox snickered and climbed onto Marshall, effectively pinning him to the bed with his body. Once there he kissed him sweetly. His flaccid cock rested against Marshall's. "It's a sad day indeed, but I don't think my dick is up to doing much of anything right now. Let's give it another ten minutes to come out of shock, okay?"

"Sure. Ten minutes sounds like just enough time."

That got Fox's attention. He narrowed his eyes suspiciously. "Enough time for what?"

"For your second Valentine's Day gift." Marshall snagged his phone from the bedside table, opened an email he'd received earlier that week, and turned the screen around so Fox could see it. "Ta-da!"

"It's... an email," Fox said flatly.

"Who's it from?"

Fox squinted at the screen. "Some attorney. I still don't understand what the hell I'm looking at."

"It's notification that the sale of my house closed." Marshall beamed. "I made the decision a while ago, but now that Kevin is officially serving fifteen years behind bars, I went for it and took the plunge... I'm not going back to California. I sold my house in Silicon Valley. At the tender age of twenty-nine, I'm now officially retired."

Fox took his phone and tossed it aside. Before Marshall could protest, Fox grabbed a handful of his hair and guided his head back, extending his neck. With a growl, Fox kissed his way from Marshall's shoulder up his neck and over his jaw, capturing the corner of his lips in a smoldering kiss before whispering his response against Marshall's cheek. "I wouldn't consider yourself officially retired if I were you—I happen to know for a fact that keeping the groundskeeper in line is a full-time job."

Marshall shivered. "Is that so?"

"Yeah." Fox kissed his way to Marshall's earlobe, which he

tugged between his teeth before adding, "I heard the pervert likes to take advantage of rich, handsome, fucking hilarious young men who look like they have too much free time. If you're not careful, he'll pin you down wherever he finds you and use you to sow a little seed."

Marshall's cock throbbed, and he arched his hips to put pressure between his body and Fox's. "Tell me how hard he'll fuck me."

"Oh, you don't wanna know." Fox reached between them, wrapping his hand around both their cocks which he started to pump. "I heard the last guy he fucked was ruined for other men—no one was ever good enough, so he never dated again."

"Never," Marshall promised. "Only you."

"Only me."

Fox kept pumping until both he and Marshall were fully erect, then pulled away to lift Marshall's leg and slot into the space between his thighs. Once in position, he guided his cock home and fucked Marshall for the second time that night. While the first time had been slow and sweet, this time the sex was urgent and primal. Fox's thick cock owned him, and had it not been for the fact that Sam was sleeping down the hall, Marshall would have let loose with a delirious cry of pleasure that would have announced it to the world.

"I love you, baby," Fox panted. He held Marshall's leg over his shoulder, his hips setting a rapid rhythm that Marshall couldn't match if he tried. "I fucking love you."

"Love you, too."

Pleasure curled inside Marshall's groin, and when Fox thrust again, it tightened in a way he couldn't shake. Muting his cry with their pillows, he came hard and fast, decorating his own chest and stomach with his spend. Fox picked up the pace, groaned, and fell still. His cum flooded Marshall, and with a few additional thrusts, Fox pushed it deeper. When there was no more left, Fox pulled out, set Marshall down, and cuddled with him beneath the sheets. Snow continued to fall outside the window, disseminating blurry starlight.

"You know it doesn't matter if you sold the house or not, right?" Fox asked once they'd gotten comfortable. "I'd follow you to hell itself if it meant we could be together. You're mine, and I'm yours, and there's nothing that's going to keep me from you. No place, no person, no thing."

Marshall knew it. He'd made the choice to stay in Bulrush not because he thought Fox wouldn't follow him, but because of what they'd found together while living there. If there ever came a time when the memories they'd made lost their sparkle, they could talk about leaving, but for now, there was nowhere else in the world Marshall wanted to be.

EPILOGUE

FOX

"You ready, kid?"

"Do I look ready?" Sam lamented. He clawed at his face, which looked to Fox the same as it always did—in other words, dainty and heavily emphasized by eyeliner. "Why did I let you guys talk me into getting braces? It feels like my teeth are gonna fall out. I can't meet my boyfriend if I have no teeth. But what if they don't fall out and I smile at him and the sunlight glints off the metal and blinds him? He's never gonna want to speak to me again."

"Hey, I'm not letting you get away with putting the whole braces thing on us. You were the one who asked for them." Fox shielded his eyes with a hand and looked across the beach in search of Marshall, who'd disappeared not even five minutes after they'd stepped onto the sand, no doubt to get up to trouble. "Besides, if you wanna lodge a complaint, you're gonna have to take it to corporate. I'm afraid I'm just a lackey. Marshall's the one calling the shots."

Sam arched a brow. "I bet he is."

Fox covered his eyes and groaned. He'd walked into that one.

"But it doesn't even matter," Sam despaired, "because no matter whose fault it was, it doesn't change the fact that it's a thing. Past me was so *dumb*."

Marshall appeared on the horizon, a few bottles of water tucked under his arm. With the way the sun beat down on their shoulders, it was a smart move. Sam in particular, who'd ditched his dark hoodies but still wore black band t-shirts and, bafflingly, a knit beanie, had to be feeling it. A little hydration would do them all good.

Sam's phone pinged with a text, and for the first and potentially only time in his life, it looked like he'd rather throw it into the ocean than check to see who'd messaged him.

"Is it him?" Fox asked.

"Yes." Sam hid his face behind his hands. "Oh my god, hide me! Dig a hole in the sand you can bury me in. Maybe you can put in a little straw so I can breathe and a phone charger so I won't get bored, but otherwise you need to pretend I don't exist, okay? If you don't, I'll die of nerves and embarrassment and you'll have to live with the knowledge that you took your boyfriend's son's life."

A year ago a remark like that would have triggered him, but Fox let it roll off his shoulders. Sam didn't and would never know what he'd been through while overseas, and Fox would never hold something like that against him. "Something tells me it'll take more than that to kill you."

"Who's getting killed?" Marshall asked as he rejoined them. He gave one of his water bottles to Fox and the other to Sam. "Did we decide Emilio is actually a murderer catfishing as a young man?"

"Oh my god, *no.*" Sam looked a couple remarks away from a dramatic teenage meltdown. "Everyone needs to be quiet about Emilio, okay? I'm already hardcore freaking out. He's on the beach somewhere *right now.* What's he gonna think if he finds us and we're all talking about him like he's some psycho killer? What would I even say if that happened?"

"Um," said the skinny, dark-haired, band-t-shirt-wearing twenty-nothing who'd approached Sam from behind while he went on his diatribe. "How about hello?"

Sam's eyes widened. He spun around and upon glimpsing the newcomer let out a startled, joyful cry. "Emilio!"

In a flash of black, Sam sprang at the newcomer and they toppled onto the sand. While they laughed and hugged and made a nest for themselves in the sand, Marshall reached out and took Fox's hand, weaving their fingers together. "You think we should let them be?"

"No. Definitely not." Fox kissed the side of Marshall's head. "We're here as chaperones for a reason. Does your adopted son's purity mean nothing to you?"

"He's going to be going off to college in a few months, you know." Marshall hitched an eyebrow. "And he's eighteen, Fox. He's an adult."

"Still." Fox eyed Sam's boyfriend—Emilio—and watched as he tugged Sam's beanie free and tossed it aside to run his fingers through Sam's silken hair. Sam whispered something to him that made them both laugh. Not long after, the moment softened, and Emilio guided Sam's head down and kissed him.

Fox looked away.

"You're thinking of asking me to move here so we can helicopter parent him through college, aren't you?" Marshall asked dryly.

Fox didn't want to say yes, but he certainly didn't say no, either.

Sam ended the kiss to glare at Fox. "Don't you even dare think about it."

"There, see?" Marshall asked. "We'll have to stay in Illinois where we won't be able to routinely watch Sam make out with his boyfriend. Tragic."

Fox glared at Marshall, although he didn't really mean it—glaring, it seemed, would be his default expression for as long as Sam was locking lips with a kid Fox hadn't been able to properly vet. As far as he knew, Emilio was a student at Cal State pursuing a bachelor's degree in biochemistry. He liked the same kind of music Sam did, and they spent most of their free time playing Fortnight together. From what Fox had gleaned from the FaceTime session

Sam had set up before they'd booked their flight to Anaheim, Emilio was honest, respectful, and seemed like a nice kid, but looks were often deceiving. Case in point, Marshall, who looked like he led a simple life working a nine-to-five, but who'd retired before thirty with more money than he could ever hope to spend.

Fox didn't have long to ruminate over Emilio's innocence—Sam dragged him to his feet and pushed Emilio in front of them, happier than Fox had seen him look in a long time. "Marshall, Fox, this is my boyfriend, Emilio."

"Hello, Mr. Lloyd. Hello, Mr. Fraser," Emilio said with a polite bow of his head. "Thank you for coming out to visit. Sam and I are really grateful you'd bring him here. It's nice to be able to meet you in person."

"Hi, Emilio." Marshall smiled. "It's nice to meet you, too."

Fox tried to loosen up but only managed to glare a little harder. "Provided you always treat Sam with respect, it's nice to meet you, too."

"Of course, sir." Emilio bowed his head. "I wouldn't dream of doing anything else."

"So, um." Sam looked between Fox and Marshall. "Can Emilio and I go walk by the water for a little? So we can talk and stuff?"

"And stuff?" Fox didn't like the sound of that.

Marshall elbowed him. "Yes."

"Afterward we can go exploring and sightseeing and all that fun stuff, but I just…" Sam glanced at Emilio, who was always watching Sam out of the corner of his eye. "Before that, I was hoping we could get to know each other a little better in private—if that's okay."

"Stay within our line of sight," Fox warned. With where Sam was at with his self-defense training, Fox had no doubt he could whoop Emilio's ass if the kid tried anything, but there was a worried part of him that was reluctant to let Sam go. He hadn't been in Fox's life all that long, but the little family unit they'd made had come to mean a lot to Fox, whose relationship with his parents continued to be toxic, and was now virtually nonexistent. Emilio was a threat to that structure, but it was like Marshall had said—Sam was eighteen and he'd be leaving the house before long to start school, anyway. Kids grew up and families changed. Fox needed to learn how to adapt.

"Totally reasonable," Sam said.

"We'll be back soon," Emilio added. Both of them waved, grinning like idiots, before Sam took hold of Emilio's hand and dragged him as far away as he could without leaving Fox's field of vision.

"You think they're going to spend the next half hour making out under the pier?" Fox asked.

"Mm. Maybe." Marshall leaned into him. "Can you blame them? Imagine if I lived somewhere far away and you only got to see me something crazy, like once a year."

"Yeah, fuck that." Fox pressed a kiss to the side of Marshall's head, and for a while they stood in silence while Sam and Emilio explored the beach. There was something about seeing young, wild love that spoke to Fox on a deeper level and made him think that, despite how he glared, everything would turn out okay. While Fox wouldn't admit it out loud, it was cute to see Sam so smitten. He'd barely known Emilio in person for five minutes, but Emilio already had him laughing so hard he sometimes doubled over. After the rough year he'd had, Fox was glad to see him like that. Sam deserved happiness.

The two young men wandered the shoreline, Sam stooping down every now and then to pluck something from the sand. Neither of them looked back.

"Hey, you think if they're not gonna go stand beneath the pier, we can?" Marshall asked. "The sun is killing me."

"Sure." Fox led the way, never letting go of Marshall's hand.

The shade beneath the pier took away the worst of the scorch. To help them cool down further, Fox cracked open the water bottle and gave it to Marshall, making sure he had his fill before he took any for himself. Between them they drained it all. Fox wedged the bottle in the surprisingly sturdy wet sand, then wrapped his arms around Marshall's shoulders to keep him close while they watched the tide go out. This was the life Marshall had given up for him—ocean views and clear, sunny days. Fame, fortune, and opportunity. What they'd found together was richer than anything Marshall had found out here. Fox acknowledged it, and he swore to himself that he'd work his hardest to keep it that way.

It felt about time he swear it to Marshall, too.

"There's been something on my mind lately," Fox admitted to the universe. From the corner of his eye, he saw Marshall turn his head to give him his full attention. "Eileen says that it's important to talk about your feelings so they don't stay bottled up. I don't always agree with her, but in this case, I do. What I feel isn't something I should keep to myself. You deserve my honesty."

Marshall tensed, undoubtedly fearing the worst. "What's going on?"

"Sam's gonna be gone in a few months." Fox followed the line where the ocean met the horizon with his eyes, committing the moment to memory. "Our little family is already fracturing. I remember before Sam came to live with us how frustrated I felt at not being allowed in to support him while he was in the hospital, and I remember how stressed you were that there'd be something wrong with the paperwork, or that your legal team wouldn't pull through and we'd end up with a different kid while Sam slipped through the cracks." Fox gave up his view of the Pacific to look into Marshall's eyes. "But I remember what it was like before, too. The kindness you showed me when I was scared and alone, the care you took of me when I needed someone there, and the laughter you brought into my life when I had nothing."

Tears pearled Marshall's lash line. He blinked them away furiously, but nothing he did could chase the sparkle out of his eyes. He was the most goddamn beautiful thing Fox had ever seen, and somehow he'd decided that Fox was worth his time.

"I don't ever want to lose what we have," Fox continued. "I don't know what I would do without you, Marshall, but whatever it is, it would make me less than what I am now. You make me someone I'm proud to be."

A solitary tear streaked Marshall's cheek. Fox let Marshall go to face him directly and brushed it away with his thumb.

"You know I'm yours forever. You know I'd follow you to hell and back if it meant we could be together." Fox's throat tightened. He swallowed his sudden rush of emotion and pushed forward. "What you don't know is how deeply I mean it, but I guess you will now."

"Fox," Marshall whispered. He didn't need to say more. The emotion in his voice carried his story, telling Fox what he needed to know.

It was time.

Fox lowered himself to one knee and produced a simple tungsten band from his back pocket. Somewhere off in the distance, Sam laughed so loudly it echoed.

"Marry me, Marshall." Fox presented him with the ring in his cupped hand. "With you, I'm more than I could ever be on my own."

Marshall blinked more tears from his eyes, then dropped to his knees in front of Fox and grabbed his hand, pressing the ring between their palms. Rather than answer with words, he kissed Fox fiercely, and Fox kissed him back. It would be like this forever, Fox realized as he fumbled to put the ring on Marshall's finger while the kiss went on. Every day they'd fall more in love.

"Gross!" Sam gagged as he approached. "Ugh, and you guys were on about me and Emilio staying within your line of sight. Guess it's up to me to be the adult, huh? This is worse than the sex pants incident."

Marshall broke away from Fox, smiling ear to ear. After a prolonged moment of eye contact that made Fox's heart race with excitement for the future, Marshall looked over his shoulder. "Says the guy who made out with his boyfriend right in front of us."

"That's different!" Sam argued. "It was the very first time we met, and we're also young. You guys are old, and you've been together forever."

Fox snorted. He climbed to his feet, helped Marshall up, then recovered their discarded water bottle. "We're still working on the forever part, kid, but think what you want." He took Marshall's hand, delighting in how the ring felt against his skin when they laced their fingers together. "If you and Emilio are done with the beach, what do you say we go sightseeing? We could take an unofficial campus tour."

Sam raised an eyebrow. "Is that your attempt to scope out the area so you can dad me from across the country?"

Fox shrugged. It wouldn't serve him to admit that Sam was right. Teams looked out for each other, after all, and there were none with as strong a bond as those that became family.

ABOUT THE AUTHOR

Should you ever find yourself traveling down the gravel street of a quiet forest community in the Midwest, you may come across Emma Alcott—suburbanite by birth, but small-towner by choice.

Emma loves all things doctors say you should only enjoy in moderation, writing the stories of her heart, and traveling. Once upon a time, she fell in love with a man from another country and moved mountains in order to be with him. They've now been married for half a decade and have far too many fur-children.

Seriously.

Do you want a dog?

If you love Emma's books, you might also enjoy her work as her alter-ego, Piper Scott!

ALSO BY EMMA ALCOTT

Small Town Hearts Series
After the Crash
Before the Call
During the Flight

Masters of Romance Series
Side Character
Bad Boy
Sweet Thing
Wild One

**Audio addict? All of Emma's books are available on Audible.
Click here to check them out!**

WRITING AS PIPER SCOTT

Rutledge Brothers Series
Love Me
Save Me
Keep Me

His Command Series
Obey
Beg
Stay
Heal
Breathe

Single Dad Support Group Series
The Problem
The Proposal
The Solution
The Decision
The Promise
The Answer
Single Dad Sundays

Waking the Dragons Series
(with Susi Hawke)
Alpha Awakened
Alpha Ablaze
Alpha Deceived
Alpha Victorious

Rent-a-Dom Series
(with Susi Hawke)
Daddy Wanted
Master Wanted
Teacher Wanted
Beard Wanted

Redneck Unicorns Series
(with Susi Hawke)
Seriously H*rny
Dangerously H*rny

Forbidden Desires Series
(with Lynn Van Dorn, writing as Virginia Kelly)
Clutch
Bond
Mate

Forbidden Desires Spin-Off Series
(with Lynn Van Dorn, writing as Virginia Kelly)
Swallow
Magpie
Finch
Peregrine

Audio addict? See which of Piper's books are available on Audible. New titles are always always being added.